GUNNING POINT ROAD

GUNNING POINT ROAD

A NEW JERSEY MYSTERY

J. N. Catanach

The Hornbill Press
New York City

Published by The Hornbill Press, New York
Thehornbillpress@gmail.com

Design by Blair Cummock
Text set in Sabon 11pt

Printed in the United States of America
by CreateSpace, an Amazon.com Company

Library of Congress Control Number: 2016938259
ISBN: 0-9706407-5-7

For A P & S

A gentleman asking one of the Proprietaries, "If there were no Lawyers in the Jerseys?" was answered "No". And then "If there were no Physicians?" the Proprietor replied "No". "Nor Parsons?" adds the Gentleman. "No", says the Proprietor. Upon which the other cry'd "What a happy place must this be and how worthy the name of Paradise!"

History of Monmouth & Ocean Counties,
New Jersey (1890) by Edwin Salter.

1

The whirr—almost inaudible—of the electric clock high on the wall, the occasional shuddering roar of the refrigerator, the squeak of the swivel chair under her slightly shifting weight; of these things she was aware. Otherwise, silence; a brittle silence, waiting to be broken. No planes, no cars, no dogs, not even wind in the trees stirred sounds to draw her mind outside. On a warm July night, not far from the Jersey shore, Bernice sat alone at a desk in a house that was not her own. When the phone did ring, she jumped; not visibly, but inside, though this was what she'd waited for, was her reason for being in that room at that hour. Automatically she glanced at the clock and jotted down the time in her log: 2:53.

"Help." She spoke evenly; not a plea, a statement, like Hello.

The voice at the other end came thin as rice paper. "Hello? Hello? I'm old an' I don't hear too well no more." Scarcely breath enough, it seemed, to squeeze the words out. "Do you hear me? Hello?"

"Loud and clear," Bernice said, not quite truthfully.

"I need help, I surely do." A woman's voice, cracked and old, countrified. "My sister's layin' over the way in her bed, sick to death. An' I wouldn't be surprised but he'll be coming for us. Any minute."

"Who's that? Who'll be coming for you?"

"The man upstairs. Any time soon. Not that I'm afeared to meet the Lord; though I sinned some, jus' like all folks, I guess."

"Do you have a doctor you can call?" Bernice spoke up.

"A doctor? Not no more. Not since Dr. Meath. He used to come ..." The voice trailed away.

Dr. Meath, a name from her childhood in this New Jersey township. "Now listen good," Bernice said. "I'm going to give you the number where you can get help right away. Do you have pencil and paper so you can write it down?"

"Not here, I don't. Least not a pencil. I'll go fetch one." She paused. "Don't go away now. You're a Christian, I can tell."

"I'm not going any place."

"May I know your name?"

"Renée." She gave her code-name. "I'll be waiting."

"If I shouldn't ..."

"Yes?"

"Well, never mind." The voice petered out, but the line stayed open.

Bernice kept the receiver to her ear. She heard muffled clanks, and a shrill buzz, like crickets, though surely? Then a swell of sound and a whoosh like a passing car. Was it an outside phone booth? Bernice waited a while, then after what seemed like an automatic disconnect, hung up.

At seven she left for home, a small, trim figure in a pale green pantsuit walking briskly along the road. A lone car passed. Perhaps the driver—a guard coming off night shift at the power plant—wondered where she was hurrying at that hour on a Saturday morning. Perhaps he'd seen her before— same time, same place, always hurrying.

At the end of the road she waited. Soon the bus came.

"Hey there, Bernice."

"Hiya, Frank." They traded pleasantries. The driver knew her name but not her business. She didn't discuss that. And if he wondered, he never asked. Maybe the button on her lapel gave it away: HELP, over two hands clasped together.

Since three o'clock that morning that frail, old voice had haunted her, though other calls had come. She hoped she'd handled it correctly. The rules were strict: on no account ask for names or numbers or try to give advice. Professionals gave advice, and a list of referrals was posted on the desktop. Had it been a matter for the police? She wondered. In three years she'd not once had to involve the police. People said the wildest things but didn't mean them. Letting off steam. Not this voice, though. It was different. Why hadn't the woman called back?

A beep-beep from the road sent Bernice scurrying around the house in search of her Bible. Most everything she did had its reason, even if on occasion the reason slipped her mind. This time the system worked: the Bible was under the cereal on top of the icebox to remind her to take cornflakes to church. And Rita, her girlfriend, was dropping her off in time for Sunday school. Grabbing the half-empty box, she ran out the back door.

The maroon Checker Marathon was as big inside as a small room. It had been known to transport a harpist and her harp, an entire cherub choir and a seniors' bocce team, not all together. Safely on the front seat, Bernice turned her back on her friend. "Zip me up, will you, Rita?" She was panting. The last minute running around had left her hot and breathless.

Rita obliged. Their friendship had survived thirty-some years, probably because few demands were made upon it. Though the same age, right down to the day, in other respects they were as different as rice and beans. Where Bernice was short and compact, Rita was long and stringy and stuck out— nose, hips, elbows, knees—everywhere but her bust. Here Bernice had her beat. Where Bernice was a nice shade of olive from the sun, Rita's skin tended to red and white and the sun did nothing but flake it. Her hair was mousy brown. Bernice's was streaked with gray.

Rita reversed the Checker out into the road so violently that the cornflakes fell off the seat and scattered. "Sorry," she glanced down, "but if I've said it once, I've said it a hundred times: this driveway's going to be the death of someone and I'm darned if it's going to me." The house, screened by bushes

11

and trees, stood at a bend in the road so that traffic from the left was invisible till the last moment to anyone leaving. For years there'd been talk of installing a mirror.

Bernice scooped the cornflakes back into the packet. "That's all right. They're not to eat."

If Rita wondered what they were for she didn't let on. She'd long since ceased asking her friend for explanations. Given patience, all would be revealed. Hurrying the process was fatal. She leaned forward and pulled a newspaper out of the rack below the dash. "Read that."

The page was folded back and a spot indicated in ballpoint. Bernice read: *Cranberry Township—Two sisters, both in their eighties, passed away Friday night probably within minutes of each other in what may have been a strange quirk of fate, according to police. Police said the bodies of Mercy Good and her sister, Annie Good, were found at and near the house the two had lived in for as long as anyone can remember, at 151 Gunning Point Road.*

When Sgt. Thomas Scaguiola, the responding officer, arrived, the Cranberry Township First Aid Squad was attending to the younger sister, Annie, believed to be a hit and run victim. Police said on entering the house Sgt. Scaguiola discovered the elder Good's body in a downstairs room.

Both sisters were transported to Franklin Wayland Memorial Hospital by the First Aid Squad, where they were pronounced dead on arrival, according to police.

Police said Sgt. Scaguiola is conducting an investigation into the matter.

The James C. Fenimore Funeral Home, Cranberry City, is in charge of arrangements.

Thinking it over later, Bernice was amazed she hadn't made the connection at once. There were so many parallels: the age, the dead sister, Friday night. Perhaps Rita's flood of reminiscence about Miss Annie Good, who'd taught her in Sunday school years ago, had sidetracked her. As it was, Bernice was standing on a chair in the church basement sprinkling cornflakes on a bunch of six year-old Israelites when the light in her mind clicked on. Revelations strike at the strangest times.

Rita never stayed for service. She wasn't among the faithful. Bernice got her usual ride home and dialed her friend as soon as she got in.

"It's me. You doing anything right now, Rita?"

"Not specially." She was watching baseball.

"I'm coming over."

"Right now?"

"That's what I said."

"How?" Rita had a bungalow in Carefree Days Village, an adult community on the other side of Cranberry City from Neptune Grove, where Bernice lived. A good eight miles away. "On foot?" There weren't any buses.

"I guess ..."

"You're crazy. Listen, Bernice, I'll be right over. I'll pick up a couple of franks on the way." It took forty minutes, battling the traffic that clogged the Jersey shore every summer weekend. The franks had gone and only a few gulps of iced tea remained in the thermos flask between them. "I don't know what you could have done different," Rita said.

"You don't think I should have called the police?"

Rita didn't answer. She stared into the trees. Bernice's house was a modest, one-story affair—living room, kitchen, bedroom with porches front and back. Her husband had knocked it together on his days off from Coast Guard duty. After Earl died—at sea—Bernice had had a proper basement added, and later, aluminum siding in a shade described in the catalog as Federal Gold, a sort of dirty mustard. While the house was a-building, the young couple had lived in a trailer on the site. The trailer was long gone, but its concrete pad, patched over the years, supported a rough wooden trellis over one end of which had been tacked a sheet of green fiberglass. A vine made of this a pleasant shaded arbor screened from the road by a bushy cedar hedge. Here the two friends sat, as they often did, swatting at mosquitoes. Bernice had changed into a shapeless patio dress and Rita had on sneakers and the same faded cotton blouse over baggy knee-length check pants she'd worn that morning.

"I don't know what you could have done different."

13

Bernice had described the Friday night phone call, omitting a few details like her code-name and the precise location of the HELP house, things that not even Rita knew.

"I don't know if Miss Annie and Miss Mercy ever had a phone. Somehow I don't think they did."

"Then it *was* a phone booth." She brushed off an inquisitive yellow jacket.

"Tell you what," Rita sat up. "We'll get in the cab and go on over there. Gunning Point Road. It's up Scoop Creek way. Not so far."

2

Gunning Point Road, on a hot summer afternoon, was shady, secretive. At least the block on which stood Number 151. Rita steered the Checker by the old house in a sort of review before making a U-turn at the intersection and doubling back. Even then, peering out of the passenger window, Bernice could hardly make out a house at all for the greenery. The trees enveloped it. No mailbox, just a broken-down gate in a wooden fence that leaned dejectedly against supporting shrubbery and, in places, had quite rotted away. "It looks deserted," Bernice said, fending off a worrying vision of herself, a quarter century hence, disintegrating behind her cedar hedge.

Rita jumped into the road. "It would be, wouldn't it?" The slam of the car door ricocheted like a challenge along the quiet street. Small, neat houses set back behind neat patches of lawn under solicitous trees proclaimed the inviolability of Sunday. A few flags, left from the Fourth of July, hung limply from their poles. "The original house on this road." She joined Bernice on the sidewalk. "They kept chickens in back, and two cows." She jerked her head at the tangled garden. "When her folks were alive Miss Annie milked every day. I remember her hands. Farm hands. All blistered and red. Rough on the outside, but so gentle."

"You ever meet them, her folks?"

15

"One time. Pair of real old martinets. I was terrified. Made Miss Annie and Miss Mercy stay with them to the end, as if that was their job; swear on the family Bible, it was said. They couldn't date, or go out, nothing like that. And they lived on well into their nineties."

Rita stepped through the gate and started up a narrow, untended path, pushing back the branches. Bernice followed, bent double. She smelled the decayed leaves and debris caked deep brown over the years and thought what terrific mulch it would make. Tread marks, coming and going, had recently scarred and scuffed it. The path snaked around to a side door across whose peeling, once green boards someone—the police presumably—had slapped a large, shiny padlock. The padlock was so new, such an alien presence in the soft decomposition of the place, that for a time it held their gaze. "They must have known we were coming," Bernice said, but the attempt at light-heartedness fizzled.

Above them rose the house; two storied but smaller than it seemed from the road, once white, now weather-washed to a wood gray. The door was glass-paneled, one frame out of the four cardboarded up, putty missing from the others. Standing on the step and pressing their noses against the glass, Rita and Bernice saw shelves loaded with rustic cans and bottles, old farm implements and piled up sagging boxes. "A bunch of junk," Rita turned away. A single red geranium in a pot gave a dash of color.

"See, through there; that's the barn, what's left of it." A trickle of a path led to an outdoor privy, and beyond that, through wavy grass and goldenrod, past a wizened apple tree, was a wooden barn. It sagged under a mass of green creeper. "The driveway used to exit on the land out back," Rita gestured. "They sold off the back lot, I guess, and didn't bother putting in a new drive." Shading her eyes, she peered for a while through a gap where the siding, once upright, had slipped askew. "My God, Bernice, look here!"

Bernice had been eyeing the privy, thinking of her childhood on her father's farm. She trotted over. "What?"

"After all these years. I'll be darned." Pale with dust, looking small and long-suffering, was a black Model A. Gingerly they squeezed through the crack into the barn and stood till their eyes got used to the gloom. Bernice sneezed. The place was filthy, mounds of rotting straw up one end and thick, dark cobwebs hanging from the rafters. Rita tried the car door. It opened as though the hinge had recently been oiled. Surprisingly, the inside looked fairly clean. Bernice retrieved a Twinkie wrapper and held it up for Rita to see. Cigarette butts were scattered about. They climbed aboard and sat solemnly, side by side, in the back. "Their old Ford." Rita patted the seat. "Miss Mercy had the driving license. She taught grade school for a while. More 'modern'. Miss Annie was like a servant, fetching and carrying, chopping wood, cutting grass."

Bernice saw a pair of eyes staring through the gap in the siding. She nudged Rita: a girl of nine or ten with blonde ringlets, clutching a skateboard. "Hi there," Bernice called softly. "I'll bet this is where you play. Don't mind us. We're not stopping." But the girl was gone already. "Looked like she'd seen a ghost."

"She liked young people—Miss Annie," Rita said. "And bright colors. I asked her once why she never wore bright dresses. Because her folks wouldn't want it, she said." She leaned over into the front. "I wonder if the horn works." Predictably, it didn't.

Out on the street, all was as before. The girl had vanished. "Let's walk down to the corner," Rita suggested.

A man came out of a garage uncoiling a length of hose. Rita stopped: "Hi." The man was in a swimsuit and nothing else and wouldn't have won any beauty contests. Bernice walked on a bit, to avoid embarrassment. But Rita stood her ground. It took more than a bit of bulging flesh to deflect her. "Too bad about the old ladies, going that way."

The man grunted. He was fixing a sprinkler to the end of the hose. Bernice rejoined her friend.

"Getting on, though, weren't they?" Rita persevered. "In their eighties, the paper said."

"Shoulda went into a home," the man growled. "OK, Stewart!" he shouted back at the garage.

Rita gestured, "I guess it got a bit beyond them, keeping the place up, and the garden and so on."

The sprinkler gurgled, twitched and started up full force, catching her in a shower of spray. She jumped back. The man yelled at the garage and watched as Rita wiped herself off.

"Place shoulda bin condemned years ago. Threw a blind eye at it, that's what they did. They shoulda went in and ordered them out."

"Who should have?"

"The inspectors. An eyesore. Vermin infested. Rats like dogs. You name it."

"Oh?"

"I seen one myself," the man protested, mistaking sympathy for skepticism. "No proper plumbing, no wiring, no terlits, no nothing. Kids get in there, smoke dope, booze it up, carry on, you name it." He warmed to his subject, the sprinkler whooshing ominously in the background. "All they gotta do now is get a bulldozer, put in a coupla Cape Cods, and every property on the block'd shoot right up by five, ten G, easy." He leered at his split-level as if expecting it to take a bow.

Rita watched a sallow-faced youth in his mid-teens with glasses and orange hair emerge from the garage. "What'll become of their place, I wonder?"

"In hock up to here, they were." The man indicated a point a foot above his head. "Couldn'ta held on much longer. Not through another winter. Blessing in disguise, if you ask me."

"Did you see anything?" Rita asked. "I mean, was it like the paper said?"

"Hey, Stewart, git over here," the man yelled. The orange-haired youth bounded towards them. "Stewart here got first prize for the *Star* newstip," he boasted. "Tell 'em, Stewart."

"Second prize, Dad," Stewart corrected. He turned to Rita. "They said I got first prize, then they said no, second. But I get to keep the whole ten bucks all the same, 'cause second prize is normally only like $7.50, see?"

"First next time," Bernice said encouragingly. Years ago she'd been a stringer for the *Star*, the county daily.

"Wanna see the exact spot?" The youth had all the savvy

18

of a tour guide angling for a big tip. "Bloodstain an' all?"

"Sure." They followed him down the road. The man in the swimsuit resumed his watering.

"Here." Stewart stopped a few yards short of the intersection and pointed a dirty sneaker at a patch of road near the curb. "See the chalk marks. That's the way she was layin'."

There were, indeed, faint chalk marks. They outlined something no bigger perhaps than a spilled bag of groceries. Rita blinked and swallowed, and blew vigorously into a tissue.

"See," Stewart indicated a dark spot. "What did I tell you?"

Bernice said, "Say, that's great about the newstip. So you want to be a reporter?"

"I coulda done better than whoever wrote it up, too. It would have made front page the way I'd have wrote it."

"How'd you mean?"

"Like, see, you gotta understand a couple of things, OK?"

"OK."

Stewart seemed to weigh how best to get across his point to two obviously dumb adults. "Like, see, I have the paper route around here, right?"

"Right."

"Saturday morning I'm off on my bike to the pick-up when I seen like this heap in the road, right. Then I see it's the crazy lady from the dump ..."

"The dump?" Rita interrupted.

"The dump. You know, where they lived." He jerked his thumb in the direction of Number 151. "So the first thing I do, I go call the newstip number. I never saw nobody like *dead* before," he added, suddenly a bit in awe of himself. "'cept on TV."

"You called from home?"

"Nah. Over there, see?"

Sure enough, across the road and just around the corner was a phone booth, a little glass and metal sentry box half hidden among the leaves. Bernice trotted off, leaving Rita and the astonished Stewart staring after her. This was where she called me from; the thought pommelled the walls of her brain. A yellowed page of newsprint lay on the floor of the booth. She picked it up: a page from the *Star* with a phone number laboriously ringed in pencil, as if by an arthritic hand. The HELP number. According to the date, three years old. But Bernice remembered the story. It was about the launching of HELP in Shore County. Reading it had convinced her to volunteer her one night a week. She slipped the folded page into her purse and walked back.

"When you went to call, was the phone off the hook?"

"How d'ju know?"

"We're detectives," Rita said. She'd been squatting down studying the spot in the road. "And another thing. This so-called blood: it's grease."

"Whatever," Stewart mumbled, but he had the grace to blush.

On the ride home, Bernice showed Rita the page. "It must have been right after she got off the phone. She was going back for a pencil. My Lord! If I'd only known."

"She said there was someone upstairs who was coming to get her, right, and she wasn't afraid to die?"

"The man upstairs? No, no. She meant God. She said she thought I was a Christian."

"That's what you assumed. But suppose there really was a man upstairs? A burglar, say; or—you heard what the man said about kids hanging out. Who knows?"

I wouldn't be surprised but he'll be coming for us. Any minute. Bernice heard the papery voice once more in her ear. *Who?* She'd asked, *Who'll be coming for you?* And the answer: *the man upstairs.* "Oh dear! I never thought of that."

"And another thing. When she spoke to you, Miss Mercy was alive."

"So she said."

"The police found her dead."

"What'll we do, Rita? Go back? Maybe talk some more to that man? Or Stewart? He seems like an observant sort of fellow. Maybe he noticed something."

"'The crazy lady from the dump'," Rita scoffed. "He's got quarters for eyes, that one." She hadn't taken to Stewart. "No, I'm not for going back. Not yet. We don't want to put them on their guard."

"What do you mean?"

"Fatso with the hose. He was happy enough to see the last of them."

"Rita, you're not saying …?"

"Maybe not *him*. But one of them on the block. Property values are a touchy subject."

"He said he didn't think they'd last the winter."

"Easy to say, now. Imagine," she gripped the wheel, "you're driving home. It's late. You've had a few. You see this old crone—from the dump—crossing the road, or maybe in the phone booth. Did you notice if the light worked?"

"It did."

"What the hell: you step on the gas, or wait a few seconds till she comes out. Well, she's eighty some. She doesn't stand a chance." They drove a few blocks in silence. Rita's voice softened: "I was six. She used to slip me jelly beans when the minister wasn't looking."

"Was there a church she still went to?"

"In those days she never missed a Sunday. Snowdrifts, floods, whatever. She'd be there, sometimes just her and the minister. They were Presbyterians. Miss Annie played piano. I guess she wasn't exactly Horowitz because when the new people started moving down they asked her to stop; got themselves some fancy woman. Didn't want any embarrassment, to remind them of their origins. Miss Annie never went to church again that I know of. Me neither. Later they pulled it down and amalgamated some place else." She paused. "I kept meaning to visit, but you know how it is."

Bernice said, "I wonder why she didn't make page one."

"It'd have been a natural, the sort of thing they usually eat up. Spinster sisters living like crows off cat-food; juicy quotes from the neighbors."

"With a photo of the First Aid Squad in action."

"Or the tumbledown house in the trees."

As soon as they reached Bernice's, Rita dialed the township police and asked for Scaguiola. He wasn't around. The duty officer asked what it was in reference to. Rita told him: the incident at Gunning Point Road. The man kept her on hold

21

for five minutes and came back on the line not at all the polite, pleasant-voiced individual he'd just been. "Well, what about it?" he demanded. It sounded like a challenge.

"We have information."

"We?" He wanted to know where she was calling from, her relationship, if any, with the deceased, all her particulars. Then, as if addressing a halfwit, he informed her that, as far as the police were concerned, the case was closed.

Rita made a face. "What about the hit-and-run driver? Have you booked someone on that?"

"I don't know nothing about that." She heard the rustle of papers. "It don't say nothing about that here."

"But it was in the paper."

"Oh, sure it was in the paper. So's Peanuts."

"But the investigation?"

"Like I said, ma'am, the case is closed."

Rita hung up. Angry. "Like I said, ma'am, the case is closed. It's like a big garbage truck came along and gobbled up Miss Annie and Miss Mercy and carted them away. He's lying."

"But the police are our friends." Bernice was puzzled. "They wouldn't lie."

"You call them, if you're so buddy-buddy."

"There'll be the funeral," Bernice sidestepped. "Will you be going?"

"Hell, yes. Pardon my French." Rita's hobby was funerals. They were cheaper than movies, and, she maintained, more fun. Real people, with real feelings, not some made-up trash. She'd work out whole scenarios as she sat with bowed head. More than once her Checker had been mistaken for the hearse. This time, though, it would be different. She'd be, so to speak, a member of the cast.

3

66"That's not Miss Annie," Rita hissed through clenched teeth. She was standing with Bernice up front in the chapel of the James C. Fenimore Funeral Home on Magnolia and Main in the old section of Cranberry City, the county seat. "What did they do to her?" Miss Annie and Miss Mercy lay side by side in open, plain $75 pine caskets, between bright green plastic palms. Their cheeks were rouged; their lips smeared a peppermint pink. They had fussy, tight little bluish curls. The embalmer had gone to town. "She never wore make-up in all her life."

"It's her own hair, though," Bernice whispered, trying to look on the bright side. "Cut and permed. It's not a wig."

"It's *tinted*," Rita lamented. "She had brown, crinkly skin and hairs shooting from her moles. Where are her moles? And look, they puffed out her cheeks. They got her, Bernice. They had to wait till she died, but they finally got her. She's 'modern'. She can play piano now."

"They put her in a nice pink dress," Bernice persevered. "Right in style."

"She'd have died sooner than wear a dress like that," Rita wailed, oblivious of the irony. "They've dolled her up like a whore."

Bernice feigned deafness. She gazed on the lifeless face through half-shut eyes, trying to decide what Miss Annie had

23

really looked like. She noted the long curve of the jaw, the sharp, slender nose and high cheekbones, the eyes deep set in dark pools, the turn of the mouth. Intelligent, she thought, a sense of humor too. Something there of what must have been. The back of the head, where the killing blow had come, was hidden. The sister's face was less remarkable, rounder, with a wary pinched look, even in death.

A young, scrubbed, chubby man in a shiny dark suit, who'd been talking to someone in the doorway, broke away with a few loud, parting words and hurried towards the altar end of the room, glancing at his watch. The minister, apparently. Bernice and Rita beat a retreat to where a dozen rows of folding metal chairs were set out. They sat near the back; then, when no other mourners appeared, moved up towards the front again.

The brief service included an eulogy in which the minister, who'd clearly neither met the deceased nor had the slightest interest in them, prattled for two minutes about what truly wonderful people they were.

A reading from the Scriptures, about 'coming down from God prepared as a bride adorned for her husband', made Rita growl; though Bernice, in her thoughts, managed to transcend the absurdity of the moment, a knack that at times like this stood her in good stead. "'And God shall wipe away all tears from their eyes; and there shall be no more death, neither sorrow, nor crying, neither shall there be any more pain'," intoned the minister.

"Like hell," muttered Rita.

When it was over, a scraping noise drew their attention to the back of the room: the folding doors were being opened. Four sleek, dark-suited men bounced forward in a haze of Bay Rum, their crepe soles squelching on the parquet floor. Expertly they whisked the caskets out to the waiting hearse.

The ranks of the mourners had now increased to three: on turning round, Bernice and Rita saw that they'd been joined by a little man with crew-cut gray hair and almost no chin. He had crept in quietly and perched, rather than sat, on a chair in the last row near the wall. He looked flustered and ill at ease. Though Bernice smiled in what, she hoped, was a welcoming way, he did not smile back. Outside, in the nearly empty parking lot, the two women climbed into the Checker. While Rita was maneuvering it into position to follow the hearse, the latecomer emerged and hovered uncertainly under the portico of the low, white colonial-style building. They looked at him.

"Did you ever see the marmoset in the Philly zoo?" Rita asked.

"Uh uh."

"Well you have now." The uncle of a high school friend had kept the monkey cage at the zoo and let her feed them once or twice. The marmoset looked small and wistful, she'd always given him extra. Either his mate had died, or he was a confirmed bachelor. She couldn't remember which.

"Perhaps he needs a ride," Bernice said. The man was clutching an incongruously jaunty green Tyrolean hat with a red feather tucked into the band. His well pressed, though shapeless, olive-green suit might have been carefully preserved from the Eisenhower era.

"Ask him."

Bernice slid to the tarmac, smoothed the skirt of her two-piece powder-blue polyester suit, patted her hair, and advanced on the stranger with quick, darting little steps. "Need a ride?" She saw momentary panic light in his eyes and pointed at the car. "To the cemetery. We're right over there. Or maybe you're on wheels?"

"No, no," he said. His voice nasal and on the high side. "Kind of you. Very kind." He followed her to the Checker.

"I'm Bernice, and this is my friend, Rita." The man shared the back seat with an enormous wreath of yellow and white lilies attached to which was a card: *From your friends Rita Bonney and Bernice Crickle.*

"Hi." Rita glanced round.

"Hi," said the man. And after a pause, "Otis."

"That's easy," Bernice piped up. "Like the elevator. Hey! Giving a lift to an elevator. That's funny."

"Bernice," Rita admonished. For all she knew the man was

25

in deep mourning. "Hold on, we're moving." The hearse lumbered out of the lot and turned right on Main. A limousine with the minister and the squad in black followed. The Checker brought up the rear.

Otis said, "It was cheaper not to bring the buggy, with gas the way it is." He seemed like a small package folding tidily into one corner of the back seat.

"You can say that again."

"Rita drives this thing for a living," Bernice explained.

"I noticed the omnibus plates," Otis said. "Just tell me what I owe."

"You got yourself a free ride," Rita said, "in spite of what they say." When she'd first moved to Carefree Days, Rita had started ferrying people around, mostly shopping and doctors' appointments. The small fee she charged helped make ends meet. Business had been brisk, and eventually, to keep on the right side of the law, she'd got a proper license.

"Pardon my asking, but you're not from around here, are you?" Bernice twisted round so she could look at the man. He didn't have the soft South Jersey accent with its hint of singsong, but with so many new people it was hard to tell residents from visitors any more.

"That's right." She caught the slight reluctance to answer.

"Don't mind me. I'm just a busybody."

"No no," he said quickly. "I'm from Orange."

"Hey, I had a girlfriend who married a boy from Orange!" A town about an hour and a half north, one of several that ran together like cookies in a pan, clogging the state's industrial northeast.

"Small world."

Rita glanced in the mirror. "You don't sound like a Piney." They drove at a stately pace along tree-shaded streets. "I didn't think Miss Annie and Miss Mercy had a relative left in the world," she threw out, keeping her eye on the hearse.

"Thought you might be, er, connected," Otis ventured. "Then I guess I'm it."

"Oh?" They both spoke together. Rita added, "I'm sorry."

"Well, I really didn't know them," he admitted. "The link's

kind of remote, you might say. Hadn't seen them in I don't know how many years. I'm sure you ladies were better acquainted."

Rita said, "Miss Annie taught me in Sunday school. That wasn't exactly last week."

"But you've kept in touch?" He sounded anxious.

"No, I'm ashamed to say."

"I saw them just now for the first time," Bernice put in. "But I did talk to Miss Annie on the phone. The last person to, we think."

Otis's hand jerked out and touched the wreath. "Gee, this sure is a generous thing, then. I appreciate it. Puts me to shame." Bernice was glad he hadn't asked about the call.

"More like a guilt trip," Rita said into the rear-view mirror.

"Oh, you mustn't say that," Otis chided.

The cars in front were slowing down, flashing orange turn signals. Ordinarily, Rita would have parked outside on the street, but with a bona fide relative on board she felt justified in turning in. *No Artificial Flowers*, a sign decreed. Soon the Checker was moving between the green verges of the new cemetery. 'New', though it was a generation old. The date on the gate was 1959. Bernice looked out at the neat plots, some flying miniature flags, some with vases of cut flowers, some with thermos flasks. "Rita, when my time comes, will you put something out for me?" She was only half in jest.

"Listen kid, we have the same birthday. We'll probably have the same death day. Like Miss Annie and Miss Mercy."

"Perhaps some kind soul will take pity on us."

A voice came from the back: "If I'm still around, I'd be glad to." They looked back and saw he meant it. "But I'm older, so the odds are against it."

"Not that much older," protested Bernice.

"Oh sure. I'm retired. This year."

"I'd never have guessed," she said gallantly.

The caskets were lowered side by side into the ground, and Rita and Bernice, with Otis helping, laid the yellow and white lilies on the grass where the headstone would go. Then doors

27

slammed, motors revved and the little procession moved off.

"Can we take you any place?" Rita offered, glancing back to where Otis was again sitting.

"Anywhere downtown, if you're headed that way."

"Perhaps we'll be seeing you this way more often," Rita said, "or will the house come on the market?"

"The house?" Otis seemed at sea. "Oh, *their* house. No, I guess the bank owns that. The bank gets everything. Paid for the funeral, too. I'm lucky if I'm not stuck with debts. They were mortgaged over their heads. Hadn't paid taxes in I don't know how long. It's a wonder they weren't foreclosed."

So the man in the swimsuit was right, thought Rita.

"Poor old things," said Bernice. "I know I shouldn't say this, but when you get right down to it, going can be a merciful release."

"You really think so?" Otis sat forward on the seat. He seemed pathetically eager. "You mentioned you'd spoken to Annie Good on the phone. When was it? Recently?"

"That same night, the night she went."

"What did she say? How did she sound?"

"She sounded," Bernice paused, "upset."

"Upset? What about? Did she say?"

"Her sister was very sick. She called a service where I work. She had death on her mind, said she wasn't afraid of it. I thought she wanted a doctor for her sister. She went to get a pencil to write the number down and never came back. It was a pay phone. I'd no idea ..." She looked at Rita, unsure about passing on what was really only guesswork.

Rita said, "But now we think there's more to it."

"Did you contact the police?" Otis asked.

"We tried to."

"They laughed," Rita said.

"Goddammit, I was right." He slapped his thigh.

"About what?" The sudden vehemence surprised Rita.

"They're in on it."

"Who?"

"The cops."

Rita pounced: "What's going on?"

Otis looked out the window. "They're after me, too." They stopped at a light. "This'll do." He opened the door. "Thanks. I mean it. It's messy. You don't want to get involved."

A car coming up on the outside screeched and swerved, narrowly missing the open door. The driver honked angrily. The door slammed, the light changed, the cars behind hooted. The Checker jerked forward. When Rita and Bernice looked back, Otis had vanished.

'What did he say his name was?" Rita asked when she calmed down.

"Otis, like the elevator."

"Otis *what*?"

"He never said. Otis from Orange."

"Otis from Orange," Rita repeated, and turned sharp right off Main.

"What are we going to do?"

"Find him," Rita snapped. "What else?" She took the next right, and the next, and emerged again on Main. The man was nowhere in sight. People walked this way and that, the office crowd going back to work.

"Bernice, check out Josey's. He might have gone in there."

While Rita waited, Bernice went in. She asked the waitress if a small man in a green suit had been around, perhaps to use the men's room. "The one that got away, huh? Sorry Bernice. Better luck next time."

"We were just at a funeral."

"I know, I know," the woman commiserated. "Grab 'em where you can at our age, right? Take 'em right out of the grave."

But Bernice had already left. "Listen, Rita, I'm late. Got to get back to work."

"Get in, I'll take you. No charge. Think I'll hang out by the bus station. You never know."

Otis did not show up at the bus station. Later that afternoon a customer—Rita preferred the term to fare—found a jaunty green hat on the floor among some white and yellow petals.

4

A car drove slowly by the cemetery, and a little while later drove by again. The man at the wheel craned his neck to see over the low stone wall. A maroon Checker was pulled up on the verge just outside the gate. The man looked at it with interest and drove on.

Rita didn't see the man. She had found what she was looking for and was on her knees by a gravestone, scribbling on the back of an envelope: *In Memory of Joseph Gaines Good 1864 – 1959 and Charlotte Phinney Good 1867 – 1959 beloved parents of Mercy 1896 – and Annie 1899 –* When she finished, she walked back to her car.

At the first phone booth she came to she stopped and made a call. And came away smiling. Thanks to her Uncle Sudeley who, many years ago, had engaged her at a nickel a stone to copy cemetery inscriptions, her morning's work had paid off. 'Logging graves', he'd called it.

By six that evening, Rita and Bernice were driving north, towards Orange. Since Ma Bell showed no listing for an Otis Good in the Orange area, Rita had set about finding the full names of the sisters' parents. She worked out the year they'd died, as near as she could, and started to and fro among the stones in the newer section of the 'old' cemetery. It didn't take long. An Otis *Phinney* was listed in Orange. The operator, asked nicely, had even supplied an address.

The house, when they found it, was a box-like brick and clapboard structure, two stories with a garage in back and a patch of concrete out front on which were set some wooden tubs containing shrubs. The shrubs had recently been watered: wet smears stained the concrete and trailed towards the gutter. Rita parked the Checker at the end of the block.

"We should have called ahead," Bernice worried. They were walking back up the street.

Rita pooh-poohed her. "Surprise is the whole idea. Remember how nervous he was? Believe me, this is the best way."

"It's me who's nervous." Bernice's shoes went click-clack down the sidewalk. "Stop a minute, Rita. Is my hair OK?" Rita had picked her up at the bank where she worked and she was still in her red, white and blue dress with the HELP button pinned to the scarf.

"Now listen, will you relax. I'm beginning to think you're sweet on the guy."

"He's kind of cuddly."

"I wouldn't trade a teddy bear for him, I'll tell you that right now."

"He'd make a good teddy bear."

"He's not a teddy bear, he's a marmoset." Rita pressed the bell. Once, twice, three times. They heard it chime 'Jingle Bells' over and over. But no approaching footsteps.

Bernice stood back. The drapes on all the windows were closed, though it was still light out. She half expected a face to appear. A white cat clung to the brickwork beside the jutting green and white striped door canopy. Plastic. "I bet he has a real one."

"All closed up," Rita said. "Looks like they're away. And yet …" She surveyed the watered plants.

"They? You think he's married?"

A concrete walkway hugged the side of the house. Next to it a low, slatted fence, then the house next door. "Let's try the back." Rita started down the path.

They had no luck there, either: a good-sized sassafras tree, its bark thick and gouged, a clump of purple Rose of Sharon, some garden furniture and a brick barbecue pit full of ashes.

Weeds were growing through the ashes. A high cinderblock wall backed onto the property, behind it a service station, perhaps, or a supermarket.

Bernice was the first to notice they were being watched. She nudged Rita, and the window of the adjacent house shot up with a clatter.

"Looking for something?"

"Someone," Rita said. They approached the fence. "Mr. Phinney. He doesn't seem to be home."

"He expecting you?" A woman, middle-aged with guarded, disappointed eyes and dyed blonde hair. The dye was wearing off around the roots.

"Not exactly. We met him yesterday, at a funeral. He left this." As Rita spoke, Bernice held up the green hat.

The woman eyed it curiously. "Funeral, eh?" Clearly she wasn't buying that. Behind her a man's voice shouted something. The woman turned and spoke into the room, then looked back. "At a *funeral*?"

"That's what I said."

Again, the man's voice. Evidently a joke. The woman cackled. "Where was this funeral?"

"Down Shore County way."

A renewed outburst followed this information, then a long altercation with the invisible man. Rita and Bernice seemed forgotten.

"Let's get out of here," Rita said. They walked back to the street.

"What was so funny?"

"Like Asbury Park, this place, where every fourth person is a mental case."

Bernice opened the mailbox and peered in. "Empty." Rita banged on the front door.

"You looking for Mr. Phinney?" A small, clear voice startled them. A little girl astride a bicycle stood watching in the road.

"Oh, you know him?"

"He's gone away. I'm s'posed to water his garden." She pointed at the tubs.

"Good girl," Bernice said. "I guess we just missed him."

"He's been gone," the girl counted on her fingers, "a week, I think."

"Where'd he go?" Rita asked.

"Dunno," the girl shrugged.

"When'll he be back?"

"I hope he ain't never coming back." She giggled. "I get a dime every day, for the garden."

"No idea?" Rita pressed.

The girl thought a bit. "On Christmas!" She added, "'Cos of he's Santa Claus."

"That's cute," Bernice smiled.

"What makes you think that?"

"'Cos of when you write Santa Claus it goes there." She pointed at the house. "My Mom says so."

"Is your Mom home?" Rita asked. Since the girl was black, she assumed it wasn't the woman at the window. The girl nodded and sped off, wheeling into a driveway two houses away. Bernice and Rita followed. A pleasant-faced young woman came out on the porch to meet them.

Bernice said, "We're looking for Santa Claus."

"Now what's Carmella been tellin' you?" She laughed nervously. A baby clung to one of her legs, its mouth a bright orange from something inside that was dribbling out. "About Mr. Phinney, is it?"

"Carmella said he left a week ago."

"Let me see now. Today's Wednesday. He left on a Friday, I believe. That'll be two weeks ago this coming Friday."

"Will he be back soon?"

"Expect me when you see me. That's what he said. He was kinda lookin' forward just to takin' off, you know. That's what I think. Not having to rush back to work Monday morning." She smiled wistfully. "That'll be the day."

"What about the cat?" Bernice asked. "Doesn't he have a cat?"

"It got run over."

"Where'd he go?" Rita persisted. Bernice was making gurgling noises at the baby.

33

"Overseas. One of them cruises, you know. I hope it's not urgent. There was two men, a couple of days ago, come lookin' for him. Said it was urgent."

Carmella had emerged from the house and was monopolizing her mother's other leg. She'd come over shy. "He's c'lecting presents. For me."

"Now you just stop that and stand up straight, you hear me, girl?" The woman cuffed her smartly and she ran off through the screen door bawling. "Round Christmastime they get a bunch of letters addressed to a certain person," she explained. "Well, he'd take it on hisself to answer them."

"That's wonderful."

"On his own time, mind you," she added. "I guess maybe he misses not having kids of his own. He's great with Carmella. Has her eating out of his hand."

"So he's not married?"

She looked surprised. "If he was it was a ways back. Tell the truth, we don't know him that well, my husband and me. Just to say hi, really. We only moved in here a couple of years ago."

"Those two men who came," Rita said, "what was that about?"

"Could have been from the club," the woman ventured. "He's round there a lot of the time. They'd know something, maybe."

"The club?"

"The Lodge. That's what he calls it. It's not far." She gave directions. "I'm real sorry I can't help more."

As they walked to the car, Rita said, "Jeez, maybe the guy is Santa Claus. Seems he can be in more than one place at a time." She looked at the little green hat, then tossed it into the back seat. "Yeah, kind of odd—for a funeral."

The Lodge, at first blush, looked imposing. It stood back from the road behind a sweeping drive and a bit of lawn boasting a flagpole and—on a concrete pedestal—a bronze stag. The green from the bronze had run down the concrete and streaked the words IN MEMORIAM and the list of names engraved there. A wooden sign nearby proclaimed:

BINGO Every Friday Nite 7:45 $1,000 in Prizes.

Rita parked on the road near a fire hydrant painted in a stars and stripes motif. Cars and trucks were crowded into the driveway and the lot behind looked full. The building—two stories in red brick—was dominated by its porch. High, white and classical, its pillars reached to the roof. The downstairs windows were of stained glass set with little shields, almost like a chapel. Upstairs they were curtained. The place had a closed look, of not giving anything away. She noted a couple of blue and white jeeps marked U.S. Mail. Otis, she gathered, had worked for the Post Office; the dead letter department, by the sound of it. She'd had an uncle in Philadelphia in the dead letter department.

Rita rang the bell. After a minute or two she suggested they try the back. Bernice recalled her Uncle Vern, a Mason, demonstrating their special knock. Knock-knock, was it? Knock – knock – knock? Suddenly the door opened, expelling the murky stench of cigar.

A pair of thick lips curled around a stub of dank tobacco held their gaze. The face in which the lips were set appeared a mask of waxy yellow build-up through which stubble had managed to force its way. The eyes, squeezed almost shut by swollen cheeks, nevertheless conveyed alarm and hostility. The sight of two women, one with bare scraggly legs, the other with a cherub-like expression of innocence, clearly did not delight this Janus. For a while nobody spoke. Perhaps the man thought that by glaring long enough he could drive them away.

The man's shirt and pants were grimy, as if he'd slept in them for weeks. "You can't come in," he warned in an incongruously squeaky, almost hysterical voice.

"We don't want in," Rita reassured. "We're looking for someone." She added: "It's an emergency."

"Wait right there," he ordered, trying to push the door to. Only Rita's foot was in the way. Fixing her with a malevolent scowl, he waddled off.

With her foot Rita discreetly enlarged the gap and stepped inside. Bernice followed. The hall was cool, paneled in dark wood. From far away came the blur of male voices, with now and then laughter and the clack-clack of a pool game in progress. Bar sounds, Rita thought.

"How can I help you?" A small, bird-like man with snow-white hair came bustling towards them. He had an air of authority about him.

"We're looking for an Otis Phinney."

"An Otis Phinney," he repeated, as if it was a species of rare fauna. He spoke with a gentlemanly drawl and his suit looked well cut. Someone to reckon with, Rita guessed. He too had a cigar, but it was long and fresh and held in his hand. "Phinney's not here, ma'am."

"Where is he?"

"On a cruise."

"He was in Cranberry City yesterday," Bernice piped up. "At a funeral."

The man looked at her with interest. "Impossible."

"Maybe he didn't leave yet."

"He left."

"When?" Rita asked.

"A week, two weeks ... One minute." He disappeared into the gloom. Rita and Bernice looked at each other. When the man returned, he was holding something besides his cigar. A postcard. "See the date on that?" He held it up to the light.

The card was stuck through with a thumbtack, its postmark partially obscured. *CRISTOBAL ... JUL 7 PM ... PAQUE-BOT ...* they made out.

"Phinney was on this boat at Cristobal at least a week ago. Go ahead. Read it," he encouraged, though he held on firmly.

Rakes Progress #1, they read. *Dear Soaks, Boarded the Stella Princess at 3pm 7/1 and due to mechanical problems remained in beautiful downtown Port Newark till 8:45 am 7/2. Once on our way we picked up to 21,5 knots. Made the Windward Passage at 7 last night. Very congenial group of passengers: six of each sex. This is a big ship—over 800 feet, and 90+ foot beam. Due to size we will transit canal during daylight. Stay tuned. O.*

"Canal?" Rita asked. "What canal?"

"Not your Delaware & Raritan," the man said primly. With a hand on the door, he was slowly squeezing them out.

"The Panama?" suggested Bernice.

The man smiled, "Top of the class."

"So where's he headed?" Rita sounded a little desperate.

"Australia. By freighter. Should be a while before we see Phinney again—in this hemisphere." The door closed firmly on his frozen smile.

Back in the Checker, Bernice said, "If they thought he was on a cruise, why come looking for him at home? Urgent, she said it was."

"See what I mean about Asbury Park."

"Maybe it wasn't them. Maybe it was about the funeral."

"And he just flew in from Panama?"

They looked at each other and began to laugh.

5

Loraine, canine beautician, graduate New Jersey School of Poodle Grooming. 8 x 10 signed glossy of Henry Kissinger, collectible, $25. Bernice's eyes flickered across the A&P Good Neighbor Free Message Board. Aha! There it was: *Kerry 13½ can babysit, cut grass, walk dogs, house sit, shop, wash windows, read for the blind, almost anything. Reasonable rates.* She'd noticed it the other day. Kerry 13½ might be the answer to prayer. Wanted: some person small enough for breaking and entering. She jotted down the number and followed her groceries through the automatic door.

To Bernice Crickle, the shopping mall on Jasper Avenue, a fifteen-minute walk from her home down Bay Road, was still something of a marvel. Long since eclipsed by bigger, flashier malls, it had been the forerunner, the harbinger of the new way of life. And Bernice could not forget that, even now when its glory had faded. She remembered when Jasper Avenue had been little more than a cart track crisscrossed by Indian trails and her uncles had farmed the land around it. Her grandpa's generation had felled the oaks to build the Methodist Church. Used as a theater in the sixties, boarded up for a decade, stripped of pews, windows and anything else of value, it stoically awaited its metamorphosis—to a Mr. Fish concession, it was rumored. In the cemetery back of the church and the annex across the avenue stood the headstones of generations of related Crickles, Barnstaples and Perts, solid English stock going back three hundred years on this land.

At one time, it seemed to Bernice, you could count the surnames of the fishing and farming families, the clammers and cranberry pickers that peopled Neptune Grove in Cranberry Township in Shore County, on the fingers of one hand. Not any more. In the thirties the summer people started filtering down from the cities to the north. By the fifties they were building year-round homes and smooth new roads. In the sixties, the floodgates opened; retirement became an industry.

Up and down the shore mosquitoes and realtors grew fat and multiplied on the infusion of new blood. Jasper Avenue became a six-lane neon, tinsel and bunting bordered highway. Hadn't her father always said never to lay at the road end of a cemetery?

As far as Bernice was concerned, life now was more fun than in the old days. No more the long, infrequent haul into Cranberry City. Farm life had its points, chiefly the memory. Running barefoot up from the bay through the woods with a bucket of crabs; watching the deer steal down at dawn to drink; walking home through the fields at night when it was so dark the lightning bugs hung like lanterns; sponge baths in the kitchen tub; her mother pulling down from a goose helpless between her knees.

Kerry 13½, slim-hipped, in an old pair of jeans and a T-shirt that said, 'I am mechanically minded', inserted herself through the missing pane in the back door of Number 151. Bernice passed through her flashlight, and after a few anxious minutes and some banging and scraping, the front door creaked open and Bernice joined her inside.

Kerry had agreed to $2 an hour, her usual charge, she said, for 'whatever'. It had sounded reasonable to Bernice who made four times as much and was nearly four times as old. They had met at a back stall at Josey's over lunch hour and Bernice had liked what she saw: a slight, freckled girl, flat-chested still, with ginger hair tied back behind her ears, which stuck out. Not a child you could hide much from—one look into her pale green serious eyes told Bernice that—but reliable. Bernice had signed her up and sworn her to secrecy.

The first thing that struck Bernice about the inside of the house was the cold, a clammy chill after the warm July evening, redolent of bats. The next thing was the mess. Someone, she thought, had beaten them to it; had rushed around the room hurling its contents about in a mad search for something, perhaps the same thing she was after. But a closer look changed her mind. No sudden upheaval had taken place, rather a slow accumulation under layers of dust. They were in what must have been the parlor, along with a whole flea market's worth of Victoriana; a mahogany sideboard, chairs backed in velveteen, a table with thick, ornate legs. The beam of her flashlight picked out the glassy eyes of a stuffed owl leaning in its bell jar at a drunken angle. In places the ceiling sagged, and the walls, once rosy red, were stained and streaked and peeling. Sheets of plastic, yellowed and torn, were tacked over the windows, and in one corner a creamy fungus had taken hold. Bernice searched out the stairs and made her way towards them, warning Kerry to watch where she trod: some of the floorboards had rotted. She sensed the child's awe.

"Wait right there while I go up. Don't move." She probed each step, expecting it to give. Upstairs, in total contrast, was hot. Paint flakes covered the floor like white petals, reflecting light from an unshaded window. Suffocating summer nights in her attic room at the farmhouse came to mind, and drenched sheets, an annual ordeal from which only marriage had rescued her. She looked up at the window—leaves, nothing but leaves—and half listened for the beep-beep-beep, which would be Rita's warning signal. But all she heard was the slow drag of a branch against the roof and the drowsy buzz of a fly. Rita, parked across the road, was pretending to read the paper. One car had passed where the man at the wheel peered first at her, then at the house, but he hadn't stopped or even slowed down. Nothing suspicious.

Bernice tried each door leading off the landing. Two were locked, though behind one she thought she heard something.

Mice, maybe. The third door opened, but the room was bare; just an iron bedstead and a chamber pot, positioned long ago perhaps to catch a drip, and the same white carpet of plaster and paint. Back downstairs, in the kitchen, she found signs of habitation. A black iron stove dominated the room. Bits and pieces of wood, some hacked from chairs, lay around. Too poor for coal, she thought. On a shelf a large, black clock, flanked by mythical tiger-like beasts, no longer ticked. Next to the stove a bed had been set up, and here, Bernice guessed, Miss Mercy's body was found. She saw where she had lain among worn-out coverlets. One had slipped to the floor. She picked it up, downy soft to the touch, laced with cat hair.

Miss Annie would have slept on the low folding cot alongside. For bathing, a tin tub must have done, filled by kettle from the stove. On a table draped with an oilcloth stood an oil lamp, its funnel gray from smoke. Bernice hadn't seen one like it in years. No sign of electricity; this had been their sole illumination. As for food, scarcely a trace of that either. A half-empty bag of meal, running with weevils, some shriveled carrots, and in one cupboard a score or more of rusty-topped quart jars of home-bottled fruit and pickles, brown with age. The nearest, neatly labeled 'raspberries 52', held a dark sediment under a pale fluid. She searched for keys to the back door and the rooms upstairs, and found none.

Kerry kept quiet, taking it all in, and Bernice as she poked around thought of the voice on the phone and felt sad to be seeing them in their shame, so to speak, as if she was violating a trust. Wouldn't it be better just to leave? Then anger shot through her like an electric charge, the anger she'd felt before, a raw sort of feeling from which, she knew, little good could come. But she didn't care. A person needed defiance in their life once in a while.

She laughed when she found it, because her mother would have had the same idea. And knew what it was, even before unwinding the frail black shawl: a Bible. Not just a Bible, The Family Bible. In the bottom drawer of the 'milk cupboard', way at the back, deep and cool, where her mother stored the milk she used to sell. She held the large, heavy book expectantly for a moment, then raised the scarred cover. Just as she'd hoped, just like she remembered: a hodgepodge of names and dates and notations painstakingly inscribed on the flyleaf in several hands and shades of ink. Had Mercy and Annie really sworn on it never to leave their parents, she wondered, and smiled thinking of the unfinished inscription Rita had found, and the graves intended for them but forgotten. An envelope slipped out and Kerry picked it up. Registered mail, typed address: Miss Mercy Good, Miss Annie Good, 151 Gunning Point Road, Scoop Creek, Cranberry City, NJ. Date stamp recent. Bernice stuck it back between the pages. Before leaving she showed Kerry how to prime the pump in the scullery and they watered the geranium. The shrill of crickets serenaded them all the way to the car.

Kerry lived in Cranberry City South, 'across the tracks', as people used to say. Bernice counted out what was owed. "We didn't keep you out too long, did we?"

"Longer the better." Kerry opened the door reluctantly. They were all three sitting up front. She added quickly, "It's not the money. I'd even do it for free. Will you be needing me again?"

A car that had been behind them passed, vanishing round a curve up ahead. One of the taillights was out, Bernice noticed. "Sure, we have to return it. It's just on loan, remember? Now run along. They'll be wondering where you got to."

"More likely didn't notice me gone." She slipped away into the shadows behind her house.

"That didn't sound so good," Rita commented.

"Good kid, though," said Bernice.

"Pity, teaching her bad habits."

"I said it was just on loan."

"I found him," Rita shouted. "I found Otis!" She'd been poring over the family tree with a magnifying glass.

Bernice ran out of her kitchen, wiping her hands. She was fixing corn beef hash, one of her staples: a can of beef, a bag of frozen hash browns and a chopped onion tossed together with an egg. She hated cooking. Leaning over she tried to follow as Rita adjusted the lamp and pointed here and there among the maze of squiggly lines.

"We start here, see, with Joseph Vannover Good, died 1867, and his wife, Hettie Bird Good, died 1885."

"OK."

"They had seven children, as far as I can see. Seven that lived, anyway." She picked off seven names with a knitting needle. "But the one we're interested in is this fellow here, see. Amos. Amos Good." The needle beat a little tattoo, and Bernice bent closer over the page.

"The eldest?"

"Right. Born 1837, died-rather young-1866, the year before his father. His first wife died in 1860, and he married the second, Ella Louise Gaines," tap tap tap, "in 1861."

"What was that?" Bernice straightened up.

"This?" Rita tapped.

"Uh uh. The back porch. There's a squeaky patch. I'll turn the outside light on." She went out to the kitchen, flicked a switch, poked at the hash, and came back.

"Vandals," Rita shook her head. "They're all over. Did you see where they let out the Strickner Dam last week and flooded Route 18? I could have drowned."

"That house kind of spooked me, I guess."

"Nice place for a Halloween party."

"Go on. The second wife."

Rita found her place. "Ella Louise Gaines. It doesn't say when she died. They had one daughter, Bertha, and one son," tap tap tap, "Joseph Gaines Good, born 1864. In 1895, he married Charlotte Phinney," tap tap, "parents of Mercy and Annie. They lived to a ripe old age and both died the same year, 1959. Probably in our Halloween house." Tap tap. "Now this is where Otis comes in. It's kind of strange."

"I'm sorry," Bernice said loudly. "Can you stop with the tapping. I keep thinking someone's at the window."

"You OK?"

"Don't mind me."

"Maybe it's them, come for their Bible."

"Who, Rita?"

43

She waved a hand over the page. "All this lot."

"It's not funny."

Rita put down the needle. "Charlotte Phinney had a brother, see, Bart. Over here. Bart married Bertha Good. Brother and sister married sister and brother. They had a son, see, Otis's father, born 1897, died ... I don't see a date. Here's Otis, only child, born 1915. Our Otis."

"So like he said, he could be the only living relative?"

"The closest. I suppose there'd be others if we traced all of Amos Good's brothers and sisters."

Bernice sat down. "I keep thinking they've caught him."

"They?"

"Whomever he's running from."

Rita scrutinized the page. "If we've got to return this, I think I'll take it home and make a copy."

"We must."

"Then the spirits will come with me."

"What about this?" Bernice smoothed out the letter. "'Curtsey, dower and after acquired interests?'" She passed it to Rita.

"Legal gobbledygook. From some lawyer in Freehold. They're supposed to sign and send it back. Then they get three hundred bucks."

"They could have used three hundred bucks."

Rita read aloud: "'all the interests they may now have, if any, in the said property, in which Joseph Vannover Good, or his wife, Hettie Bird Good, may have had an interest of record at the time of their deaths, situate, lying and being in the Township of Cranberry, in the County of Shore and State of New Jersey, including any interests in the below described parcel of old bog swamp and meadow shown on the Cranberry Township tax map as one thousand, two hundred and thirty five and one quarter acres.' And so on and so forth. I wonder if Otis got one of these?"

"Should we go on up to Freehold, do you think? See the lawyer?"

"Before we go charging off any place," Rita said, "I wonder if maybe my Uncle Sudeley ..."

"What?"

"Expert advice. You know lawyers. We don't want to immolate ourselves like a couple of dumb moths on a bug zapper. Talking of which ..."

A smell of burning had been building steadily. Bernice scampered into the kitchen head down like a linebacker facing an intercept. Rita heard low moans and pan banging. She gathered up the Bible and the letter, re-wrapped them in the shawl, and shouted, "Bernice, check with you tomorrow."

"It's OK, some of it." Bernice ran back, but Rita's hand was on the door. "I can fix us some eggs." She didn't want to be left alone.

"I'm fine, Bernice. Honest."

Bernice walked her to the Checker. It was a clear, soft night and she stood for a minute after Rita left, drinking in the smell of honeysuckle and locust. A car passed. Its single red rear light disappeared in the direction Rita had gone.

When Rita got home her phone was ringing.

"Thank goodness!" It was Bernice. "You're home."

"Where else would I be?"

"I called already a couple of times."

"I stopped by the clubhouse to make those copies. What's the matter?"

"Nothing."

"You sure you're OK?"

"Sure. Take care now."

"You too." Rita hung up.

It was a little while before Bernice went to bed, and even then her mind kept working. The upstairs room, the man upstairs; was it mice, or? She got up, found the phone and started to dial. No, it could wait till morning.

6

Stewart was walking on air. He couldn't believe he'd done it. Won first prize in the *Star* newstip contest less than a week after coming in second. True, they hadn't run the story the way he'd written it. But still, there it was, with a picture—not his, but they'd have never got it without him—and, most exciting of all, his name. Stewart Krabbowicz. On page one.

Now that he'd finished his paper route he paused at the side of the road, legs astride his bicycle, and gazed narcissistically at the headline. *DEATH HOUSE IN MYSTERY BLAZE.* Not up to his headline, FIREWORKS ON GUNNING POINT ROAD, but not bad. It was still early morning. The few commuters in their passing cars stared stonily at points six inches beyond their noses, unaware of their proximity to greatness. Perhaps they too had been up half the night watching the flames, fearful they might spread.

All around him on the road was the evidence. His father's gouged front lawn where a thousand-gallon pumper had backed up to turn (three volunteer fire trucks had answered the call); the leaves and branches, wet still and trampled, spilling over the crumpled fence into the road; the woody, strangely pleasant burning smell; and central to it all, the hacked out cavity where the house had stood: a green and black morass from which, here and there, swirls of gray smoke still plumed. Like a war movie, Stewart thought, regretting he'd not played up that aspect in his copy. *Apocalypse Now, now.* For the firefighters had literally hacked their way though a jungle to get at the blaze, felling trees and trampling undergrowth.

The house was leveled. There'd been no real attempt to save it. The barn, miraculously, was still there. Stewart, with a journalist's instinct, had hung about near the fire chief and picked up the radio traffic. The talk was of containment, isolation; the place was coming down anyhow. At first, before the trucks came, it seemed like giant lightning bugs were cavorting in and out among the trees. The crackling and hissing suggested something chained, or caged, getting madder and madder. Then as the first truck roared up the street, flames and sparks in a great bound reached above the tree level and set the watchers stumbling back, calling to their kids to "for chrissakes get outta here". The night was filled with flying gray particles, like moths' wings.

"It wouldn't surprise me if he set it himself. For a lousy ten bucks." Rita was driving south.

Bernice, beside her, also was thinking of Stewart. "No," she said, "he wouldn't." And she was right. Stewart had been upstairs in his room with his earphones on listening to Billy Joel, with the window open. He'd smelled something, gone out to investigate, rushed back and called the police, just like it said in the paper. Except that, first of all, he'd called the *Star.* First things first. Years back, when Bernice was a stringer and a neighboring farmhouse went up, she'd been so busy helping douse the flames she forgot to file the story. It was after that they let her go. Stewart reacted like a pro.

"Vandals, just like I said," Rita sighed. "Everything these days is vandals."

"Just the two of them lived there, right?" Bernice needed reassurance. The thought that behind that upstairs door someone had met a fiery end kept butting in.

"There's always spontaneous combustion. All those needles. It's been awful hot."

"Well it sure wasn't electrical, like it suggests here," Bernice thumped the paper. "They weren't hooked up."

It occurred to them both, though neither voiced it, that the fire, coming so soon after their own visit, might somehow be laid to them. Stewart's eagle eye, for instance, might have spotted the Checker. But apparently it hadn't. Or surely they'd have heard.

The Garden State Parkway followed the coast, but inland a few miles. After half an hour Rita turned off the landscaped six-lane highway and headed inland on a much smaller road. "I hope he's still alive."

Bernice looked to see if she was kidding. Her friend, at times, had a very deadpan sense of humor. "You ever *meet* Uncle Sudeley? Sewerage Authority. Surveys. Stuff like that. Worked for the township all his life, so he knows his way around." There'd been no way to warn him of their coming.

The road ran fairly straight through flat, sandy country. Scrub pines and cedar, three and four feet high, dotted the landscape as they headed into the Pine Barrens, a vast tract of bog and pineland. Up ahead a car's headlights flashed, then another's and another's. It was just after six, still fully light.

"Darn," said Rita. "We're too late."

"Not him, surely?"

"Who else lives out this way? It's protected land."

The cortege—sleek, black sedans, churning the dust—hurtled towards them along the narrow road, led by a police escort. Responding to a warning beep, Rita slowed down and pulled over as far as she could.

"The Governor!" Bernice swiveled in her seat. "That's the state flag."

"What was the other one?" The lead car flew a flag from each front fender. Two men reclined importantly in the back.

"You got me." They looked wonderingly at each other. "Seems like Uncle Sudeley's had company."

"Oh, sure," Rita scoffed. It seemed an unlikely spot to meet the Governor.

A few miles further on they bumped off the road down a rutted track. "This was a weekend place he had," Rita volunteered. "Partly, I suspect, to get away from Aunt Sadie, who

48

hated the country with a passion. After she died and he retired he moved down for good. Now the state's trying to get him out because it's a wilderness area where nobody's supposed to live. Uncle Sudeley's fighting them every inch of the way. He needs to have at least one good fight going or he'd drop dead. But the state doesn't know that."

The Checker lurched to a halt at the entrance to a small clearing. The only sign of life was a brown hen, which had hopped onto the chassis of a derelict vehicle and was watching them, its head cocked at a questioning angle. At the end of the clearing sat a trailer. Fifties vintage with frilly lace curtains in the window and steps out the back. Beside it was a wooden shack with a complicated-looking antenna attached to the chimney. It was very quiet in the clearing.

Rita peered in the windows while Bernice eyed the old chassis which, fenced in with chicken wire, was doing duty as a henhouse. She pulled the heads off a spray of tiny white flowers that were growing through the wire, and squeezed them so they foamed. "Soap weed. Look."

Just then, close by, two shots rang out in rapid succession, followed by the roar of an engine being furiously gunned. A minute later a battered Rambler edged past the Checker. From the sound, it should have been touching sixty. Its actual speed was more like three. Contrastingly, the man who jumped from behind the wheel and trotted towards them radiated energy.

"Wild dogs," he announced from several yards off, as if picking up the thread of an interrupted discourse. "Goddam so-called pet lovers. Come out from Philly, "'Lantic City, let 'em loose here. Took all my hens bar one."

"Get any?" Rita eyed the gun Uncle Sudeley was waving.

"Not a one. They get wise, fast." Their visit didn't seem to surprise him.

"This is Bernice, Uncle Sudeley. Crickle."

"Crickle, Crickle." He scratched his head. "Knew a Samuel F. Crickle sat behind me in class at Cranberry High. Some darn debater. 'Cackle' we used to call him. KIA D-Day in forty-four. Nice fellow." He shook his head.

"We're all related," Bernice said. She could see that Uncle

Sudeley was nobody's fool. The Governor had his work cut out. Behind a smudged pair of glasses, one side of which seemed held together with Band Aids, bright eyes gleamed. High cheekbones suggested the Indian blood she knew ran in Rita's family. A flattish oval face, flecked with white stubble, gave him an owlish cast. His hair, still more black than gray, stood up in patches. The collar of his shirt was tucked under, baring his neck, and here his age showed in the flaccid texture of the skin, like a turkey's gill.

"Passed the Governor and a fleet of limos heading real fast out of the Pines. We thought perhaps you'd had company."

"Lucky for him, no." Uncle Sudeley shook his gun in the rough direction of Trenton, the state capital. "Magpies, the lot of them." He was about to spit, but reconsidered.

"We stopped by for some free advice," Rita began.

"Most everything I eat these days is canned," he looked worried. "Can't live on teaberries and skunk cabbage like Indians. 'Course, if you don't mind pancakes and molasses ..."

"We're not stopping," Rita put in. "We just want to pick your brains." She didn't relish driving back after dark.

He looked relieved: "Pick away."

"It's about some land," Rita said, baiting the hook. Uncle Sudeley's nickname was 'Snoop'. He was what, in the business, they termed a 'land snooper', someone who ferrets out the title to a parcel of land that's in doubt or unrecorded. Had it down to a fine art. Everybody called him Snoop.

"You can't eat land," he cautioned. "But land can sure eat you." They were walking towards the cabin, the door of which Uncle Sudeley now flung open. "This in here's all land." He gave the final word a sort of verbal caress.

The women peered past him. Apart from a desk and chair, an armchair, a television under a dustsheet, and a lamp still in its clear plastic wrap from the store, the room was a clutter of boxes and cabinets with papers pinned up and strewn around in heaps and rolls.

Uncle Sudeley transferred books and papers from one pile to another, blew ineffectually at the dust, and waved his visitors to seats still loaded with files and clippings. Rita produced the letter. Holding it just beyond the tip of his nose in the light from the window, grunting and growling, he moved it back and forth so that it occurred to Bernice that he might at any moment eat it.

"Couldn't say how many of these I've seen in my lifetime. Any number. It's a quitclaim deed. Means just that, too. You sign here," he stubbed a finger at the paper, "and quit any claim you might have to a particular piece of real estate. "In exchange for," he consulted the letter, "in this case it's three hundred bucks."

"For all that land?" Rita protested.

"You could get nothing. Zilch. You're not selling the land, just any claim you might conceivably make on it as a potential heir. Folks get it into their head they can hold out for thousands," he was rummaging under the desk and pulled out a roll of blueprints, then another, and another before tossing them away, "Son of a gun, where did you say you got this?"

"I didn't say yet." With Bernice embellishing, Rita told him all she knew.

Uncle Sudeley eased a hand round the back of his neck and pushed his glasses up to his forehead. "Son of a gun," he repeated, "this could be interesting. You gals any notion at all what kind of hog-wallow you're getting into?"

"Why?"

"I'll tell you this. If I were you and you pleaded with me from hell to breakfast, I wouldn't put a toe in there." He chuckled. "But I'm not you. I happen to know a thing or two about that particular parcel. Did a little business with them myself not so long ago."

"An easement?" Rita guessed.

"Good girl. You haven't forgotten. Yep, for eighteen hundred. Needed right of way onto a road. Just a few feet. So happened I owned it. Had 'em over a barrel. Right there's where the industrial park's going. Biggest milch-cow to come down the pike since the Garden State Parkway acquisition in the fifties. The township's stashed away hundreds of acres so as to transfer clear title to the developer. Word was they had it sowed up tight, but seems like maybe they don't." He planted a resounding smacker on the quitclaim letter. "Can't get financing with any sort of cloud hanging over a property. I wonder, …" His eyes gleamed. "Tell me some more about them old gals of yours, the Good gals, let's call 'em."

Rita produced her photostat from the Good Family Bible.

"By Jiminy." Uncle Sudeley exhaled, after an extended silence. "We may just have something,"

They crowded closer.

"Happened to me, once," he observed unhelpfully. "Had title to a piece of land in the bag; sewed up fair and square, so I thought. Then out of the blue comes this fellow, all the way from Frisko. Didn't know him from Adam. 'I own that land,' he said. And, to cut it short, he did. Buying out that claim cost me, I can tell you. Soon as they contest, along come the lawyers, sniffing like hound dogs. And that means everything gets held up. A developer trying to turn over his money'll get madder than a wounded bear. And generally they'll settle for a pretty good whack to get a holdout off their back." He chortled, perhaps recalling times he'd done exactly that. "Land. You've got to know soup to nuts on land. Mind if I keep these? Do some research?"

"He's hooked all right," said Rita, as they bumped back towards town.

7

They were in the car, in Bernice's driveway. Rita was looking back at the road, judging the opportune moment to step on the gas. Bernice was hunting in her purse for her ID to show at the station house. It was a fool's game, they'd decided, getting any sort of traction with the police over the phone. They would have to beard the lion in his den. The tapping, rather timid, on the window, startled them. Otis Phinney popped up among the cedars like a jack-in-the-box.

Rita wound down the window. If he hadn't looked so vulnerable, she would have bawled him out. "Well, hello there stranger."

Bernice fumbled under the dash and came up with the green feathered hat. But when she tried to pass it across, Rita pushed her hand away. "Get in," Rita indicated the back seat.

Otis obeyed.

"No tan?"

He looked puzzled.

"You were on a ship in the Panama Canal, last we heard. How come no tan?"

Otis's pallid face looked as if it had been cooped up indoors all summer. "I'm no sailor."

"You know about knots and beams." The handbrake creaked as she set it. "Who are you?"

"You were at the club." It was an accusation. "What did they tell you?"

"They flashed a postcard purporting to be from a ship in the Canal Zone. Signed O for Otis Phinney."

"Rake's Progress?" His mouth cupped into a smile.

"Mailed a week ago."

"But not by me."

"You wrote it but you didn't mail it?"

"Mail it? How could I? I was up here, at a funeral."

"Yes. How stupid of me."

"I couldn't be in two places at once."

Bernice knelt on the seat and poked her head over. "Hi there, Santa!"

His reaction threw her: "You went to the club; you went to the house; you asked questions. Where else did you go?"

"Sure we asked questions," Rita was aggressive. "You left this." She tossed him his hat.

"I warned you. I said, Stay out." His small fingers kneaded the green felt. "Now I'm telling you again."

"You ever hear of reverse psychology?" Rita threw out.

"I was never in college."

"You were a child though."

He almost screamed. "It's not a game! They don't fart around, these people. You seen what they did already, to a couple of old ladies. You seen what they're putting me through. I'm telling you, once they get your number there's no stopping them."

To cheer him up, Bernice said, "We've something for you. Shall we tell?"

Rita shrugged.

"If not for the fire we'd have put it back. But it's yours now anyway. The Family Bible. Oh, and a letter was in it."

"You got it here, their Bible?" He sounded incredulous.

"Not exactly," Rita said. "You've got to level with us. We were just off to the police. We maybe still are."

To soften what seemed unnecessary harshness, Bernice said, "We just wanted to help, that's all." She looked round to where Otis sat in the vastness of the back seat, and caught his expression. A worried dwarf out of Snow White. Bashful perhaps. No, Dopey.

"OK, I'll do my best," he said.

She felt like hugging him. Had she been sitting next to him, she probably would have. Rita or nor Rita.

Instead of going to the police, Rita drove off in the direction of Carefree Days. Bernice glanced back. No Otis. He'd been there a minute ago. Then she saw some shirt and, by straining a bit, most of the rest of him crouched down in the space between the seats. "Everything all right back there?"

"Don't pay no attention. Act like I'm not here. I'll explain later." He sounded aggrieved.

"No time like now," Rita called out. "Spout. We won't look round."

The voice came small and self-pitying. "Some of it, I guess you know. I'm just a retired postal worker from Orange. Simple as that. No wife. No kids. Not much put aside, either." It seemed like a plea. "Don't have many memories."

"That's all right," Bernice said soothingly. It was like HELP-link: talking without seeing.

"Let him get on with it."

"Sure I wrote that card. Gave it to a fella on that boat to mail. It'll soon reach Australia. Wanted to go there ever since I was a kid."

"Why, for God's sake?" Rita interjected.

"Australia? Well ..."

"The card! Why go to all that trouble?"

"Buying time."

"For what?" She slowed down, thinking 'It's going to be like pulling teeth.'

"To stay alive. To try to get what should have bin mine. That letter, the one with the Bible, what was that about?"

"A quitclaim they were supposed to sign, on some property." Bernice was aware Rita was trying to tell her something.

"But they didn't, did they? They didn't sign?"

"The deal is for you to tell us," Rita boomed, "not the other way round."

"I got one too, you see," he confided. "That's what started

55

me off, looking into it. Three hundred bucks, it said. If I signed." He laughed, a peculiar, tinny sound. "Three hundred! Give me a hundred thou, I said. Take it or leave it." Perhaps sensing skepticism, he resumed the pleading tone. "This is my main chance, you follow? I won't get no other."

"Who did you say all that to?" Rita was aloof.

"Who'd I say that to? The lawyer, the one that sent it, that's who. The guy's a nothing—I know that—a front for the higher-ups."

"What higher-ups?"

"You wanna know what's going on?" Suddenly he was shouting. "Well, I'll tell you."

"Thank you," Rita breathed, so only Bernice could hear.

"It's a billion dollar deal, that's what. A brand new industrial park in the works. I found out all about it. They been buying up land like crazy, securing title, the whole enchilada. But guess what they didn't reckon on? Guess what's the spoke in the wheel? You're darn tootin'. Otis Phinney, that's what."

"Whoa there, boy. Hold your horses," Rita said. "I want names and addresses. I want facts."

"So I don't have all the answers," Otis's voice rose dangerously. "I'm working on it. Believe me, the best I know how."

For a moment Rita wondered if he was armed. He had an edge to his voice, a tightness in the words as if he was under strain. It brought to mind the time she'd had a man in the cab who'd escaped from the Center for the Criminally Insane at Matawan. Of course she hadn't realized till later who he was, but she recalled the voice—scared, and at the same time defiant—when he said he wouldn't pay.

Bernice said, "We believe you."

"Like I said, they got it all set, all systems go, 'cept for one thing. Some signatures on a piece of paper. Mine. And theirs."

"Miss Annie's and Miss Mercy's."

"They gotta have guaranteed clear title before they touch the place. And they don't. No title, no insurance."

"You're right," said Bernice, "They didn't sign."

"So I figured, why not? Bin playing safe all my life, where did it get me? Here's my big break. Call their bluff. A hundred thou or nothing. Peanuts, to them."

The Checker stopped for a light. Rita looked at Bernice who put a finger to her lips.

After a moment, Otis spoke again. He seemed calmer. "A few days later I'm at the club and I get this call. Guy says, 'Check the obits in tomorrow's Shore County *Star*.' That's it. No more. I'm left with a dead phone. So I buy the *Star* and right away I get the message: Otis, you just got invited to your funeral. You better run while you still got legs."

"But you went to the funeral."

"Yeah," he said sadly, "I went. Had to. Every year I'd send a card. My only living relatives."

Rita said, "And you guessed it was about the quitclaim?"

"Seemed obvious."

"So who's behind it?"

"On paper an outfit calls itself KAY-LEE Enterprises." He spelled it. "That's the developer."

"KAY-LEE," Bernice mused. She'd heard the name somewhere, or seen it. "So then what?"

"Thought of the furthest place I could away. By slow freight. How'd you like that?" A little flash of pride. He was no longer crouching but sitting on the floor, his short legs braced against the back seat, caught up in the tale.

He was—Rita had to admit—making more sense. The furtive manner that had raised her hackles at least now seemed justified. Amply so, if all he said was true. And they could check. "So what can we do?"

"Stay out of this. You're raising more dust than a twister. They got telescopic vision, these people. From one end of the state to the other. I don't want to read no more obituaries."

"We can't stop looking for whoever did that to Miss Annie," Rita said, "At least I can't."

"Me neither," echoed Bernice.

"Godammit." It was a whisper, but distinct. Otis got up on his knees and peered over the back of the seat. "You're crazy. You don't stand a chance. A couple of turkeys on a wall. No way they can't pick you off." Getting no response, he said somberly, "Whoever got Miss Annie, whoever's after me, they got the whole county rooting for them. Including the police, the paper, and the banks. Nobody's going to stand in the way of that industrial park. And especially not on account of a couple of crones who were next door to dead anyway. You follow me?"

Rita said, "So, to all intents and purposes, you're in Australia?"

"There's the state police," Bernice suggested brightly.

"I'm not getting through," Otis groaned. "I'm not getting through. The state's as deep in this as anyone. They even got foreign money in it. This is gonna be what's gonna revitalize South Jersey, you see what I'm saying? The governor's looking for another term. He's gotta take South Jersey."

"Then I guess it's going to be me and you and Bernice against the revitalization of South Jersey. They'll have to do it round us, or over us, or something."

Otis held his head in his hands. His body—tense with the strain of recent weeks—felt jarred and sore from the ride. "You heard of the 1-80 overpass at Saddle Brook?" The question was presumably rhetorical. "You know what they got in a concrete stanchion there? A man, that's what. The way the two of you are talking, you gonna get a whole industrial complex all to yourselves."

"What about you?" Rita said.

"Myself, I can handle."

"But we're just a couple of dumb broads who can't safely cross a road, right?" Rita lashed back. "Wrong, Mister. We aren't buying that. You got in the wrong cab. This one goes all the way."

Otis said feebly, "Just stay out of my hair." Bernice smiled: the man had a crew cut and not much of that. "I wash my hands. I'm not responsible. Whatever happens, just don't forget that."

They passed an organ outlet that could have been an antebellum mansion, and a sign saying 'Auto Parts Kingdom'. Traffic headed east across Bay Bridge to Island Beach was backed up for the usual mile. "Who was that fella ..." Otis began, and answered himself. "Custer. Custer's last stand. Well, that's me. Figure I'll go out with a bang, 'cos what's left?

58

Why stick around? If I can't get my money, at least I don't have to hand it to them on a platter. Make 'em sweat, heh. That's what I'll do."

He's psyching himself up, Bernice thought. But the prescribed HELP-link responses seemed inadequate: get them talking about anything; get a handle on their lives, any little hint. They like to drive? Build on it. Up their sense of self-worth. "Isn't there anything we can do? We might come up with something."

"If I think of it, I'll contact you."

"Don't call me, I'll call you, huh?" Rita pulled into Carefree Days past the sign, white on green, with 'active adults over 50' in small letters underneath. She went into a building. A car slowed on it's way out, grandma up front with the driver, kids squashed and cheerful in the back. Bernice was glad Otis couldn't see.

"I know it's tough, but did you ever feel anything for any one, like love or anything?" A crumb of food to a bird she hoped wouldn't frighten away.

"Don't we all, one time or another? Only with me it's been a long time."

"That little girl—the one who's watering your plants who thinks you're Santa Claus—that's not so long ago."

His response was sort of a stifled squawk. It dawned on Bernice that he was crying. Kneeling on the front seat, she reached over and patted him, first on his back, then, when he didn't resist, on his head. She might have been patting a dog.

Rita emerged with a parcel, which she handed to Bernice. "They kept it for me in the safe."

Bernice passed it to the back seat. "It's hard to believe. A burglary that did some good."

"Where to?" Rita called out. "I guess it's no use asking where you're staying."

"Anywhere in town. And let me pay." He pulled out a wallet. "I guess it's no use asking what you're gonna get up to next."

"Keep you money," Rita said. "Whatever you say, we're in this together."

After he'd gone, swallowed up in the crush of tourists at the boat basin, they found a five-dollar bill on the seat.

"Well," said Bernice.

"Well, well," said Rita.

"What do you think?"

"He's a paranoid schizophrenic."

"Then maybe we all are."

"Unlikely."

"Let's find out."

8

The gladioli lay on the back porch, professionally wrapped in cellophane and green tissue. No note. Bernice found them when she got back from work later than usual, having stopped off at the firehouse for a meeting of the Ladies' Auxiliary. The flowers were limp, she noted. Who on earth could have left them? Inside the house it was mercifully cool, with the shades all down and the windows open two inches at the top. She ran cold water into the kitchen sink for the glads and herself took a shower. The walk from the bus stop left her hot and sticky. She'd hurried because it was Friday and she was due at the HELP house for her overnight.

As her heartbeat slowed under the calming flow of water, Bernice's mind cleared and it occurred to her who her anonymous admirer might be. She pictured him sitting in the Checker beside the lilies. Perhaps it was his way of saying thank you. Perhaps her name on the wreath had given her away. She slit the stems and arranged the flowers in a vase. They perked up and so did she. Even if it wasn't Otis, the thought agreed with her. May as well admit it, though not to Rita. Rita would laugh. It would be her own private fantasy. Though perhaps Rita had glads too.

The clock on the wall showed past midnight. Bernice again sat in the HELP house alone—or lay rather on the couch—the phone cupped to her ear. From it came noises, but no voice. Bernice ignored the noises. She was hearing voices of her own, catching up with her thoughts. Little else to do. Calls like this—she suspected a masturbator—could keep the line tied up for hours. It was against the rules to hang up.

At the firehouse a strange thing had happened. The upcoming Chinese auction dealt with, talk at the meeting had shifted to the fire on Gunning Point Road. A big woman in a low-cut peasant blouse and purple cowboy boots, who often did the calls on Bingo nights, piped up: "Hey, girls, you're not going to believe this one!" Gradually everyone stopped talking. She was usually good for a laugh.

"Guess I've been saving this for Christian," she bellowed, "'cause it's her department." A few titters ensued, heads turned. Christian was the name they'd pinned on Bernice after her election the previous year. The Ladies' Auxiliary was a bunch of tough-talking individuals who, in the words of one ex-member, "could rip shreds off you quicker than a half-starved piranha fish". And the language some of them threw around would make a bouncer blush. Bernice steered clear of the bloodletting by just keeping quiet. And her swear words smelled of soap. So they tagged her, and it stuck. Though when they got to know her, the suspicion that induced it wore off.

"I was down at the beauty parlor yesterday," the woman was saying, "and I'm right next to that Mrs. O'Connell whose husband has the dry cleaners. 'Morning,' I says, 'Nice day.' She just stares at me. 'You seen a ghost, or something?' I ask. 'He was looking right at me,' she says. 'Who? Jesus Christ?' She gives me this strange look, 'Do you believe in the Devil?' She was at that house, she said, the night before it burned. Gone looking for her daughter who creeps through the hedge to play though she's told her often enough not to. And there he was, in an upstairs window, black as pitch, leering down at her.

If this was the punch line, nobody laughed. The woman went on: "Said she felt bad. Only a couple of days before she'd packed her girl off to bed without her dinner for telling tales about seeing ghosts in the old barn."

Bernice could have added a better punch line but didn't.

The story left her speechless and depressed. The phone was back on the hook. Then it spoke again, sharply. She caught it on the first ring: "HELP."

The voice was slurred, male. "I'm outside. I could come in. If I did, it'd be all over. Nothing against you personal, see. You're probably a nice lady. But you and your friend, you're in over your heads. So don't say you weren't warned."

She held the receiver in frozen silence after the line went dead. The manual said: In an emergency, such as a medical emergency or persistent nuisance caller, contact your backup person. What about a death threat coupled with a break-in? She thought of her backup, asleep miles away. The manual hadn't reckoned on that.

Bernice groped for her shoes and put them on. She checked the back door and scurried around the house drawing the blinds, making sure the windows were shut, double-checking the bolts on the front door. The nearest phone booth was a mile away, on the avenue. She didn't really believe anyone was out there in the darkness. Not yet. If a car pulled up, she told herself, her first call would be the police.

Back at the desk, she waited, lifted the receiver, replaced it. If somebody called and tied up the line, she wondered what to do. 'Bernice, you scaredy cat.' She said it out loud and laughed. Funny, how she could think of death so rationally. Like a person, almost. A long postponed visitor. When Earl died and she felt the tug of despair pulling her down, part of her was for surrender, part resisted. The resistance began to wear thin. Then one night, walking around the side of the house, there he was, standing on the path between the cedars. "Earl!" Surprised, yes, but not scared. And he'd beckoned; just stood there, beckoning. And she'd shaken her head. "No, Earl; not yet. I'm not ready yet." And he'd gone. But from then on she'd known that death—and being ready to die— were one and the same thing for her. And she wasn't ready to die. Not yet. So she wouldn't.

For an hour, perhaps two, Bernice sat by the phone in the dark. Several cars passed. Once she heard sounds like scuffling at the back door, and lines memorized in eighth grade sprang to mind: *While I nodded, nearly napping, suddenly there came a tapping, As of some one gently rapping, rapping at my chamber door.* A raccoon, surely, into the garbage.

When the phone did ring, it was a child, and Bernice hadn't the heart to cut her off. The minutes ticked on. It began to get light. She got up and opened the curtains. Sure enough, the garbage pail lay on its side by the back door, clamped shut. On the way to the bus, a man she didn't know offered her a ride. As soon as he was out of sight she wrote down the license number, just in case. Somebody wants me out of the way, she thought, puzzled. It would take a bit of getting used to. 'Don't mind me', almost her mantra. But now, it seemed, somebody did.

Rita received neither flowers nor phone call. "Flowers, Bernice? Without a card?"

"Glads, orange. They go perfect with the living room curtains."

"Glads, orange glads! Why didn't you say so? My God, Bernice, you never heard of the kiss of death?" She dropped her voice. "This goes to the cops. I don't care how, but it goes. Stay there, I'm coming." She hung up.

Bernice hadn't made her usual call at the A&P, and her standing Saturday morning hair appointment had gone by the board. She'd called Rita the moment she got home. And her friend's reaction puzzled her. She seemed more disturbed by the flowers than by the call.

Rita made it in record time.

Cranberry Township Police Headquarters stood back from Jasper Avenue in its own landscaped setting, clusters of silver birch on rolling green lawns with evergreens in back flanking the parking areas. The Stars & Stripes hung slackly from a tall metal pole. Since its move from downtown a couple of years back it might have been taken for a Junior College or the flagship office of an insurance company. It even had a new name: Law Enforcement Center. Inside, loitering men in blue and posters for the Police Athletic League reassured a perhaps wondering visitor that she was in the right place.

A woman with glasses slipping down a pointed nose was sitting at a desk to the right of the entrance. "Can I help you?" Rita asked for Sergeant Scaguiola.

"Hey, Buddy, Scag in yet?" she yelled at an officer who happened to be passing nursing a cup of coffee.

The man glanced at the clock. "Scag? Give the guy a break, willya, Denise?"

"I guess that answers the question. Anyone else do?"

"When's he due in?" Rita asked.

"When's he due in?" the woman shouted. "Scag."

The officer disappeared into a room down the hall, then backed out, minus coffee. "Scag's got the Magic Hours, midnight to eight." He looked at Rita and Bernice. "In reference to what was it?"

"He'd have had the same shift last Friday, would he?" Rita asked. "Midnight to 8. No, I guess I mean Saturday."

The man took a few steps towards them. "Sure, sfar's I know. Hey!" he clapped a hand to his forehead. "What am I saying? This is Saturday, right? Fridays and Saturdays he's off."

"Then he'll be in Monday?" Rita asked.

"Sure thing," said the woman at the window.

"We'll come back."

"Better be here by eight sharp," the officer advised. "He comes in, see, from patrol, turns in his keys, and goes home."

They were back in the Checker with the engine running when Bernice exclaimed, "Wait a bit. If he wasn't working the night shift Friday or Saturday, how come he was the officer at the scene the morning they found Miss Annie? That was a Saturday."

"It was early, too. Perhaps he wasn't off that night."

"I'm going back to check."

"They'll only start asking questions. *Bernice*." Too late, she was gone.

"It was a snap." She was back in a flash. "She checked the log for me."

"What did you do, bribe her?"

"Told her she looked like Carol Burnett. He finished up last

Friday morning at eight, then he didn't go back to work till midnight, Sunday night; for the Monday morning shift."

"So he wasn't even on duty!"

"Does he work alone?"

"They're all single-officer patrols. I asked."

"Let's try him at home."

They found three Scaguiolas in the phone book. One was a pizza parlor; one was in a leisure village. Only one seemed likely. "Camelot Mews," Rita said. "Isn't that that new development? Up beyond Gunning Point Road?"

9

Uncle Sudeley chortled a good deal on the way back from town. "Son of a gun," he repeated. "Son of a dog garn gun. Who'd have ever believed it?"

The inside of his head felt like an oven where the door needed opening to let out some heat. Same way it felt at tax auctions just before the deadline expired on a piece of property and it was his. He gave the wheel a friendly punch, and the Rambler shuddered its response. He knew the old car's every noise, every tremor, like he knew his own body, which is probably why he hadn't long since junked it. You don't junk an old friend, not if you're a certain kind of person. Uncle Sudeley could easily have afforded cash down on this year's Cadillac or even a Rolls Royce, and the knowledge that he could, but didn't, gave him pleasure.

The sound of scuffling from the back seat made him look round. Dog garn hen! Cage must have shaken open. At any rate, the bird was loose. He probably shouldn't have brought it along. But he had, and they were nearly home. This was one meal the wild dogs wouldn't have, he'd promised himself. With a mighty flutter the fowl made it to the back of the front seat where it perched and peered around, eyes blinking white. Uncle Sudeley whistled some bars from 'The Halls of Montezuma'. "No sirree", he addressed the bird, "they don't call me Snoop for nothing!"

He turned off the main road and bounced along between scrub oak and dwarf pitch pines, lit copper by the rays of the sinking sun. Any day now Rita and her friend would be back. Tomorrow was Saturday. Maybe they'd come then. He had something for them. Boy, did he have something for them.

Bernice woke with a start. The Checker had pulled off the road and was bumping its way into the clearing. The first thing she saw was Uncle Sudeley's Rambler. "We're here," Rita announced. They'd decided to save Sergeant Scaguiola till later in the day when he was more likely to be up and around. Bernice, protesting she wasn't tired, had nodded the whole way.

As usual, Uncle Sudeley lost no time on preliminaries. "We're going fishing," he announced. "Deep sea fishing. I got the bait, so thread your lines. It gets pretty choppy out there. You'll need strong arms and a strong stomach. Rita'll be all right, I know. She can stand with the best of them. Like her daddy." He looked inquisitively at Bernice: "You got sea legs?"

Bernice, who got horribly seasick, nodded.

Uncle Sudeley pulled what looked like—and was—an old rolled up window shade from the back seat of the Rambler, and spread it over the hood. Scrawled in magic marker were names and dates, his version of the Good family tree. "This here, all of this," he swept an arm almost the entire length of the sons and daughters of Joseph and Hettie Good, "we can forget. Watertight. Shipshape. But here, see," he drummed a finger on a particular spot, "here's the leak." They leaned closer. "Amos. Interesting fella, this Amos. Eldest son. Born 1837. Died 1866. Twenty-nine years young. Twice married. Your old gals, see, Mercy and Annie, they were descended from the second marriage. So was your pal, Otis Phinney. Well, forget that too. It's his first marriage that interests us. That's where our boy is."

"Who's that, Uncle Sudeley?"

"The one that got away." Had he been able to crow, Bernice thought, he would have done so now.

"Here's where we tie up the machinery of state and get all the flunkies and bureaucrats dancin' and hollerin' and cussin' like the nigger who sat on the anthill." He threw a glance, disconcertingly shrewd, at Bernice, and winked. "With a bit of luck. You've got to probe, see, till you find a soft spot." His hands kneaded the air. "And this here, I bet my barnacles, is it." He brought his index finger down insinuatingly on the window shade, then stood back.

Rita took her cue. "Jennie Eliza Machonochie," she read, peering closely at Uncle Sudeley's squashed, old-fashioned writing.

"Amos Good's first wife," Uncle Sudeley intoned. "Married:"

Rita did the responses: "1859."

"Had issue:"

"None."

"Died:"

"1860."

"Now look to the left, all the way over. She was married before, am I right?"

"It doesn't say to whom. Just an M."

"M for married," Uncle Sudeley said. "Now take a look at this." From his shirt pocket he produced the copy Rita had made from the Bible. It had acquired a soft, tattered look. He pointed to a spot. "Here it is, here; right underneath. See the arrow?"

Rita twisted her neck. He handed her the paper. "Obed, born 1855, took name of Good on adoption."

"Go on." He almost pirouetted with excitement. "Three letters."

"GTT." She frowned. "GTT?"

Uncle Sudeley surveyed his audience with the air of a conjurer who, having produced his rabbit, awaits the applause. "Stands for *Gone to Texas*," he said. "The missing heir. Now all we have to do is find him—or rather his descendants, if any—before *they* do. As of now, I doubt they're even looking. So grab your gaff poles, girls, 'cos when we hook him we've still got to land him."

It took a certain amount of backtracking for Rita and Bernice fully to appreciate Uncle Sudeley's coup. He had gone up to town the day before with the quitclaim deed and discovered that the title search on the proposed industrial park was conducted by a local firm of insurers he'd done business with over the years. This saved him days of hunting for Wills, deeds and death certificates, the raw material of the chase. Sure, the boss would talk about it. He was keen to. An open and shut case. He challenged Uncle Sudeley to find a hole. He even helped him look.

The insurers had checked title back to 1682 when the land was conveyed—along with all New Jersey east of a diagonal from Little Egg Harbor to the Falls of the Delaware—to William Penn and eleven associates, the first Board of Proprietors. It had come to them from the executors of Sir George Carteret, sold to pay off debts. Sir George had it from the Duke of York, who had it from his brother, King Charles the Second. If anyone had it before that—as the man told Uncle Sudeley—it was a bunch of Indians. And they'd have a job to prove it.

In his Will, old Joseph Vannover Good had left everything to his wife, and his children after her. That much was clear enough. When, eighteen years later, Hettie Bird Good died intestate, the estate was divided among the six surviving children. Amos, the eldest, by then of course was dead, and his widow had moved away or lost touch with the rest of the family. "Some sort of coolness in there, seems to me," Uncle Sudeley said, rubbing his hands together. At any rate, they hadn't cut her in on what should have been, by rights, if not her share of the estate, at least her children's and their children's.

In 1928, or thereabouts, the U.S. Government put it about that a large tract of flat land was required near the ocean on which to build an airfield. Cranberry Township, eager to expand its meager tax base, acquired what was thought at the time to be clear title to the entire original Joseph Vannover Good estate. But the airfield was never built, or it was built some place else, and the land, scrubby and largely unproductive, was leased out for a variety of uses, mainly chicken farms, but never sold. So when, some fifty years later, the state came nosing around South Jersey looking to build an industrial park, Cranberry Township was waiting. And the factor that eventually tipped the scale in the township's favor was the clear title it could serve up on all those acres, worth pure gold.

KAY-LEE Enterprises won the main contract to develop the site and, as a matter of course, set in motion its own title search. This turned up the flaw in what came to be called 'the Settlement of 1928': the exclusion of Amos Good's heirs from their rights under the terms of his father's Will. His sole living descendants were found to be Mercy and Annie, his grand-daughters, and Otis, his great-grandson. KAY-LEE's lawyers sent them quitclaim deeds to sign, and since word on the deal wasn't yet generally out, no problem was anticipated. And when the sisters suddenly died, that matter became *de novo*. Uncle Sudeley's ace in hand was that he knew, and KAY-LEE didn't, that Amos Good had adopted a son. Assuming a living descendant could be found, here was a claim that could tie the deal up in legal knots for years. Yes, he reiterated, they sure were going fishing.

Bernice had a way of reducing things to manageable proportions. "Gone to Texas, you said? I have a cousin did that. Well, more than a cousin, really."

"Bernice," Rita squelched, "that's terrific. That'll solve everything. Texas is only forty times as big as New Jersey."

But Uncle Sudeley didn't scoff. "Well, we've got to start somewhere."

"You did say Texas?"

"Gone to Texas. Kind of a catch phrase they had back then meaning wherever you'd gone, you likely weren't coming back, and perhaps your people wouldn't be too happy if you did. 'Went West', we might say. 'Course it may well have been Texas. You've a relative there, you say?"

"Well, he is but he isn't. I'd a hand in raising him. His folks … Well, he was kind of an orphan for a while. He's a lawyer now."

"Lawyer, eh?" Uncle Sudeley perked up. "Where at?"

"Houston. I think."

"Well, we'll keep him in mind. Meantime we've got to scratch our brains, see if we can't come up with a clue or two as to who this young fella Obed Good was, and what he did and where he GTT'd to. Rita, you were always good at clues."

"I've no idea, Uncle Sudeley."

"Sure you have. Ideas flow like water, if you just turn 'em on. For instance, if the lad was born in 1855 and his mother—if she was his mother—married Amos Good in 1859, and Amos adopted him, my hunch is he was living with Amos in 1860. So where's be the first place I'd look?"

Rita drew a blank.

"You forgot already, everything I taught you?"

"Already! Uncle Sudeley, that was forty years ago."

"Thing about living out here," he muttered, "time gets away from you. Well, first place I'd look is the Census of 1860. Then I'd say to myself, 'If the lad's mother passed on in 1860, and Amos followed her in '66, could be our Obed stayed with wife number two—he'd be eleven, though that was older then than it is now—and was brought up along of her own son, born 1864, the father of your two old gals. I'd check that out too."

Uncle Sudeley clattered along like an express. "I'd also see if I could find a Will. Amos might have made a Will. Adoptions in those days were a pretty casual affair. With a Will, well ... You know what they say: where there's a Will there's a way."

"Otis might know something," Bernice exclaimed. She described their encounter.

Uncle Sudeley pulled a long face. "He's an interested party; the only known living heir. If I were he, I wouldn't want some last minute interloper barging in on my claim. Let him pan his own gold and we'll pan ours."

Bernice disagreed. Why wouldn't he be glad? It would draw some of KAY-LEE's fire. Besides, he had the Family Bible. He could see for himself.

"So let him." Life had taught Uncle Sudeley who to trust

and who not to trust. They'd met the fellow. He hadn't. The least he could do was warn them. Man and the land had nursed each other over the centuries; it was a fool or a lover—which amounted to the same thing—who came between a man and his land.

It was getting on for six-thirty, with rain threatening, when Rita and Bernice found the address listed under the Scaguiola name in the phonebook. 'Camelot Mews', the sign said, 'A new concept in patio living.' A half dozen four-unit apartment blocks were grouped around a cul-de-sac. The Sir Launcelot was the second building on the right. Telltale signs of shoddy workmanship abounded: some of the siding shingles had slipped, a gutter hung loose. As they climbed the outside stairs to Number 4, various scrawled messages urged them to commit unspeakable acts. "Weren't there pine trees over there," Bernice pointed east, "and a view across Island Beach to the ocean?" All they could see now were houses, and an enormous sandpit.

The woman who answered the door was no Guinevere; in her mid twenties, she had the unhealthy pallor of a junk food addict who orders out. "He's at work." She betrayed her northern origins, rhyming work with oik. In the background a baby kept up a steady bawl.

"Oh," Bernice sounded surprised. "They said at the station house he was off weekends."

The woman maintained the door at a defensive six inches. Her eyes flicked back to take in Rita, who smiled encouragingly. "He got other work," she said grudgingly. "It don't pay good, police work. Not down here, it don't."

"It's rough these days, particularly starting out with a family," Bernice sympathized. "How old is he, or is it a she?"

The woman ignored this overture. "We're getting outta here. Getting us a house. Ain't never lived in a place like this before, not me." She lowered her voice. "They got welfare livin' here. Know what I mean? My husband, he won't let his folks come down, mine neither."

"Nothing wrong with a weekend job," Bernice said.

"Where? The new mall?" A lot of policemen—especially the younger ones—moonlighted as security guards.

"Down the Furnace." A night spot a ways out of town catering to the young rock crowd on weekends. It had come under fire from elements in the community as a trouble spot. There'd been a stabbing in the parking lot. Perhaps they were trying to clean up their act, hiring off-duty cops.

"When's he finish up?"

"Two, three, depends."

"Last Friday night, was he there?"

"Ask him. You from the church?" She clamped down her guard.

"Not exactly," Rita said. But the door was already shut.

Back in the Checker, "How do you like that?" Bernice asked.

"I can't wait to meet this character."

"What are we waiting for?" Bernice was having trouble balancing her head on her shoulders.

"You can sleep all day tomorrow."

10

Sentry duty in the moist boredom of a Saigon summer night. It wasn't just the rain that eddied across the half-full car park making the lights seem to flicker like gaslight. It was his whole life up to now, all the breaks he hadn't had. Sometimes he wished he could scrap it and start over. The F.B.I. could set you up with a whole new identity. He'd heard about that. If they liked the sound of your squeal. He tightened his lips against his teeth in a grim smile. Fantasy? It might just come to that. Except his folks were getting on. He was all they had. He couldn't put them through it. So he'd hang on. A year. Two years. Five. Sergeant Scaguiola's mood was bleak.

A bunch of kids came towards him running like gooks, bending against the rain, screaming. Under the awning they tugged fake IDs out of tight jeans and patted their hairdos. Scag glanced at each 'proof', not taking his hands from his pockets, and gave an upward jerk of his head. Contempt, it was supposed to signify. The kids piled on into the barnlike building from where, each time the door opened, the thud of the music reached out grabbing hands. New Wave Rock. Scag winced. A far cry from the rock 'n roll he'd grown up with, even if some of the hairdos looked the same. At least he wasn't working the floor tonight. Apart from the din, it was warmer and wetter inside than out, and his uniform wasn't exactly tailored for the tropics. The bosses liked the uniform. They got all the pull and heft of the Cranberry Township police for a lousy fifty a night. Not that it made any difference. In Scag's opinion, kids these days had no more respect for a police uniform than they did for anything else.

A car pulled in, all swirls of purple and gold, and little black bubble windows, kids dropping out before it had even stopped. Troublemakers, Scag thought, noting the Pennsylvania plates, and already into the booze. They started popping the tops halfway across the Delaware because the drinking age was lower in Jersey. You could smell it on them as they went by. He distrusted vehicles he couldn't see into: more than drinking went on in the back, he knew that. A beer can clattered to the tarmac. "OK, pick it up," he intoned wearily; and, when nobody moved, more deliberately, "Pick it up or get outta here." The can was retrieved. Scag frisked a couple of the guys, sniffed at a pack of cigarettes, and let them pass.

Punks, he thought. Punks and vandals. Parasites. Sometimes he felt like knocking their greasy heads together or grabbing them by the balls and twisting. You could do that in Nam. 'Don't think you'll get away with it,' he'd have liked to shout. 'You're gonna have to pay. Just like everybody, in the end.' He'd paid. And how. He'd like to see them in five or ten years time, soured up marriage, kid or two, trying to hold down a shitty job or perhaps still looking, payments coming due. And all the expectations people had. Oh sure, Uncle Sam had gotten him a BA in sociology from Bloomfield College; a lot of fancy jargon was swilling around inside his head. Christ, he'd learned more about human behavior in a week on the force, or a weekend here at the Furnace.

Two females were approaching. They must have got out of that maroon Checker that had pulled in. He sized them up: white, fiftyish, one short and plump, the other tall, raw boned. They walked fast, sheltering under a yellow plastic slicker. If Scag half closed his eyes, the impression was that of an erratic camel wending its way towards him over the shining tarmac. Not your regular Furnace clientele. Yet where else would they be going? The Furnace stood alone in its parking lot. Once an old barn, part of a defunct farm, it had been fixed up a few months back by a couple of out-of-towners looking for a fast buck.

The tall one spoke first while the other shook out the slicker in the relative dryness of the awning. "Sergeant Scaguioli?"

"Scaguiola," he corrected. "Like in Ayatollah." It usually brought a smile. Not tonight.

For Rita, the uniform was the giveaway. Undoubtedly, this was their man. She was relieved they didn't have to go inside literally to face the music, which sounded from where she stood as if strong palms were squeezing and molding it into a missile to zap whoever opened the door right between the eyes. Boom, boom. Thud, thud. Twang, twang. Without rhyme or reason to her ears. At least out here they could hear themselves speak. He looked different from how she imagined. Dark hair, thinning in front already. Pale face, on the narrow side, made more so by neatly trimmed, three quarter length sideburns. With those deep-set eyes, haggard almost, long lashes and a slightly protruding upper lip, he should have been a poet, she thought, or a priest in one of the soaps. Though he did have long ear lobes, a criminal trait according to something she'd read. Son of Sam had them. So did Attila the Hun.

"I'm Rita, and this is my friend, Bernice."

"Hi," said Bernice.

They'd agreed that Rita do the talking. "We want to ask you about last week. The old lady who was run down on Gunning Point Road." She was suddenly nervous, falling over herself, rushing it.

"Pardon me, ma'am." Scaguiola stepped over to intercept a fresh bunch of teenagers clattering in under the awning. Carefully, he checked proofs, and waved them through with a crisp, 'Thank you.' One or two glanced up at this unaccustomed show of civility. Then, seeing the women, understood, or thought they did. Scaguiola took his time. He needed time to think. The door opened and closed to truncated bedlam.

Rita began again. "She was killed early Saturday in a hit and run, right?"

"I don't know nothing about that, lady."

"You were the responding officer."

"What if I was? There was nothing about a hit and run." Dammit, he thought, he shouldn't even have said that. "Who you are, or what your interest is, I don't know or care. As far as I'm concerned it's water across the bridge." The words held a sullen challenge. Cool it, Scag, he thought. He could hear the roar of motorcycles broaching the crest of the hill, and for once wished they'd hurry. "I got my job to do just like you, so if you want to make any sort of statement, you go right on down to the station house and make it there."

She didn't trust this man at all, Bernice thought. He had the brittleness, under the surface, of something you handle very carefully or it explodes in your face. Likely a wife-beater, too. She prayed Rita's temper wouldn't get the better of her. But Rita, even now, was saying something wild. Bernice could hardly believe her ears.

"You're goddam right we will, buster. 'Cause we've got evidence." The roar of the bikes made her raise her voice.

"Oh yeah? What kind of evidence?" the gloves were off.

"You'll find out."

A wave of kids hit the entrance. Tough looking. Levis and black leather. To the thud of the music and the splatter of the rain, Scaguiola checked proofs.

"Time to go," Bernice whispered. "Go," she repeated, when Rita cupped her ear.

"We just got started."

"What's the point? He's dug in."

They sat in the car with the wipers going, breathless from the short run. Bernice mopped her face with a Kleenex. Just us well she'd skipped her hair appointment. Scaguiola, in his tent of light, looked small and insignificant.

"Whatever possessed me?" Rita moaned. "I must be crazy."

"Not crazy, just ..." Hotheaded, she was going to say.

"It just slipped out, Bernice. Sorry."

"I guess now we'll know for sure."

"What?"

"If he's involved."

Rita released the break and the Checker moved gently forward. "Oh, he's involved all right. It's written all over him."

"Evidence. You said evidence."

"I know."

"We better get some."

"How?" They were back on the road, moving fast.

"Stewart," Bernice said. "We should talk some more to Stewart."

Scaguiola watched the Checker till it rounded the bend beyond the school bus depot. Couple of old hens scratching around, he told himself. Nothing to get excited about.

The sign was there, just as he said on the phone it would be: 'To the Haunted Barn. Tours.' And a white hand, dripping blood. Once again it was Sunday morning on Gunning Point Road. The trees, the little lawns, the summer lethargy. Only the void was new, where the house had been. The outhouse was gone, the grass singed to within a few feet of the barn. Amazing it hadn't caught.

Stewart's head appeared in the gap in the siding. "You want in?"

"Sure," said Bernice. She'd stayed over at Rita's for safety's sake, and felt better for a night's sleep. They'd parked the Checker out of sight around the corner.

"That'll be a buck. Each."

"Wait a minute." Bernice pointed to a sign nailed to the siding. "I can read." 'Admission: 10 cents,' it said.

"Yeah. For kids."

"Truth in advertising," she wagged a finger. "You could lose your license."

"We're gonna make a playground. For all the kids on the block."

Had he dreamed it up, then and there? The way he was ogling the dollar bill Bernice had in her hand said it all. She deftly whisked the note to safety. "When we're through."

Inside, one reason why the barn hadn't burned became obvious. It was soaking wet. And surely not just from last night's rain. The firemen must have doused the place. The damp and chill and smell of mold and decay enhanced the ghostly aura Stewart would be after.

"How's business?" Rita asked.

"It'll pick up. Bound to." He pointed. "See over there?" They strained their eyes.

"Hanging from the beam." Something was, indeed, hanging from a beam. It looked like an old coat. "Wanna feel its toes?"

A moan came from the direction of the coat, distinctly unfrightening. "OK, Ollie, you can come out," Stewart called. A small boy, his face smeared, straw sticking to his clothes, stumbled out of the shadows. "My assistant," Stewart announced. It was his kid brother, and from the look on his face he took his job as spook in residence seriously. "Stand guard, OK? And don't let anyone in. Tell 'em the next show's at noon. And peel more grapes for the eyeballs."

They climbed aboard the old Ford, Stewart at the wheel. "Where to?"

Bernice was ready. "Back in time."

He found reverse. "How far?"

"Ten days, maybe nine, around the time the old ladies died."

"Some time warp."

"You're an observant sort of fellow. Did you notice anything unusual around then? Or if you didn't, perhaps one of your pals did?"

"Pals?" he sniffed. "Like what, for instance?"

"People. Cars. Unusual coming and going?"

He peered into the streaked windscreen, seeing his own dim reflection and perhaps theirs. His hands caressed the wheel. "S'pose I did see something?"

Rita controlled an urge to clobber him. By agreement, Stewart was Bernice's territory.

"Could be a story. If it breaks, you'd have first crack."

"I already won the *Star* newstip. First prize, you know."

"So I saw. And between you and me, this would make the newstip look like last week's leftovers."

Stewart considered. "Maybe I did see something. Yeah."

They waited. Finally Bernice said, "Well?"

"How about a car?" He turned round. "How about if I saw a car?"

"Depends. Did you get a number?"

"A playground's sure gonna take a load of dimes," he leered.

Absent this remark, his glasses might have stayed put. As it was, the swipe Rita dealt him with her purse squashed them against his cheek and the frame bent out.

"Oh, Rita!" Bernice was angry.

Suddenly Ollie was there, dancing around the car, screaming, "He's coming, he's coming! He couldn't stop!" He tugged at the driver's door, then pummeled on it. Stewart was too busy trying to straighten out his frame so he could see, to pay much attention. In the process, they snapped. He had to hold them up to get a proper look at the dark shape filling the gap in the siding.

"Goodness," Bernice exclaimed, "It's Otis."

"Is everything all right?" Otis advanced, hands outstretched, in a blind man's shuffle. "Saw your buggy and thought I'd better check."

"We're having just a fine time," Rita said. "Get in, there's room up front."

"I heard the commotion," Otis puffed. He was out of breath. "Who's this?"

Stewart was explained. Outside on the street Bernice related what had happened. "Let me handle it," Otis said. "Give me a minute."

Waiting for him, Rita asked, "Do you have the same feeling I do?"

"What?"

"The guy's following us around?"

"He probably thinks we can't look out for ourselves."

"My question is, can he?"

"My feeling is he's pretty good in that department."

Rita soon had to swallow her words. A few minutes later, Otis reappeared. He glanced nervously up and down the street and climbed in behind them. "That's that," he patted his breast pocket. He was wearing the pants of his green suit and a brown golf shirt several sizes too big. "I got it."

"Got what?" Rita demanded. The tinge of smugness in his voice alerted her.

"Plate number of suspect vehicle."

"O, boy!" Bernice whooped.

He talks like he's in law enforcement, Rita thought.

"Nice kid. Had him eating out of my hand. Treat 'em right, they respect you."

Go on, rub it in, she thought.

"Says he saw this vehicle in the vicinity a day or two prior to the crime, then again the night it happened. It's a habit with him, jotting down plate numbers."

"Was it a maroon Checker Marathon with omnibus plates?" Rita asked. No one laughed.

"It wasn't late model, he says. Darkish. Green or blue."

"Keep your head down," Rita said. "I'm driving by Scaguiola's. That's our prime suspect." It was less than a ten minute ride.

Cars were dotted around the Camelot Mews cul-de-sac. "Bernice, call the numbers."

The fourth number belonged to a dusty, dark blue Impala. "Check," Otis said. "That's it."

Bernice said, "Do both its tail lights work?"

"How should I know?" Rita's mood should have been ecstatic now they finally had a break. Instead, she felt irked.

"Why?" Otis called out.

"Oh, I guess it's not important."

"You never know," Otis persisted.

"Just that a couple of times a car seemed like it was following us. It was missing a tail light."

"Which side?"

She tried to visualize the scene. "The left."

"So how much did the little SOB hit you for?" Rita couldn't resist.

"They want to make a playground. It was a contribution. The kid showed me his notebook, right where he'd written it. Then there were the glasses. They were broken."

Touché, Rita thought. "It was his own damn fault. I'd have settled with his father. Now he'll claim twice."

"Say, we make a pretty good team," Bernice put in determinedly, "the three of us. And you were right about the police, Otis, not going to them. Who'd ever have imagined? I reckon it was money well spent."

Precisely, Otis thought. He was careful not to mention the actual sum. No way they'd have approved.

11

"Just listen to this!" Bernice was sitting on the floor in Rita's small living room reading the paper. The pages snapped angrily in the breeze of an electric fan. She battled to control them. "Governor Serenades Mexican Pesos. So *that's* what he was up to."

"Say again." Rita came in from the kitchen.

"The other flag on the car on the way to your uncle's. '*The Governor and his guests paid their respects at the memorial to the fallen Mexican air ace, Emilio Carranza, who crashed to his death in the Jersey Pines July 13th, 1928, during a severe thunderstorm while on a goodwill mission to this country.*'

"They've got all this oil money to invest, and some of it's coming to Jersey," Bernice went on. "And guess what?" She wrestled with the page and eventually subdued it, "Right over here: *A proposed industrial park for South Jersey.*" She stumped on her knees across the carpet to the couch where Rita was sitting and plunked the folded paper on her lap.

"He said there was foreign money involved. I guess he was right."

Outside, a series of small explosions broke the evening's calm, followed by a resounding bang; like a gas leak in somebody's basement. In the rush to the window, Bernice knocked over the tea.

Rita wrenched open the front door. Up and down the street

people were peering through their gauze screens and lacy curtains, curious, frightened. "Lordy, Lordy!" A tell-tale haze of smoke drew her gaze to where, about three houses down, a familiar looking vehicle had come to rest. Walking rather quickly in Rita's direction came Uncle Sudeley, seemingly unaware of the diversion he was creating. On the far side of the road flapped and squawked a brown hen, its little legs pumping the tarmac. "Guess who's getting lapped by a road-runner?" Rita called to Bernice.

"Abandon ship!" Uncle Sudeley cried, cutting across the lawn. "Bad business, bad business." Sweating and heaving, they managed—the three of them—to push the car to the curb. No offers of help came, though Rita guessed twenty pairs of eyes were watching. It was that sort of community. She looked around for the hen, which had vanished.

"Uncle Sudeley—that bird yours?"

"She'll be back. Just stretching her legs."

"You can say that again," Bernice laughed.

"It's going to scratch up flowerbeds and it's going to be reported," Rita warned.

He teased: "And be lynched by the vigilante committee."

"There's a rule about poultry."

"There's a rule for everything here." Uncle Sudeley mopped his brow and looked around at the neat bungalows with their pink cast iron flamingoes, wishing wells and names like Xanadu. "Give me Alcatraz any day." Next thing they knew he was scattering chicken feed from his pocket over the lawn. "She'll be back."

"Want to call the garage?"

Uncle Sudeley winced. "A garage is to a car what a hospital is to a man. First rule of the road: don't go near one unless you're looking for trouble." He looked affectionately at the Rambler. "We traveled a ways together today. Trenton. She's a country car; doesn't hold much with towns. Then coming in here got us all turned around. Must have put on ten miles. She's just thirsty. Needs a rest and a drink. We both do. We've earned it." He held up a tattered copy of Search magazine with a flying saucer on the cover. It was scribbled all over.

Whatever her uncle had come about, Rita knew it must rate. He didn't make social calls, and 'leisure villages' were his idea of hell. It had been Aunt Sadie's great object in life to move to one. She'd had it all picked out for years and steadfastly hacked away at his resistance. Uncle Sudeley hadn't visited in the year Rita had been at Carefree Days. "'Cording to the address I had, you're on Russel Road, Rita. Now what's all this whatyoumacallit?" He consulted the flying saucer. "Demo something?"

"Demosthenes Drive. They changed it after one of the committee read through the philosophers—which is who the streets are named after. Turns out this Russel was a Commie. They got up a petition."

"Well it hardly fits on the sign." They were back inside with fresh iced tea.

"Try to find a safe one with a short name. Anyway, next time look for Ruby Road. I hear they voted for precious stones." She pushed the paper across the table. "Did you see in the *Star* about the Mexicans and the industrial park?"

He squinted at the small print. "It's getting about then. Watch how they put the squeeze on your friend for his John Hancock." He chuckled. "They're in for a surprise. If they knew what I'd turned up today they'd give me a turn on the rack too."

"In Trenton?"

"We hit pay dirt, girl, in the State Library." He slapped down the newspaper. "We can put a name to our missing heir; a name, a face, and maybe even a destination." He chuckled again. "Some face, though. I'll tell you that."

"So tell."

Uncle Sudeley pushed back his chair importantly. He'd looked forward to this. "Some laddie, that Amos Good. Ahead of his time, shall we say. Not bad for then. Not bad for now, come to think of it. "According to the census of 1860, taken in the month of July in Cranberry Township, Amos Good had a five-year-old male living under his roof along of his first wife, Jennie Eliza. That youngster was our friend Obed. Obed Good. And after the name, in the column marked color, there was an M. M for Mulatto."

"He adopted a colored boy?" Rita made sure she had it right.

"Which may account for that coolness in the rest of the family. Heck, the Klan was founded in '66, and the White Camellia the year after. Those were rough times. My own father joined the Klan, your grandad, Rita. And probably his father before him." He looked at her slyly. "It wasn't long after they were married your grandma found his robe. Told him he had one hour to burn it up, or he'd seen the last of her. He burned it, or I guess we wouldn't be here. As it was, he'd have been hounded out for marrying a Democrat. There were no Democrats in Cranberry Township in those days. They were all hard-working Republicans."

"Obed Good," Bernice nudged.

"That was the easy part," Uncle Sudeley continued. "I went to the census of 1870. Nothing. Not a word. He was gone. Amos was dead and Obed gone. Either of you gals got a pencil?" He turned a fresh page of the magazine and began to scribble, scrutinizing scraps of paper he pulled from his pockets. "Best get it down while it's fresh." Bernice and Rita watched. After a minute or two, he peered at them over his glasses. "Know something? I haven't had this much fun in years. No, sir, they don't call me Scoop for nothing. What's the time in Texas?"

"A little before five," Rita said. "They're two hours behind."

"That lawyer of yours," he looked at Bernice. "Can you get ahold of him?"

"Cousin Harrison?" She reached for her purse. "Oh gee, the number's at the house. Let's see ... Gee, it's been a while."

"No matter," Uncle Sudeley said, "Ask Ma Bell."

"Now?"

"We want to get him at the office."

Bernice talked to a Houston operator and the next thing she knew the phone was ringing in Cousin Harrison's office. "What'll I ...?"

"Just put me on." Uncle Sudeley joined them in the kitchen.

"I haven't talked to him—oh boy, it must be five years."

Cousin Harrison, to her considerable relief, was in a meeting. A woman told her in a warm Texan drawl that sure thing, if it was urgent she'd get him to call back just as soon as he could. Rita poured more iced tea and foraged for snacks in the fridge.

"This here's what we know so far," Uncle Sudeley shifted a saucepan and smoothed out his magazine on the drainboard.

What, he'd asked himself as he sat in the library in Trenton, would have become of that little colored boy? The lad would have been eleven when his adoptive father died, scarcely old enough to strike out on his own, though there were lads not much older who'd ridden the railroad west and made do by herding sheep or as a tinker's helper or an hostler. But a colored lad? With slavery so recently flourishing? Heck, out West, even the Indians had slaves. Times were turbulent in those parts after the war. Most likely if the second Mrs. Amos hadn't kept him—and, for whatever reason, she apparently hadn't—he'd have been farmed out to relatives. But which ones? Surely not the Goods who later did her out of her inheritance under Joseph Vannover Good's Will. Then perhaps the Gaines, her own people? And what would take a New Jersey person out west around the year 1866? There was business, like cattle ranching; there were the missions; there was adventure and pure fortune seeking; and then there was the Union Army. With the war just won, the army was manning forts all through the West, nailing down the country's unruly frontier.

Uncle Sudeley had got out Stryker's *Record of the Officers and Men of New Jersey in the Civil War* and looked up Gaines. No one fitted the bill. Then he looked up Machonochie, because that was the maiden name of Jennie Eliza, Amos Good's first wife. He flicked through the pages of the big book, ran his finger down the column, and, yes, there it was. Even in the retelling, his heart jumped a bit: Machonochie, Napoleon B., Lieutenant. A rundown of the engagements he's taken part in ended with his posting, in 1866, to Fort Concho, Texas, with the 4th Cavalry. A brother, perhsps, to whom an orphan child might be entrusted? It was a shot in the dark.

Fort Concho wasn't on any modern map. Uncle Sudeley

found it eventually in an historical atlas and figured out the county it was in. He needed the county so as to request the right microfiche of the 1870 census in Texas. He fitted the reel onto the machine, focused and started winding. Fort Concho was near the end. He wound slowly, squinting at the names, which didn't appear to be in any particular order. Machonochie, Machonochie. Perhaps he'd been posted away in the four years since 1866. But no. Luck held. *Machonochie Napoleon B. 40, Male, White, Captain 4th Cavalry. Born New Jersey.* Then the names of two lieutenants, presumably billeted with him, and then, in the looping, graceful band of the census taker, *Good, Obed, 16, Male, Mulatto, Domestic Servant.* He made a copy.

The phone rang. Rita looked at Bernice.

"Harrison? Hi!" Her nervousness evaporated at the sound of the voice. There seemed to be an extra boom to it.

"Hey! Mom! Great! Gee, do you mind if I still call you that? How are you? Hey, how's it going back there?"

"Oh, pretty much the same ..."

"Know what, I'm fixing to get married. I was going to call you."

"That's wonderful."

"Coupla weeks. Listen, tell you what, come on down."

"To Texas?"

"Sure thing. You'll be a witness. It'll just be Melanie and me and ..."

"That was your Grandma's name."

"I'll send you a ticket."

Rita was gesturing with her eyes at the ceiling. Bernice ignored her. She couldn't get off work, she said.

"We'll make it a weekend."

"All the way to Texas?" The nearest she'd come to flying was the Ferris wheel at Great Adventure.

"Mom, listen. I've got to do something for you special, after what you did for me. Will you let me do that? Please?"

One of the things about Harrison, she recalled, was his Texas-sized impulsiveness. Sometimes it took the form of generosity, which was one reason, she supposed, she hadn't kept in touch. Still, maybe now he could afford it. "Well, maybe there is something, Harrison; something you could do. Remember Rita? Rita, the one who ..." She laughed, "You got it."

After a brief introduction, she put Uncle Sudeley on. "Knows his onions," he grunted, when he hung up. Harrison's secretary had taken down the details. A copy of the quitclaim deed in the mail, express, was promised. "Naught to do now but cool our heels. If there are descendants, and if they're still in Texas, I reckon he'll drop a net on them."

"Let's hope." Rita sounded doubtful. She had her own memories of Harrison.

"He'll come through, I know it," Bernice said. "You never had the patience ..."

"The guy's about to get hitched."

A dreamy look lighted on Bernice's face. "I sure wish I could go."

Uncle Sudeley was filling a battered tin flask from the tap. "One for the road." He never traveled without his Japanese water bottle, retrieved on the beach at Saipan. On cold nights he filled it from the kettle and took it to bed to warm his feet.

"There's something out there." Rita was staring. She had sharp eyes. The kitchen looked out on a steel mesh fence some thirty yards off, the Village boundary. Beyond was a stretch of weed-tufted sandy ground, and beyond that sea pines against the evening sky, which flared a bright orange so the trees looked like they were on fire.

Straining her eyes, Bernice saw a figure ducking back towards the trees.

"Let's go." Rita grabbed her keys and ran out the front door. They piled, all three, into the Checker.

"Was he looking our way?" Bernice gasped.

"Not for the first time, either."

"There's a track turns off that way a couple of hundred yards up," Uncle Sudeley puffed. "It's a dead end so if we get a wiggle on we may catch the son of a gun; bottle him up." The sewage plan for Carefree Days had been drawn up in his time.

"Then what?" Bernice asked. She didn't expect an answer.

Dusk was falling. They hurtled past the startled guard and

turned left out of the gate. Uncle Sudeley tensed forward as Rita flicked on her beams. "See that sign, POOLS? It's across from there." He might have been in his landing craft, cresting the beach at Saipan.

Off to the left fast-moving headlights flickered among the trees. For a few seconds it seemed that the two cars were on a collision course. But the other pulled out ahead, barely hesitated, then hared off up the road. The left rear light was out.

Rita floored the gas pedal. "See that? It's him." It did resemble the car they'd seen outside Scaguiola's on Saturday. She urged the Checker on till it rattled and shook so much something was bound to fall off. But the quarry had spotted them and slipped away. In the gathering darkness, they hadn't seen the number.

"You'd think they'd have pulled him over by now, driving like a maniac with his light out," Bernice said.

"Cops," Rita growled, recalling the times she'd been booked for lesser offences. "They get away with anything."

"Not with murder." Bernice's small fists clenched in her lap. "We'll see."

Getting back, they found Uncle Sudeley's hen tucked up for the night under the Rambler, just as he'd predicted. With a fearsome clatter, the car steamed down Demosthenes Drive, along Pascal Parade and down Schweitzer Boulevard. They heard its consumptive cough all the way to the gate.

"He should junk that thing. It's a deathtrap," Rita said. "Did you see what was keeping the gas in? Cling wrap and a rubber band."

They drove to Bernice's to pick up some clothes she needed for work next day. In the gap between the screen and the back door someone had stuck a sheet of cardboard; on it, daubed in white, was a grinning skull.

"Don't touch it," Rita snapped, staring with a mixture of disgust and amazement. There were no signs of a break in. "We're going to the police and we're laying the whole thing out. I don't give a damn what they say. If something happens to us, on their heads be it."

12

Detective Gus Biswekki of the Cranberry Township Police Department uncoiled himself from behind the wheel of his unmarked Torino and looked about. The women from the Checker were already mounting the steps to the back porch of what, to him, seemed like a ramshackle small house, one of the older ones along Bay Road. He wondered if it might be coming on the market any time soon, and made a mental note to tip off his brother-in-law. A smart agent could make an overnight killing on this type of property, if it was handled right. He'd thought a lot recently about going into real estate himself. Seemed like these days you couldn't lose. Biswekki lit a cigarette and tossed away the match. From the sound of it, all was not well on the back porch. He wondered again why the boss had ordered kid gloves.

"It's gone," Rita yelled. "It was here last night. Right in here." She was holding the screen door ajar and flapped it to get the detective's attention. "And now it's gone."

"What about the glads?" Bernice made as if to enter the house, but Rita stopped her.

"Let him see for himself." She appealed to Biswekki.

He eyed the door languorously: "Nothing there no more." He was a large man, running to plump, in his early thirties. His sport coat, lightweight in a heather check, had breast pockets with button-down flaps and a half belt at the back.

His shoes boasted gold buckles. On his right pinkie flashed a large signet ring set with his birthstone, topaz, a present from a girlfriend that wouldn't come off. His school ring graced his middle finger. From his upper lip drooped a chestnut mustache.

Inside, in the kitchen, Detective Biswekki obediently surveyed some wilted gladioli, while Bernice explained how she found them. He took a long drag on his cigarette and, not seeing an ashtray, used the sink.

"Wait right there, Officer. I'll get the wrappings." Bernice bustled out to the garbage and reappeared with an armful of green tissue and cellophane.

Biswekki took it all in: the wrappings, Bernice, Rita, the flowers. He sucked long and hard at his cigarette and exhaled slowly. They watched expectantly. "So what am I supposed to do?" he said, finally. "Dust it for fingerprints?"

Already, at the station house, Rita and Bernice—who had managed to get off from work—had laid the whole thing out, just as Scaguiola had challenged them to do: the phone call from Miss Annie, the threats against Bernice after they'd first called the police, the feeling they were being watched, the car with the broken tail light; and finally, their suspicion of Scaguiola himself. Bernice even mentioned the woman who'd seen the devil the night before the fire, which itself, they insisted, was suspicious. They kept quiet about Otis Phinney, and about the family Bible, the quitclaim business and Uncle Sudeley's historical research.

The duty officer had listened politely, made no notes, and even managed to keep a straight face. And when the complainants seemed not about to get up and walk meekly away on the promise that it would all be looked into, indeed showed signs of staying put till the alleged perpetrator, a brother officer, be dragged in and booked for murder, he did some fast thinking. Biswekki's loud guffaw in the hallway proved the detective's undoing. A quick consultation, and he was deputed to lure them away on the pretext of a preliminary investigation.

Standing in the kitchen of the house on Bay Road, even Rita

was forced to view the detective's obvious ennui with sympathy. She tried to see it from his angle: disembodied phone calls, missing tail lights, flowers and skulls and diabolical visions. A clear case of paranoia. They needed something concrete, something for him to see and turn over and over in his large, fleshy hands. Something to get his attention.

"There is another thing." She said, half looking at Bernice and unaware that in her next breath she might be signing somebody's death warrant. "This kid on Gunning Point Road; his name's Stewart. About 16. I don't recall the last name, but he lives near where they did. He got the number of a car that was in the vicinity around the time it happened. It was Scaguiola's." She waited for a reaction. It didn't come.

Biswekki took out a notebook and wrote, 'Stewart, no last name, Gunning Point Road.' To all appearances, he was still dying of boredom. "I'll look into it," he said.

Rita knew there was a risk: Stewart might bring up Otis. It was Otis he'd given the number to. Yet he wouldn't know Otis's name or anything about him. It was what he'd seen, not who he'd told about it, that mattered. "We could go along; show you the house."

"Na," he snapped shut the book. "I gotta report back anyway. I'll find it. Better that way."

After he'd gone, Bernice discovered the paper with the piece about the fire. "Krabbowicz." She tapped her head. "I had it filed under seafood." They decided to drop it off at the station house on their way through town.

While Rita waited in the car, Bernice ran up the steps. The receptionist wasn't at her post. Bernice started off down the hall, then stopped at the sound of a voice booming from an open door: "Get out the cuffs there, Buddy boy. Looks bad for Scag!"

"Hi there?" a voice behind her enquired.

"Oh, hi." It was 'Carol Burnett'.

"I just wanted to leave this—for Detective Biswekki. He'll know what it's for."

"Alrighty."

She handed over the paper with the name circled, and left.

The tone of Biswekki's voice and the answering guffaw said it all. It didn't look bad for Scag. It looked rosy.

Rita clanged down the phone. "Some consolation, but if anything happens to us, Bernice, like I said they're going to look pretty darn stupid." For two days they'd been getting the runaround from the police. 'He's out.' 'He's looking into it.' 'They're working on it.' Not even, 'He'll get back to you.' "It's the herd instinct: one's threatened so the whole pack bands together."

"I guess ..." Bernice didn't finish. Her confidence in the forces of law and order had all but evaporated. It was a bitter pill.

"What?"

"Looks like we're it, then."

They decided to make a start by shadowing Sergeant Scaguiola in his off hours, on the theory that he'd lead them to his boss or bosses. He was, in their eyes, a hit man, nothing more, in it either from fear or greed. If they could tie him to KAY-LEE Enterprises, they might have themselves a case. Otis might get his money. Miss Annie's death might be avenged. The immediate problem was the Checker. Otis had said it stood out a mile. He was right. The alternative—renting—was too expensive. It might be weeks before they turned up anything. In the end, Rita decided to risk it, but be extra cautious.

Friday night, after failing to persuade Bernice to drop out of HELP, Rita stayed with her, against all the rules. She stretched out on the couch and was soon snoring. She slept better than might have been expected: Bernice didn't know, but in her purse, within easy reach, was a .22 caliber revolver, loaded.

Midday Saturday Scaguiola's car was parked at the curb where they'd seen it before. The windows of his apartment were closed and curtained. At four, when they checked again, the car was gone.

Rita swore. "We lost him already."

Instead of driving into Camelot Mews and risking a close encounter, they had chosen a vantage point some hundred yards away across rough ground in the parking lot of a pet

95

care center. Bernice was rummaging in a bag of groceries for something to nibble on, mainly to keep awake. "If we hang around, maybe he'll come back."

"Holy Moly!" Rita whipped out her binoculars and adjusted the focus. "It's him. He's parked the car. Now he's getting something out of the back seat."

"Is he alone?"

"Yes. Oh my God, it's groceries. We could have run into him in the aisle. Three bags."

"He's in a blue T-shirt, right?"

"Some angling club. There's a fish on it. He's walking across the gravel, up the stairs. He's getting out his key. Oops! He's dropped something. He's kicking the door half down. Christ, what a swine. Talk about a short fuse."

There was a tap at the window. They both froze. "'Scuse me, would you like four Himalayan kittens?"

"What?" said Bernice.

A small face eyed them intently. "Four Himalayan kittens."

"Thanks anyway."

"What's she doing?"

"Cop watching."

"OK. Bye."

"He must have gone in," Rita said. "The door's open. Oh oh. She's coming out; in her nightie still, by the looks of it."

"A housedress could be."

"She's picking stuff up. Her hair's falling every which way. I wonder if she ever gets out of there." She put down the binoculars. "Well, that's that little bit of excitement."

"What if he won't let her out?"

"You mean she's a prisoner? Uh uh. She's alone most of the day. She could leave."

"I don't mean physically," Bernice said. "mentally. Particularly if she doesn't have friends around to talk to. A woman called up one time who said her husband beat her every night. Every night. So I said the same thing: 'Why not leave?' She couldn't, she said. There was like a chain binding her to him. She couldn't explain. It was just there."

"Why not get her to call HELP? We could slip a note under

the door with the number. Maybe she'd talk. I'll bet she suspects he's up to something, even if she doesn't know for sure."

"Rita!" Bernice hoped she was joking. She pried open a packet of pop tarts and passed one over.

"He's off again." Rita grabbed the binoculars. Heading for his car. In uniform." She turned the key in the ignition, suddenly nervous. Trailing a cop was easy enough to talk about. Doing it was something else.

The Impala turned left out of Camelot Mews. The Checker followed. They barreled along, separated by a single car. Rita took her foot off the gas, hoping the car behind would pass. She'd be happier with a two-car spread between them. It didn't. After a few minutes, the Impala made a right. The car behind kept going. Rita, in a dither, also made a right, but at the last moment so that the car behind her hooted irritably. They were on Gunning Point Road.

The road wound gently inland. At the bay end, the houses were larger and more settled looking than those further on where the sisters had lived and development taken its toll. The Impala was out of sight now. Around every turn Rita expected to see it pulled over and Scaguiola standing there, flagging her down. Would she stop, she wondered, or pretend not to see? Why was he going this route anyway? Sure, it was one way to the station house, but unless he's changed his schedule he wasn't on duty today. And it was too early for the Furnace. My God, she thought, another block and they'll go right by Miss Annie's. "He's got some nerve," she said out loud.

Bernice had been thinking the same. "Maybe he turned off already," she ventured.

Now they were on the block itself and could see clear to the intersection where the phone booth was. Approached from this direction, the charred gap was on their right. They were amazed to see that since their last visit almost a week ago bulldozers had moved in. The scorched surface had been partly skimmed away, leaving level, reddish earth. Only the barn and two or three big trees remained alongside the yellow hulks of the machinery. A sign said, 'Desirable Tract: For Sale Half Acre Lots'.

Bernice saw him first. He'd parked his car and was getting out. "Keep going," she cautioned. "Don't look round."

On reaching the intersection Rita turned right and stopped. "Did he spot us?"

"I'm not sure. His back was to the road." They circled the block, left the car on a side street, and reconnoitered on foot. Apart from the occasional Saturday driver, Gunning Point Road was quiet.

Stewart's house looked deserted. Rita stopped, grabbing her friend's arm. An awful thought had struck her. "He couldn't be," she dropped her voice, "after Stewart?"

The chirping of crickets, unnoticed till now, filled their ears like a warning. The house, behind its newly scarred lawn, stared back impassively. The garage door was closed. Rita had an urge to cross the road and peek through its little window, just check if a car was there. She didn't.

At the edge of the sisters' land they paused. Scraggly bushes and clumps of Queen Anne's lace had survived both fire and bulldozers, affording scanty cover. Not thirty yards off, moving with an odd, jerky stride, eyes down as if searching for something, Scagiola came towards them. Suddenly he stopped, dug in a heel, and drove what looked like a steak into the fresh earth. Then, turning at right angles, he moved away across the land where the old house had stood.

"The nerve." Rita let out the breath she'd been holding. "What's he up to now?" They didn't stay to find out. Back in the Checker she found herself shaking uncontrollably and clutched the wheel for support. "It's times like this I curse the day I stopped smoking."

Bernice, too, was seething. "I've been thinking, Rita. What you said about the wife."

"The HELP line?"

"No, but talking to her."

"How'd we get her alone?"

"Well, she's alone right now."

They looked at each other. Rita turned the key. The Checker moved forward. "Problem number one: getting in the front door."

98

Twenty minutes later a diminutive figure could be seen climbing the stairs to the Sir Launcelot, preceded by a large fern which gyrated at every step like a flamenco dancer. Bernice rang the bell. Anyone looking through the peephole would have seen a plant standing there. "Welcome wagon!" As the door opened, she lunged, fern first, for the gap. In seconds the plant had changed hands.

Rita, downstairs, kept watching the now closed door, at any moment expecting it to disgorge her friend. Amazingly, it stayed shut.

"I felt bad, the other day, about your not feeling welcome down here. I said to myself, Bernice, you've lived here all your life, there's got to be something you can do to help make that nice Mrs. Scaguiola feel at home. So I thought and thought, and I thought the best thing to do is be a friend, stop by once in a while for a chat, see if anything needed doing ..." Bernice rattled on while the woman, still holding the fern, fastened her with the uncomprehending gaze of a child, as if she was watching TV with the volume off. A set was blaring from a room down the hall.

Bernice took in the shapeless housedress, frayed carpet slippers, unkempt hair, the black and blue marks on the carves and a nasty-looking rash across one side of the face which the woman tried, with her free hand, to hide. How long, Bernice wondered, before some spark of fellow feeling lit in those frightened eyes. Or would they stand here in the cramped, stuffy, vestibule forever? She decided to risk an opening. "Don't mind me. Here I am, going on and I don't even know your name."

As they stood, silently eying one another, Bernice's smile began to wear thin. Then—one low word—it came. The ice-breaker. "Doreen."

"I'm Bernice." Still the woman didn't move.

With a crash the potted plant hit the deck. Doreen wasn't far behind, and the sobbing wail that accompanied her descent turned Bernice to gooseflesh. From down the hall, an infant joined its screams to the hubbub.

Rita had been standing in the stairwell at the second floor

level of the Sir Launcelot for twenty minutes, eyes glued to the road, before she saw the blue Impala turn into the cul-de-sac. On the whistle hanging round her neck she blew a blast loud enough to wake—if not the dead—then anyone in the building. Then she waited, watching the car park, and listened for the closing of the fourth floor door and light footsteps padding along the balcony and down the concrete stairs. Another blast. She listened again. Bernice was cutting it pretty fine if she wanted to make it down three flights to the hideout they'd scouted round the back by the trashcans. Already Scaguiola was edging into his regular spot.

Rita took the stairs two at a time. She didn't knock on the fourth floor door, she pounded, cracking—as she later discovered—one lens of her binoculars. Then she ran back to the stairs and started walking down with all the composure she could muster. Already steps were ascending. Angry steps, she thought, of a man in a hurry.

Once the woman opened her mouth, there was no stopping her. Bawling and sobbing, sobbing and bawling. Bernice lost track of time. Somehow they made it the few yards to a couch in the living room, but each attempt—however gentle—to elicit information about Scaguiola brought on a fresh squall. And the TV blared. It was the battering at the front door that did the trick: Doreen leaped to her feet. "He'll kill me." Grabbing Bernice, she propelled her into a closet in the room with the baby. She was beginning to get her bearings when the potted fern joined her.

Then came a voice, Scaguiola's. "So you bin entertaining, eh?"

"No I ain't."

"Oh no? Who was that then, going down?"

"Who?"

"That woman."

"I wouldn't let her in. I wouldn't let nobody in."

"You wouldn't, eh? You better not. What's all this here, then?"

"All what?"

"This right here."

100

"Look at your muddy boots," she retorted, "You bin rolling in it?"

Bernice heard sounds of a scuffle. She winced. "That's enough outta you. Now get these cleaned up. And don't try nothing."

Bernice felt around. The place smelled of mingled sweat and perfume. Clothes, shoes, purses, belts, all higgledy piggledy . Why hadn't Rita blown the whistle?

Ten minutes in a packed closet was about Bernice's limit. Then Doreen's bruised, puffy face bent over her. "He's gonna kill me. Now get outta here. And don't come back. Please."

"Will you be all right?" Bernice looked at her anxiously.

"*Please.*"

The baby's face was scarlet. She'd have liked to comfort it. "So what's he mixed up in? What's his problem?"

"I don't know. I don't wanna know. 'Wait and see,' he says." She handed Bernice the fern.

Outside the sun shone. Bernice blinked. Rita was walking towards her. But for the fern, they would have embraced out of sheer relief. The Checker was at the pet care center; they stumbled over the rough ground towards it. "He looked a real mess," Rita said, "running up those stairs. Mud. Sweat. It makes you wonder." She put a hand on Bernice's shoulder. "I thought for sure you'd come out feet first. He had murder in his eye."

"I was worried about you."

"Me? I just walked on past him, cool as a cucumber."

They had driven through town and were within a mile of Carefree Days in heavy traffic when a smattering of hoots made Rita look in the mirror. A big car was flashing its lights; then the car swerved into the center lane to overtake. "What the?"

"It's Otis! He's signaling. Slow down, Rita."

"Who does he think he is? Rip van Winkle?" Otis's now you see me now you don't act was getting to her.

Otis had pulled ahead. His right turn signal came on and he abruptly reduced speed. Rita applied the brakes and followed him into the parking lot of a Monarchburger concession. Behind the wheel of what looked like a brand new Eldorado, Otis appeared even more dwarf-like than usual. "You win the lottery or something?" Rita eyed the car.

He walked over. "If I'd have played your number backwards I'd have made the millionaire's draw."

"So what's the occasion?"

"The Caddy? They're giving them away,"

"I mean why did you pull us over?"

"Saw you pulling out of where that cop lives."

"You following us around?"

"You're hard to miss."

"We've been doing some following of our own." Bernice described their adventures with Scaguiola.

Rita leaned across. "And we did go to the police. They put this complete dodo on the case. We had to dangle some fresh meat to make him pay attention, so we threw in Stewart: how he got the plate number. Don't worry, you're safe. We didn't mention you."

Otis had a way of wiping his hand along his upper lip when agitated, like a chipmunk. He was doing it now. "You OK?" Bernice asked.

"You're crazy," he spluttered. "Plum crazy. You wanna get that boy killed?"

They stared at him.

"Well, you're going the right way about it."

Rita recalled her panic as less than an hour ago they'd stood across from Stewart's closed up house. In hindsight, it seemed melodramatic. "I doubt they followed it up. They weren't very interested."

"Let's hope not; for his sake—and yours." Otis sounded ominous. "And another thing: chasing after cops, in that of all things. You *looking* for trouble?"

"As a matter of fact, yes. You know what?" She turned to Bernice. "We should follow that son of a bitch tonight when he leaves the Furnace. That's the time to watch him."

"Not in this you don't," he slapped the Checker. "It's a red rag. He'll lure you off some place and that'll be it."

"Any suggestions?" Rita said archly.

"Lemme think here." After a minute of apparent intense concentration, he said, "I got it. This is a 24-hour joint, right?"

Rita nodded. "So?"

"When does the Furness let out?"

"Two. Thereabouts."

"I'll meet you back here then. Say quarter of two. We'll take my car. It's rented."

The Eldorado—grass green with gold trim—swung back onto the highway in a squeal of rubber. "Talk about standing out a mile." Bernice watched till it was out of sight. "Still, it's not what you'd expect." Otis was full of surprises.

13

There were other cars, but few and far between.

The Garden State Parkway snakes north along the Jersey shore, twin ribbons of asphalt curving through banks of foliage lit jungle-green by intermittent arcs of orange. In the front seat of the Eldorado an overtaking motorist might have glimpsed an older couple, Munchkin-like, seemingly comfortable in their silence. A third passenger might also have been observed hunched in the back and staring up the road ahead. The one incongruous note, perhaps, was the lateness—or earliness—of the hour. 3:30 a.m. Their shiny conveyance notwithstanding, these people didn't look like high rollers on their way home from the green felt tables of Atlantic City.

Rita wore a red wig—from a one-time suitor who liked redheads—and lipstick to match. Bernice had on a little flowery bridesmaid's hat (also Rita's), and blue-tinted shades with slanted mother of pearl frames out of a grandmother of the year contest. Otis boasted a natty gray mustache, which, Bernice thought, gave him a rather dashing continental air. If not quite Maurice Chevalier, it did offset his weak chin. His gaze swept the dashboard. "Six way power seat adjustor, automatic climate control, side window defoggers. You name it. State of the art." He leaned back comfortably. "How sweet it is."

When Scaguiola swung his Impala into the northbound

104

entrance to the parkway they had felt the adrenalin surge in their veins. He wasn't heading home. Up ahead, his one red taillight appeared and reappeared with reassuring monotony. They'd been waiting for him, not at the Furnace but at a junction beyond the school bus depot where he'd have to pass. The lone red light had become their guiding star. "Still hasn't fixed it," Bernice exclaimed. "He's a cop," Rita reiterated. Otis agreed: "All they're gonna see is the uniform." Still, to Bernice, it seemed odd.

Rita broke a silence. "So is he a loner, or is he a hired gun?" Getting no response, she went on, "Right up till we saw him today, pacing that property like he owned it, I'd have sworn he was just a hatchet man. Now? What's the deal? What's he playing for?"

"That's maybe what we're going to find out," Bernice said. The tinted glasses were giving her a headache. She took them off.

Otis shook his head. "A nickel to a buck he's working for KAY-LEE. He's gotta be."

"KAY-LEE, KAY-LEE, KAY-LEE," Rita blurted out. "What is KAY-LEE when it's at home?"

"More like who," Otis said. It's one guy, basically, name of Taffelbaum. Felix Taffelbaum. Has a whole mess of corporations he controls. Trucking to oil to chicken farms. KAY-LEE is construction."

"That's where I've seen it," Bernice said. "Up on billboards."

"Up north mainly," Otis said. "Taffelbaum's worth more money than God. But nobody ever heard of him. Not like say your Charles Engelhard. He plays possum. Holes up on a 300 acre estate and pulls the strings from there."

"Where exactly?" Rita asked.

"North Jersey someplace," Otis sounded vague.

"Like where?"

"Somerville. Around there." He added quickly, "You can't get near it. Like an armed camp." Words they would remember.

"You tried?"

"Negative," he admitted. "But it's common knowledge."

"You just said nobody ever heard of him."

Bernice noticed they were gaining on the red light. She touched Otis's arm and he eased up. "Maybe he's going there now." But before the Somerville exit Scaguiola turned off. They'd been close to an hour on his tail.

Some of the tension seemed to drain out of Otis. "I was beginning to think he was headed for the city." New York wasn't that far off. "We'd have lost him over there."

They crossed the Raritan River at its mouth by the Victory Bridge. The tires sang on the metal grid of the narrow, steel drawbridge. To the right the bay opened into the Atlantic. The night was clear and they could see storage tanks gleaming like giant, silvery vats at the water's edge. "All Taffelbaum," Otis jerked his head. A slew of messy factories lined the shore.

"Welcome to the city of Perth Amboy," Rita read, wrinkling her nose. It wasn't just that the town had seen better days— as capital of the eastern half of the state back in the seventeen hundreds, for instance. It literally stank. At the first light after the bridge, Scaguiola made a right and was lost to sight behind a long, white, crumbling building ringed by weeds and a high wire fence. Otis put his foot down and the Eldorado responded like a mountain lion. A smell, like synthetic bread, filled the air: they were passing a lye factory. The street was lined with pumping stations and taverns, all ghostly still. Side streets, crammed with tiny houses, rose to the left. The Impala had slowed to a crawl, dangerously narrowing the gap between them. Surely he's seen us, Rita thought. But if he had, he made no sign. Biding his time, perhaps.

Right again across railroad tracks. The place looked increasingly rundown: factories on the river side, old houses, many crumbling and empty, to the left. Where's he taking us, Rita wondered, but nobody spoke. Otis pulled over and they watched the red light till it vanished round a bend before moving forward again. Mountains of scrap iron towered against the southern sky, black on lighter black. Dead ahead they saw the glint of water and specks of distant light: the bay. The road veered sharply to the left and the smell became pungent and somehow familiar. ("Municipal Sewage", Bernice read.) It curved along beside the bay, past trees and houses, all of a sudden a boulevard. But no red light glowed ahead.

A van shot past in a clatter and whirr, its headlights piercing the Eldorado like a laser. Bernice ducked involuntarily, fumbled for her glasses and put them on. "Hey, you're a good driver," she turned to Otis. She was afraid they'd lost the Impala and didn't want him to feel bad.

"After fifteen years with a mail van, something should rub off."

They eyed the cars parked here and there along the curb. When they saw him, all three at once, Otis, to his credit, didn't speed up, or slow down, or stop. He drove sedately by. Scaguiola had doused his lights, but his engine was running. He sat behind the wheel, staring out to sea. Bernice caught the brief red glow of a cigarette; then they were past.

"You don't suppose he came all this way to look at the sea?" Rita whispered incredulously.

Scaguiola took a long, hungry pull on his joint and felt the magic begin to work, soothing his jarred psyche, smoothing out the crinkles. Normally he didn't care even for cigarettes, but these were not normal times. His job at the Furnace gave him access to a variety of goodies—one of the perks, he supposed—and tonight he'd turned up a couple of reefers on an unsuspecting kid and confiscated them. Good stuff, too. More like he remembered from Nam than the garbage going around these days. No wonder the kid was sore. He stared out past the masts of a flock of small boats to where, in the dark mingling of sea and sky, a single light blinked. A ship, perhaps, or the lighthouse at Sandy Hook. But his thoughts stayed where they'd been all evening: should he or shouldn't he? Like tying and untying a knot. Only all the time knowing it was too late, because he'd crossed the line. If the answer was no, why had he come? Why was he sitting there? He took another drag, a fierce one, and felt the heat at the back of his throat. A van passed, then a car, along the road behind him. He looked at his watch. A few more pulls and he'd go. Everything was going to be all right. Everything was going to be cool.

From where they sat they could just make out the house: clapboard, two stories, with a stoop and a railed balcony. Scaguiola had backtracked all the way to the street of filling stations and bars. The house stood on a side street, one of several that descended steeply to the factories. They'd seen him go in. Otis gave him two minutes, then disengaged the gear and the car rolled silently forward. The house looked yellow-gray; everything did in the faint glow of the streetlamps, even the trees. Small, plain, working class, much like all the others. No light in any window, though the door had opened quickly enough at his knock. Apparently, he was expected.

"Ten to one it's his folks'," Rita voiced her disappointment. "Or relatives."

Bernice thought of his wife. The puffy, bruised face: *He's gonna kill me.* North Jersey people, both of them.

"So what now?" Taverns stood guard either side at the bottom of the street. Otis turned right and pulled in behind a parked semi trailer.

More minutes passed and they still hadn't decided anything when car tires sounded from the hill. The Impala took the corner, barely slowing, in a protesting squeal, flashing past them in the direction of the bridge. Otis swung the Eldorado into pursuit. "Home already?"

But once over the Raritan, Scaguiola crossed under the parkway, instead of rejoining it. A mile or so further on he wheeled into a roadside parking lot. In the lot were two tractor-trailers and a pickup, and a ramshackle hut of a building under a lit-up sign: 'Café a Go-Go. Girls. Girls. Girls.' A martini glass emitting bubbles was picked out in bulbs, but only the bubbles worked, a spastic stream of neon fireflies. Otis kept going. "Either he's trying to shake us, or …"

"He's looking for love." Rita helped him out.

"Or a bit of both," Bernice suggested sleepily.

They passed other, similar establishments in quick succession: a sort of local cottage industry; then pulled into a deserted gas station and stopped. "What say we give him a couple of minutes and go back for a look?"

Other vehicles now were about, and but for the fact that it was Sunday, there'd doubtless have been more. The eastern sky showed telltale signs of dawn. It was more like ten minutes before the Eldorado doubled back and nosed in behind a truck. The Impala hadn't moved. If he came out now, at least they'd be hidden.

Bernice yawned. Rita too. And after a while, so did Otis. The minutes passed. Five, ten, then, beyond the truck an engine rattled to life and beams from headlights fanned out across the lot, throwing bits of rock and gravel into relief. Soon they were heading south on the parkway, focused again on that single red light.

"Watch out for cops," Rita cautioned, oblivious of the irony.

Otis glanced down. With the smoothness of the ride and their fixation on the car ahead the needle had crept up unnoticed, registering twenty over the limit. He had barely jerked his foot off the gas when the low moan of a siren sounded close behind.

"Just our luck," Rita groaned. "What the ..." Not only was Otis slowing down, he'd swerved over to the shoulder and was stopping.

Bernice was equally dumbstruck; the more so when, in a tone she'd not heard before, he barked out, "Get over here. Quick, take the wheel." Almost before the car had scrunched to a halt he was dragging her towards him along the seat, then scrambling frantically over her. "You got a license, don't you? You got a license?"

Sure, she had a license. It was in her purse at Otis's feet. For I.D., year after year, she'd renewed it; though she hadn't driven since the Edsel. All this, however, quickly became moot. The flashing white monster, which had seemed about the devour them, whizzed past. They watched numbly as it disappeared. Rita recovered first. She opened the rear door and stepped into the road. Walking round the car, she opened the driver's door. "Bernice, move over."

"Jeez, I ..." Otis shook his head in apparent disbelief. "I

guess I lost my cool there for a second." Silence. "It's just that once they catch me, that's it."

"The highway patrol?" Rita didn't sound particularly mollified. "I don't get it."

"I told you," Otis raised his voice, "I'm a wanted man. KAY-LEE, the police, they're hand in glove, the lot of them."

"I'll drive," Rita said firmly. "If that's all right with you." Without waiting for an answer, she eased the Eldorado into the outside lane.

Just around the bend, the patrol car had pounced. Scaguiola stood by the trunk of his car, which was open, talking to the trooper. They seemed both to be relaxed, even smiling, and the sergeant was holding something at arm's length. As the Eldorado passed, gathering speed, its lights caught the cardboard skull painting that, a day or two before, they'd seen stuck in Bernice's screen door.

The women gasped, but Otis spoke first. "It was the tail light he was after, see? What do you know, an honest cop?"

Forget the taillight, they told him, and explained about the sign.

Otis whistled. "If I had any doubt, which I didn't, I don't now."

Bernice's right hand dropped to his left knee and gave it a reassuring little squeeze. He brought his hand over and gave hers a pat. As they sped south, leaving Sergeant Scaguiola behind, dawn broke over Jersey.

It didn't take long to fix the light: a wire that had jiggled loose. That skull, though? Well, it had saved him from a ticket. As soon as the trooper left, he flung it as hard as he could into the bushes.

14

Some people have a very low tolerance for alcohol, Bernice among them. They laughed for months about the rum punch at the office Christmas party: it takes a certain level of inebriation to call out, 'What's cookin', Good Lookin'', to the President of Shore County Bank & Trust while belting out a risqué version of *Good King Wenceslas* with the girls in Loans. Only later did they tell her it was artificial flavoring.

Texas, it seemed to Bernice, had a similar effect on Cousin Harrison. He had quite lost his head. Bernice always felt that Harrison had it in him to be someone, even when he first came to her as a skittish, white-faced nine year old, afraid of his own shadow. As her mother had once observed, bending over the kettle after a morning's crabbing, "The paler they come, the deeper they redden." Bernice had done what she could with him and when, after four years, he'd left without even a proper thank you, she'd not found it in her heart to blame him. The time will come. He'll redden. And the time had come, with a vengeance. The second call from Houston changed everything. For Bernice, the very course of her life.

The most Bernice and Rita had hoped to gain from Uncle Sudeley's odyssey into the past was time. It was in their minds that KAY-LEE Enterprises, faced with proof of another claimant to the Good Estate—perhaps more than one—would ease up on Otis. It wouldn't be just him any more between them and their greed. And Otis, out of hiding, would be a useful ally in nailing Miss Annie's murderer. For there was no doubt now, in either of their minds, that Scaguiola was guilty. If KAY-LEE was behind him, the link must be laid bare so that the police would have to act—industrial park notwithstanding.

Cousin Harrison had indeed traced the descendants of Obed Good. The one-time 'domestic servant' of Captain Machonochie of the 4th New Jersey Cavalry at Fort Concho had had his career cut tragically short. Some fifteen years after he'd gone to Texas, the North Concho River had flooded its banks and swept him away along with two of his offspring and half the population of the little town he'd settled in. His young wife and one child survived the flood and moved to nearby San Angelo, as the town a few miles upriver came to be called. Eventually she married again, but Obed Junior kept the name of Good and in his turn married and had issue. It was these children—the four that were still alive, and the three children of the one who'd died—who were joint (no longer missing) heirs, with Otis, to the Joseph Vannover and Hettie Bird Good Estate. Uncle Sudeley's hunch had panned out.

Except that they were now no longer heirs. As of a couple of days ago, Bernice Crickle, of Neptune Grove, in the Township of Cranberry, was the heir. How Cousin Harrison had managed to deliver seven quitclaim deeds in her favor, signed and witnessed, inside a week, didn't bear thought. Whether he'd persuaded, cajoled, bribed, threatened, tricked or blackmailed, the fact was the documents were legal and on their way east, air express.

"Could be worth something," Harrison drawled. The drawl was new. "Never know. Time I started paying you back, eh, Mom? Mom, you there, Mom?"

Bernice opened her mouth, but not knowing what to say, said nothing. She was standing in Rita's kitchen, and Rita, sensing catastrophe, gently pushed a chair under her. It flashed through Bernice's mind that yes, it might be worth something: her life, and that she should tell that to Harrison and tear up those bits of paper when they came. But Harrison had moved on to the topic of his wedding. Something about a conference call so she could hear the vows from the horses mouths. ("hah hah!")

As soon as she hung up, Rita shouted, "Well?"

"Oh boy." Bernice ran into the living room, flushed and confused. Anxiety jumped like sparks between them.

Rita, piecing it together, was forced to look through new eyes at her friend, eyes filled with something approaching awe. She imagined the whole KAY-LEE apparatus mobilized to 'zap her dead' as the bug killer commercial put it. Otis too. Perhaps she'd been too hard on him.

"The first thing I'm going to do is make a Will," Bernice announced, warming to her new role. "I guess leaving everything to you, Rita."

"Thanks. A lot."

They collapsed on the couch, laughing.

Cousin Harrison was as good as his word. The following day a thick packet arrived for Bernice at Rita's. They photocopied the contents and, after work, drove down to Uncle Sudeley's.

"Gone to Texas, eh? What do you know!" He greedily perused the documents. "Seems like that lawyer's been having himself a turkey shoot. Picked off the ones on the edge first so as not to scare the others." Clearly, in his book, Cousin Harrison was all right.

Bernice asked him to keep the originals. "No one would think of looking here." Even if they did—she eyed the piles of paper—they'd have their work cut out. She could have used a safe deposit box at the bank, but something told her not to.

"And what do you gals plan on getting up to now?"

"Going to have to claim my inheritance, I guess."

Uncle Sudeley liked the sound of that. "Like I said: you can't eat land, but land can sure eat you. Take care now."

The first thing they had in mind to do was break the news to Otis. So far they'd followed Uncle Sudeley's advice and kept the Texas connection to themselves. But now, the sooner he knew, the sooner they could make plans. But how to find him?

"We should have set up a signal for emergencies."

"Well, we didn't," Rita snapped.

Next day, as they went about their business, they half-hoped his worried little face would bob up beside them, as before. Rita caught herself peering into the back of the cab if she'd left it parked somewhere. Bernice, instead of her usual sandwich in the basement lunchroom, took a yogurt down to the boat basin and ate it slowly, sitting on a bench looking across the inlet, hoping every footfall might be his. The thought of his face, when he heard the news, made her smile. In a sense it would put the two of them in the same boat, share out the load. Perhaps he'd relax a little, look less worried. But night came, and Otis didn't, and the next morning something happened which convinced Bernice they'd have to go ahead without him.

It was a little after seven. Bernice, now a regular on Rita's couch, heard a plop as something hit the screen door. A well-aimed copy of the *Star*. She shuffled out to fetch it. After fixing herself an orange juice, she sat down at the table and cast a sleepy eye over the headlines. Stewart, once again, had made the front page. This time, with his picture. "Rita!" she screamed. "Rita!"

A bubbly squawk from the bathroom indicated that Rita was brushing her teeth.

"Listen," she called through the door. "Stewart Krabbowicz, 16, of 148 Gunning Point Road, Scoop Creek, has gone missing from his home. He was last seen leaving home Saturday morning wearing black cotton jeans, a green T-shirt and sneakers. Anyone having information regarding this person should contact the police. There's a number to call, and a headshot." As Rita opened the door, Bernice thrust the paper into her hands. "Look."

"Saturday?" Rita was spitting toothpaste. "You don't think? You don't suppose …?"

"What?"

"Is this some prank he's pulling? I wouldn't put it past him." The alternative was too awful to contemplate.

Bernice shook her head. "Uh uh. He wouldn't, any more than he set the fire. You've got him pegged wrong, Rita."

Rita sat down at the table and closed her eyes. She was back on Gunning Point Road with Bernice, looking at the shut-up house and closed garage door. It was Saturday. Then a voice—Otis's—said: *You wanna get that boy killed? Well you're going the right way about it.* "Biswekki! That was Friday, right, when we told him about Stewart seeing the car?"

"Yes." You told him, Bernice thought.

Rita had grabbed the phone and was dialing. "Detective Biswekki. Yeah, I know it's the special line. I want Detective Biswekki, on this line. Well then, give him a message. Tell him Rita called. From Carefree Days. R I T A. He'll know." She hung up. "I just want to know one thing: did Scaguiola find out about Stewart from Biswekki. Because if he did, and Stewart doesn't show, you'll know who to thank."

"Scaguiola?"

"Me."

"Rita!"

"I opened my big mouth to Biswekki, didn't I?"

Bernice fetched a glass of juice from the kitchen and set it down beside her friend. "What about Otis? We'll have to tell them, won't we, if they come asking? That he was there; that it was Otis who got Scaguiola's number out of Stewart."

"We'll say he gave it to us. Who's to know?"

"The little brother."

"Damn." Rita recalled the boy's panic as he rushed to Stewart's side in the barn. "With any luck he's young enough so they won't pay much attention." She added, "For his own sake, I hope."

Bernice leaned back among the couch cushions and stared up at the chandelier, which sparkled in the early sunlight filtering through the curtains. "Oh boy." She shook her head.

"You think I shouldn't have called?" Rita was having second thoughts.

"No, it's not that. I'm glad you did."

"I feel like this time we've got to shake them and rub their noses in it," Rita said fiercely, "And if they don't see it, or pretend they don't, then there's only one conclusion to come to: it's their own damn shit."

"Rita."

"That's just how I feel."

Bernice said, "I wonder where he is?"

"Stewart?"

She didn't mean Stewart. She meant Otis. But she nodded anyway. "Lost time, lost lives." She pulled the phone towards her and dialed. It rang and rang. "Is there stuff you have to do today, Rita?"

"Not specially." The usual parade to the beauty parlor, a couple to the shops, someone's family she was supposed to meet off a bus. Nothing she couldn't get out of.

Bernice hung up. "I guess it's too early yet." She looked at the clock. "Oh, sure it is, Bernice."

"For what?"

"I'm going to do something I only did once before, and that was when the basement flooded after Hurricane Agnes." She smiled conspiratorially. "Call in sick when I'm not. We're going to find out where this Felix Taffelbaum lives, and we're going to tell him a few things to his face. Like who he's got to reckon with over title to a certain piece of real estate. Oh boy, get ready for Daniel in the lion's den."

When it came to the Old Testament, Rita was, to say the least, rusty. Several times that day she found herself wondering if Daniel had emerged from the den intact, or indeed, at all. When she came to wonder in earnest, it was too late. Bernice was not around to ask.

15

The sign said, 'Private. Proceed At Own Risk'. Rita stopped the Checker, looked at Bernice, and looked back at the sign. "You're the boss."

"I guess this is it," Bernice ventured. It was two in the afternoon. They'd spent the morning cruising in the Somerville area, up and down leafy creeks, along wooded lanes, being ogled by horses and bayed at by hounds. And it was hot, the hottest day of the summer, so far. Rita's back felt like the run-off from the Grand Coulee Dam. They'd asked here and there, in stores, at gas stations, trying to be discrete, but the Taffelbaum name elicited only shrugs and stares. Rita would have thrown in her hand an hour ago. 'An armed camp,' Otis had said. There wasn't any camp, only a wild goose chase. And his half-hearted attempt to deter them—he'd no doubt remind them of that—just made it worse. In his absence, her wrath devolved on Bernice. And Bernice had retreated into a sort of dogged mysticism; it was here, it was there, it was just around the corner.

Then they'd come upon a mailman. He was sitting in his jeep at the roadside having a contemplative bite. Oh sure, Taffelbaum. They'd stopped delivering to the house eight, ten years back. Why? He'd no idea. At the customer's request, he supposed. There'd been talk: a bomb scare, or was that some place else? He wasn't sure. "You wouldn't believe some of the stuff that goes on." He glanced around at the pastoral peace, then winked at Bernice standing on the newly mown grass verge. "I could write a book."

"Confessions of a Mailman," she joked.

"Hey, know what? That's good. Confessions of a Mailman." Waving in the air the remains of his sandwich, he traced the route they should take, managing at the same time to outwit a small phalanx of flies.

Rita drove past the cautioning sign with the shrug of one who has abdicated responsibility.

"He said there was no name." Bernice tried to reassure herself.

Rita said nothing. She could see, up ahead, a second sign, and waited perversely for Bernice to see it too. 'Not responsible for Damage incurred by Unauthorized Personnel'.

"I guess that's about how you feel." Bernice was half apologetic.

"I'll tell you what this is," Rita retorted. "One of those top secret army depots. That's what it is." She kept going. The trees reached to within a few feet either side of the narrow strip of tarmac. Trees behind and trees in front. They were encircled, the leaves filtering the sun so that it almost felt cool. The ground was a tangle of huckleberry, laurel and poison ivy. She looked in the rear-view mirror. "There's someone behind us."

Bernice turned, but saw nothing. "Let's ask them."

"They're keeping their distance. Slowing down whenever I do." She brought the car to a gentle halt. "See?"

It wasn't exactly a car, and it had stopped some thirty yards off on the edge of a bend in a patch of deep shade. "It's a kid!" Bernice exclaimed.

Rita wasn't so sure. "It's one of those mechanized tricycles, for cripples." She reached for the binoculars.

"Oh Rita, no."

"Talk about the enchanted forest. It's a dwarf."

"You're kidding."

"Take a look."

Bernice quickly abandoned her scruples. "Maybe it's him. Taffelbaum." Whoever it was eyed them dispassionately

118

from under the awning of a shiny black tri-ped.

"I'm backing up," Rita announced. She found reverse. As the Checker moved, so did the tri-ped, till it vanished from sight around a bend. "This is ridiculous!" She stopped, and then started forward again.

Bernice kept looking, but the tri-ped with its mysterious driver didn't reappear. And soon they saw another sign: Final Warning! All Unauthorized Vehicles Turn Here. The road bulged, underlining the point. Rita kept going.

"Kind of long for a driveway," Bernice commented. A doubt tugged at the edge of her voice. From the position of the sun, they seemed to be making a circle. "Can you believe snow-plowing this?"

"There must be a shortcut." A throbbing drone sounded faintly above the trees. Rita peered up through the windscreen. "A chopper. I guess that answers that."

They were quiet now, increasingly watchful. Rounding a bend Rita jammed on the brakes. In the middle of the road sat an armored jeep, a light flashing desultorily from is roof. Two men in uniform were ambling towards them. Everything about them from their gait to their bulges and badges said Security. But for their height, they might have succeeded in looking menacing.

"Jesus, what is this? A Munchkin retreat?" Rita murmured.

Bernice got the fat one. His well-pressed khaki shirt was splotched with sweat and the walkie-talkie at his waist crackled impressively. The one on Rita's side, older and tougher, was evidently in charge. "You are trespassing, you know." He opened the door, an invitation to Rita to get out, which she chose to ignore.

"I'm driving a cab and I have a customer to deliver," she said. "Is that against the law?" They'd agreed on a story.

"You have an appointment?"

"Sure. With Snow White."

Bernice leaned across. "Excuse me, Officer. It's in Mr. Taffelbaum's best interests to see me." He flicked a look of surprise in her direction. "And he's going to be mad at you for stopping me."

"State your name and the nature of your business, ma'am." The man had evidently made a decision.

"It's about that industrial park he wants to build down south. I'm claiming title to the land."

"Your name?"

"I'll tell him when I see him."

They watched him walk to the jeep. "Smile, Bernice, you're on candid camera," Rita pointed. A camera was mounted on the roof. She called to the fat man, "Hey, John Wayne. We on location or something?"

"Rita!" The other man was coming back.

"Everybody out," he commanded. "Line up over there."

"Chief!" the fat man called excitedly from the Checker.

Bernice gasped at what she saw. The chief was walking back towards them twirling a tiny silver revolver from his pinkie.

"Sorry." Rita was embarrassed.

"Right here is the parting of the ways. You," he pointed the gun at Rita and made a circling motion, "Home." Then, indicating Bernice, "The other lady can come with us."

It didn't take Bernice long to make up her mind: "What are we waiting for?"

Rita shook her head. "No deal. Either way we stay together."

"Suit yourselves." The guard turned. It made no difference to him.

"We've got to do what he says, Rita. It's our only hope."

Every cell in Rita's brain screamed a warning. She stared at Bernice, and out of her mouth, by some freak of nature, came the single word, "Fine." Bernice's mind was made up.

The guard emptied out the gun and tossed it to Rita. "Follow me to the circle, then head back the way you came. Don't try nothing. You're under surveillance. And if we ever catch you round here again, young lady, you'll be prosecuted to the fullest extent of the law."

Bernice said, "Don't worry, I'll call."

"Or I'll send in the Marines." Rita managed a grin.

"How about the fare?" the fat one smirked, pleased with himself. "Or was it a free ride?"

Rita stowed her pistol back under the dash. She didn't regret bringing it, only that she hadn't told Bernice.

The car at the curb in front of her house looked vaguely familiar. As Rita pulled up the door opened to disgorge a bulky occupant: Detective Gus Biswekki. She watched him smooth down his jacket and check the pleats on his pants. He should be selling pools, not chasing criminals, she thought.

"Phone's been going ten, fifteen minutes already," he jerked his head at the house.

Rita slammed the Checker door and ran across the lawn. Strange that in the last stretch of the return trip, in the few seconds she hadn't been worrying about Bernice, she should get such a sharp reminder. "Hello?" She was out of breath and had left the front door open.

"Rita. Thank the Lord." It was Bernice.

"I just got in."

"Do me a favor, will you? Call up the bank and tell them I won't be in for a day or two; I've taken a turn for the worse. And call HELP about Friday. I'll make it up next week. Sunday school too. Oh yes, and the Chinese auction. And Rita, don't tell where I am. Not anyone. I mean it."

"Well, where are you?"

"I'm all right. Everything's fine. We can talk later."

Through the door Rita could see Biswekki, head down, apparently contemplating a patch of grass. In a low voice, she said, "Aren't you going to wish me a happy birthday?" It was a code they'd worked out. 'Happy Birthday' meant distress.

"Not now. I'll call. There's a phone right here."

"What's the number?"

"It doesn't seem to have one. Anyway, it doesn't matter. Just don't worry. Bye." She hung up.

Biswekki had edged his way to within inches of the door. "Come on in," Rita called. He did, stooping. "Beer?"

"Don't mind if I do."

She fetched a couple of cold Schlitz's, opened hers and

drank thirstily from the can. "There's no moisture left in me, I declare."

"Busy day?"

"You could say so."

"I been trying to get back to you since morning. Figured I might as well stop round in case you weren't answering the phone."

"Like some people." She gulped down more beer. "So how's it going? Come up with anything?"

"On the kid, you mean?"

"I meant on the old ladies."

"Oho," he said, "So that's it; that's why you called."

"Why else?"

"I thought it might be on account of the kid."

"You mean Stewart? Yes, I saw about that. It's all the same case, though, isn't it?" She was looking at him steadily now, hands on the table clenched around her beer.

With his pinkie Biswekki eased an imaginary lash from his left eye. He wished he'd not accepted the beer. It put him at a disadvantage. He tried flashing a winning smile. Biswekki was proud of his winning smile, which he rehearsed in mirrors whenever he could. He'd once been accepted in news casting school on the strength of it. Girls had been known to light up in the afterglow. Not this one, though. It occurred to him that perhaps she'd not had—what did they used to call it—carnal knowledge. Too many angles, probably, like fucking a trapezium. "So what's up?"

"What's up? That's for you to tell me." They held each other's gaze. "All right. Stewart. Did you talk to Stewart?"

Biswekki stretched out a placatory hand. "Believe me, it wasn't for lack of trying. On the Friday, I was there. No one home. Saturday morning, I was there. Talked to his old man. 'Stewart's with his mother,' right? 'North Bergen for the weekend,' right? As I see it, looking between the lines, there's not a lot of lovey dovey in that situation. She's Irish." As if that explained everything.

Rita thought back to that first encounter with Stewart's father on the lawn. No sign of a mother then, either.

"So Tuesday, around five, I'm in the vicinity and I stop by again, and you're not going to believe this. The guy says he's still in North Bergen. So I say, 'Can I reach him there?' 'Sure, go ahead,' he says, 'use the phone.' Well, as it turns out he never was in North Bergen that whole weekend. His kid brother was in North Bergen; got off the bus alone. So I say, 'Why did you think he was in North Bergen?' You know what he said? You're not going to believe this. He said, 'Where else would he be?' The guy's a slob. Guys like that should be serialized."

"Tell me something else. It's important. Did you talk to Scaguiola about Stewart before he disappeared?"

Biswekki wiped one hand across his mouth and tugged at his collar. "I may have done."

"Did you? Yes or no?"

"What can I tell you? It's not a yes and no situation. Guys sit around, shoot the breeze ...'

"OK, you did." They sat for a while, each glumly eyeing the table. "So you've no leads at all? You checked out the barn, for instance?"

"We finger-printed the place. The kid was all over it. But he's not there now."

"And you searched his room, obviously?"

"Sure we searched his room. We searched the whole house."

"Did you find his notebook, where he wrote down license plate numbers and stuff?"

"Notebook? There was no notebook," he said, feigning patience.

"What did I tell you, dummy!" Rita almost shouted. "It is so, one and the same case. Find the notebook and you've found Stewart."

Biswekki looked at his watch. Past five already. He wondered if he could claim overtime.

In a calmer voice, Rita said, "There was a notebook." Then she lied. "I saw it."

Biswekki looked up sharply. "You prepared to go on oath with that?"

"Why not?" she replied evenly.

"What sort of a notebook?"

The only person who could answer that was Otis, if he ever reappeared. "Let me ask you something first, OK?"

"Be my guest."

"If Scaguiola isn't a suspect here, and apparently he's not, how come he was on Gunning Point Road on Saturday, the day that—according to you—Stewart went missing?"

"You're getting off into a tangent."

"How come? Just tell me how come? He was there, by the barn, getting awfully muddy."

"Who says?"

"We do. Bernice and me. We saw him."

"Well, it's hardly surprising, considering he's building a house there."

"He's what?" Rita didn't believe her ears.

"He bought one of the lots." Immediately he cursed himself for saying too much; but Rita wasn't about to let him escape.

"He's building a house there, right there where they died?" Rita shook her head in disbelief. "I told Bernice he had some nerve. I didn't know how much. Oh, and another thing; find out where he was the night the place burned down."

"OK, OK. Tell you what." Biswekki rubbed his large palms together. He was sweating, and would have taken off his jacket if it hadn't been for his gun. "I'll ask him." He turned to go, then turned back. "But there are some things about Stewart Krabbowicz I need to get from you."

"You got yourself a deal," Rita said.

He ducked out the door and she closed it, and through the lace curtains watched him getting into his car. A feeling grew in her that at last there might be traction. Thanks to Stewart. She hoped, wherever he was, he was safe.

16

'Whippoorwill Motel. Vacancies. FM – Clock Radio.' It was the sort of temporary roadside lodging that draws people with something to hide, without the means to do it stylishly. A yellowish peeling blockhouse of a building bisected by a driveway to an inner courtyard. Tacked on to the sign, like an afterthought, were the letters, 'TV'.

Otis Phinney conveyed the last slice of scrapple—the everyday breakfast special—to his mouth, withdrew the fork, and chewed with rabbit-like absorption. The warm meaty taste dissolved the years, and suddenly he was at his mother's kitchen table, bare legs dangling from the wooden chair, gobbling nervously, an ear cocked for the backfiring of the school bus as the driver geared down to take the corner. Scrapple. They always had it at home. Dabbing his lips with a napkin, he glanced furtively about. She was there again, the same woman, at the corner table, crying, just as his mother had cried years ago. They left her alone like they'd left his mother alone. And though he was a good student, his teacher said, he'd had to go out and get work because his father had run off, God knows where to. Story of his life: missing the bus.

Otis got up, put down a quarter tip, and went across to the office. Payment by the day—that was the rule. Passing the woman, he wanted to comfort her—at least say something—but he knew he wouldn't. Three days now, she'd sat there. And like the others, he'd pretended not to see. Story of his life. Run off? Run off? Dad had blown his brains out.

125

"Howdy, Mr. Olds." That was the name he'd registered under. Olds, Arthur Olds. His driver's license said Olds. So did his checks and his credit cards. Clever, the way he'd worked it. No one knew him as Phinney.

The rooms flanked the courtyard, beyond which was a seldom-used railway track, all weeded over. More than once it had crossed his mind that if they came for him, it was a short hop out of his window to the tracks; and if he lay down and waited long enough ..." If, if, if. He crossed the yard to his car. Not the Eldorado. That had served its purpose. A green Pontiac he'd gotten cheap in Freehold. Rentals were risky. Cash down to a dealer—that was safest. Something with some mileage on it. And if you knew a bit about what makes them go, so much the better.

A twenty-minute drive brought him within sight of the Carefree Days signboard on its manicured shrub-green island. He was early. A quarter of eight. But he didn't want to miss them like he had the day before, and driving past the guard was risky. Otis settled down to wait at his usual spot. A half-hour later his patience paid off: a maroon Checker Marathon nosed into the road and turned towards town.

Rita let off her last passenger—a man in a wheelchair who worked part-time at the library—and sat for a moment, considering what to do. It was too soon to start badgering Biswekki for the answers he'd promised. She'd give him a day or two. As for Bernice, all those calls had made her late. What was she supposed to do now? Sit by the phone and worry? Her feelings about her friend ranged from irritation to guilt to fear, with some grudging admiration mixed in. If she hadn't brought the gun ... No, speculation was useless. What she should really do was find Otis. Seeing Biswekki again would be more productive if she had some answers for him on the notebook, her side of the bargain. To give inspiration a chance to strike, she stopped off at Josey's for coffee.

She was on her second cup, with inspiration still in the wings, when opportunity knocked. At least, to Rita, it seemed that way. There, across the street, glued to the window of the Clarissa Charm and Modeling School, was Otis. Slapping down a dollar, she made for the door, not taking her eyes off him.

"My, aren't we hungry today." The waitress watched Rita almost collide with a moped as she greeted the little guy with enthusiasm. "The long and the short of it," she observed to no on in particular, and went back to wiping tables.

They were in the Checker, heading north, retracing their steps of the weekend past. Otis hadn't balked at using the cab this time, to Rita's surprise. In fact, he'd encouraged it. The entire trip had been his idea. Not that she hadn't jumped at the chance to hold him more or less captive for a few hours. Things needed saying on both sides, and as long as they were on the parkway traveling at 55 mph and she was driving there was less chance he'd do his vanishing act. "Where's Bernice?" he'd asked, and she'd lied. "At work, where else?" The entreaty to silence presumably covered Otis. "Kind of busy yourself, I guess?" "Nothing special." "I been thinking: we should check out that house in Amboy." "Any time." "No time like the present." "So long as I'm back by three. I got a guy in a wheelchair to take care of." "No problem." And that was that.

Otis glanced back. "Yeah, there's room for a wheelchair. What do you do for a ramp, though?"

"Couple of guys."

"Suppose you didn't show?" he mused. "What'd happen?"

"You always do. You've got to."

"But just suppose …"

"They'd call an ambulance, I guess. Or the police."

"You got a pretty good thing going." He seemed to lose interest.

"Not at the rates I charge."

For a long stretch they didn't talk, then it was Rita's turn. "How about Stewart?"

"The kid in the barn? What about him?"

"The cops don't know anything; not that you saw him or had anything to do with him."

"What's he done?"

"Don't you see the papers?"

127

"I guess not."

"He's missing." She glanced at him wondering how he could possibly not have heard.

"Missing? What happened?"

She expected reproach—an I told you so—but none came. Had he forgotten his prediction? "Family troubles. That's the official word. His Mom and Pop don't get on so he cut out. I'll tell you what we think." Scaguiola's newly acquired half acre, his weekend activity and Stewart's notebook: she ran through it all. Otis listened. "Now what I need from you is a description of the notebook so I can swear by Almighty God I saw it in his hand." Bernice would hardly have approved, but it was her own fault for not being there.

"It was just a notebook. Nothing special." Otis rubbed his chin. "About three by five. I think—yes, I'm pretty sure it was ruled for cash. He listed plate numbers at the back. Not the last page, near the back."

"What color?"

"Color? It was dog-eared, dirty. Some pale shade, originally. Pink, maybe green."

"But mainly grubby?"

"And curled over, like a wallet."

"Like it lived in that pocket?"

"Yep."

"And now for the good news," Rita announced. He glanced at her, warily, as if no news could possibly be good. "You've got company on the KAY-LEE front. Someone to stand beside you, to guide you, and get blown to pieces with you."

"That's what I bin telling you I don't need."

"I'm not talking moral support, here. I'm not even talking retribution. I'm talking about where it will hurt them most: dollars and cents. Suppose I told you that Bernice, as of last week, is co-heir with you, with paper title to the Good Estate?"

"I'd laugh."

"Then laugh. I'm telling you."

Otis didn't laugh. He didn't even smile. As Rita caught him up on the details, he seemed to sink into a reverie. She wasn't even sure he followed her. His responses became monosyllabic, and glancing over at his crumpled countenance, it seemed he'd aged ten years in as many minutes.

"You OK?" It occurred to her that he'd had a stroke.

"Me? Sure." He made an effort to sit up.

"Something on your mind?"

"Yeah, well, Bernice as a matter of fact. She's a nice lady. I'd feel bad if something happened to her."

Rita thought: And how much worse you'd feel, little man, if you knew where she was right this moment. "We've been pals a long time, Bernice and me. She may look small and kind of passed-over, but she takes a lot of putting down. Believe me."

"Which goes for me too, I hope." He gave a queer little high–pitched cough and relapsed into silence.

Small and passed-over. Maybe he took it personally. She'd not spent time alone with him before. He had that sort of fifties smell—Mennen aftershave and mothballs—almost of someone who'd died. As the minutes and miles passed, his presence began to weigh on her. Almost like driving with a corpse. Odd, that feeling, because—though neither of them knew it—they were on their way to a funeral.

Otis's idea of gathering information was to knock on the door and ask, specifically for Rita to knock on the door and ask. She discovered this as they crossed the Raritan. And, on reflection, saw his point. Sure, they could dig up records at City Hall, perhaps find the owner's name, or sit in a corner bar pumping the locals. Chances were they'd only stir up suspicion and make their task harder. Small communities could be hard nuts to crack. She worked up a flimsy tale of a great-aunt who might have lived in the house. It might get her in the door.

An overnight rainstorm had dissipated the worst of the heat, if not the smell, and the bay sparkled in the breeze. The street, by day, seemed innocent: red, white and green houses, brick and clapboard, patches of lawn in back. Rita glimpsed lines of washing, puffed up and straining, as if a whole school was learning to fly, the big things instructing the little things. The tree trunks were swollen with age, and in places roots had heaved up the paving. She sniffed mown grass and passed a decal behind a rose bush—the crucifixion with two white plastic swans perched on it. Three old people shuffled about their business.

The door was three steps up from the sidewalk. She knocked and waited. Then listened. Nothing. There didn't seem to be a bell. She knocked again, louder. Something soft against her ankle made her jump and almost cry out: a black cat had sprung from nowhere. Rita didn't much care for cats, but she bent down and made a fuss over this one in case it went with the house; all the while keeping an ear to the door and an eye on the street behind her. Otis, out of sight a block away, stayed with the car.

She felt vulnerable on her perch, sure she was being watched. Why hadn't Scaguiola stayed longer? All that way. It hardly made sense. Out of the corner of her eye she saw a woman descending the hill dragging a carry cart stuffed with something. Rita strolled towards her, followed at a distance by the cat. The woman was hefty. The cart clanked and bounced behind her like a gun carriage in the wake of a tank.

"Hi there." Rita waved. "Good morning."

The whole caboodle wheezed to a halt. "There won't be no one home, not this morning." The woman crossed herself.

"Do you suppose they'll be back?"

"Not him, he won't." The woman screwed up her eyes, "You one of *them*, are you?" Rita looked puzzled. "Reporters and such like."

"Reporters?"

"From the city," she added darkly. Her face was white and swollen and the fat on her arms rippled unpleasantly.

"Oh my, no." Rita laughed. "I'm from down south."

"It's St. Mary's you'll be wanting."

"They're at church?"

"Giving him the Christian burial he deserves." Her look of incipient defiance convinced Rita that she was still suspect. "Should have seen how he helped my Brian. A saint, that's what he was. Not that they'll put that in the paper or the TV." She gave directions.

Rita walked back to where Otis was waiting. "Seems like some kind of local philanthropist lives there, but we just missed him."

The street in front of the church was jammed with limos, sleek and black, one with three sets of doors, another with a 'State Senator' plaque on the fender. Chauffeurs stood around smoking, and old people in little groups chatted as if something noteworthy had just happened. A crew was filming the bumper sticker on a beat up Volkswagen: *Mafia Staff Car. Hands off*. Rita parked a couple of blocks away. As they turned to walk up the church steps, a man hurried forward. "Do you have a relationship with the deceased?" he demanded.

For some reason, probably because she was a veteran funeral crasher and he was a novice, Rita had taken Otis's arm firmly under her own. Now she felt a panicky tug. The man had his notebook out and was clearly from the press. Just as a voice behind them called, "No cameras inside!" Otis managed to break free and scurried up the steps.

Rita said, "Just curious, same as you. Who is this guy, anyhow?"

"Hanratty?" The man laughed. "You from Mars or something?"

"Cranberry."

"Figures." He turned away, then glanced back. "Frank Xavier Hanratty. Hood of Hoods. He stole from the poor to give to the rich. Frank the Bank."

In the gloomy interior she didn't at first see Otis. The coffin was up front, draped in the flag, and the pews were less full than the scene outside had suggested. Before the altar a priest was intoning. Strange sounding words. A spotlight picked out the colors of his vestments: pale blue and green and gold, all of shimmering silk. The priest was brown and young, perhaps of Asian origin. "The souls of the just are in the hands of God …" Rita enjoyed Catholic funerals: the chanting, the incense, the gaudy statuary, votive candles flickering, and the sense of mystery. She could live with God the Mysterious: to Mystery its due. It was the God Next Door she objected to, who at any moment might stop by for a cup of sugar. She suspected this latter God was Bernice's though, by unspoken agreement, they didn't talk religion.

At last she saw Otis, cowering off to the side behind a pillar. "I think it's the *Mob*," she whispered." Frank Xavier Hanratty. Mean anything to you?"

"My God. The Man with the Golden Garage." He flicked his tongue around dry lips. "Is *he* still around?"

"No," she pointed. "He's over there."

Otis didn't smile.

"A man who is dead has been freed from sin ..." The priest's singsong voice rang out. Otis seemed suddenly transfixed by the scene at the altar. His Adam's apple worked up and down as if he was trying to swallow. Rita remembered when she'd first set eyes on him, also at a funeral, also cowering at the back.

When, at last, the pallbearers moved forward and took up their burden, Rita slipped along the pew to the aisle. She half expected to see Scaguiola among the mourners, then reflected that if he 'had a relationship with the deceased' it was more likely a business one. In the tight little knot of close family she counted five: in front the widow, petite, well-dressed, sixtyish, face lined with hard work, no makeup to speak of under her veil; she was supported by an older woman and a much younger one; then two men, one old, one fortyish. The rest were strung out behind: in raincoats, leather jackets, jeans, city suits, leisure suits, shirtsleeves, an odd assortment. A tall, tanned man in a sleek pinstripe strode down the aisle with a much younger, heavily painted blonde on his arm trailing a boa. Rita recalled the plaque on the limo, and two crones in front of her, who kept up a running commentary, confirmed her hunch.

They drove back in a hurry. Otis had skulked inside the church till everyone had left. Not anyone to get mixed up with, this Hanratty, he warned, dead or alive. For years he'd controlled the numbers racket in North East Jersey. If that was the crowd Scaguiola was running with, they better be sure their cemetery plots were all paid up. The glads, the painted skull, it all fitted, he warned Rita. Maybe—even for a hundred grand—it wasn't worth it. Maybe he'd sign. If KAY-LEE was playing games with the Mob ..." And so on, and so forth, down the Garden State Parkway.

It was a much-chastened Otis that Rita let off in town. Before parting she managed to pin him down to an emergency means of contact: if he saw the Checker parked outside the library at noon, he was to walk by Josey's. The Monarch-burger, the one they'd used before, would be the rendezvous. It was a long shot, but all she could think of at the time.

On a shelf at the back of the closet, wrapped in dry cleaning bags, under a newspaper, was the Good Family Bible. The first thing Otis did when he got back to his room at the Whippoor-will from Perth Amboy was fetch it down. Rita's report that a branch of the Phinneys—or more precisely the Goods—had been swept under the carpet and rediscovered was quit a shock. The Bible confirmed it. GTT. He bent over the page. Yes, there it was. Even if he'd found it, would he ever have guessed what it meant?

Stretching on tiptoe, Otis returned the book to the shelf, pushing it as far back as possible. Then he sat on the edge of the bed. At first, all the old doubts assailed him. Not that he was about to quit now. Whatever he'd said to Rita, he was too far in to think of that. No, it was Bernice that troubled him; the thought of what might happen to her.

Gradually, as he sat, his mind cleared and courage seeped back. Perhaps it was for the good: it tied up some loose ends quite neatly, in fact. And what was the use of a new life with-out someone to share it with? He wouldn't be taking Otis Phinney along, that was for sure. He'd just keep on being Arthur Olds. They'd go away, of course: California, Hawaii, Europe. He'd always wanted to see Europe. Away from all the memories. Yes—he slapped his knee in what passed for a deci-sive gesture. He'd ask her. The worst thing she could say was no; in which case he'd think of something else. He felt his heart vibrating and clutched at his breast pocket for his pills. The feel of the tiny white tablet nestling under his tongue calmed him. He wondered which he'd run out of first: pills, cash or luck.

17

Each time the phone rang Rita thought it was Bernice. On Friday—the day of the funeral—she waited up late and dozed off watching *The Jungle* with Rod Cameron and Cesar Romero. Saturday morning she stayed home, more and more anxious for Bernice and more annoyed at herself for being anxious. About midday she was in the kitchen fixing a tuna salad sandwich when the doorbell chimed. She didn't even bother to wipe her hands. It was Biswekki. At the station they'd said he was off.

"Lemme ask you something," he stood on the welcome mat in what looked like a brand new pair of designer jeans. "How d'you know it was me?"

"I didn't."

"Then do yourself a favor, will you, er, Rita? Mind if I call you that? Don't open the door till you know who it is."

"What is this? The South Bronx all of a sudden?"

He bridled: "We don't want nothing to happen. Nothing untoward."

"I was expecting ..." She was about to say Bernice but thought better of it. She stepped back to let him pass.

"I did what I said I would."

"Good boy. He gets a nice cold beer."

"I wouldn't draw too many conclusions. Let's just say you made the bullpen."

135

"Scaguiola? You questioned Scaguiola?"

"I asked him. Man to man."

"Aha." Already it didn't sound good.

"He didn't deny it." Biswekki sat down heavily on the couch. En route to the kitchen Rita stopped dead and looked at him. "He *didn't* deny it?"

"First off," Biswekki grabbed his left pinkie and jerked it back, "He drives down Gunning Point Road to and from the station house eight or ten times a week. Less traffic that way. He saw the billboard the day it went up and got his deposit down right away. What he was doing Saturday was figuring if he could fit his house in and still keep the barn"

"He gets the barn, too?"

"For a hobby center. He tinkers with vintage cars."

"And the car?"

"Second off: the kid. Any kid on the block could have wrote down his number. Kids do that all the time. Playing cop, what have you. I did it myself. It don't mean a thing if Stewart did or not."

"In other words, forget it."

"You said it." He popped open his beer.

"And what about the fire?"

"The only time in his life Scag was ever in that house was right after they deceased."

"He says."

"And I believe him."

"That's another thing: how come he was the responding officer? I thought he was off weekends."

"He was first on the scene. On his way home."

"At seven a.m. on a Saturday. From where?"

He shrugged. "What can I tell you? It's his life. He's over the age of consent. We each got our own lives to live the best we can, right?"

"Yes and no. He's a public servant. Supposing he was, say, up to his ears to a loan shark?"

"Rita, Rita, Rita." Biswekki held up both hands in a gesture of protection. "Look, I'm doing my best for you, right? You wanna start slinging crap, go work on a hog farm."

"It's facts I'm slinging, Mister," she retorted. "You ask your good buddy—man to man—who it is he sneaks up to Perth Amboy after hours to visit. See if you get a straight answer to that. And if he tells you it's his old auntie, you tell him bullshit— from Rita." She stalked out. "Unless his auntie's married to Frank Xavier Hanratty, which somehow wouldn't surprise me."

Biswekki swigged some beer, looked at the can, grimaced, belched, and swigged some more. "Frank the Bank Hanratty?"

"Mean anything to you?" she called.

"I wouldn't call him Humanitarian of the Year, not the one I got in mind."

"That's the one."

"Adult bookstores. What's that gotta do with Scag?"

"Is that what he's into now?"

"You ever bin in one?"

"Sure. For gag gifts."

"From the Hudson to the Delaware," Biswekki spread his arms. "He's got sexual paraphernalia all tied up."

"That aspect I never went for," Rita said, emerging from the kitchen with her sandwich. "Care for some?"

"Sure, why not." He sat up and burped again.

"Ask him. I'm serious."

"You usually are."

"Any leads on Stewart?"

"The standard three hundred witnesses who've seen him between here and North Bergen. Plus a sighting in Honolulu." He bit into the sandwich, and held it up. "Yummy."

She watched him munch. "You come out here on a Saturday. You act almost human. At least some of what we asked you've looked into. But two people have died and one person, who could have seen something, has disappeared. I don't get a sense of an active investigation. What's going on?"

Biswekki waved the remains of the sandwich in the air. Bits fell out. He observed them gravely. "I'll be up front with you, Rita," he said at last. "Don't loudmouth it around, OK? Something came down the pike. Somebody, and I mean somebody, wants this whole thing looked into and cleared up."

137

"Oh, you mean end of cover-up?"

He fixed her with a despairing look. "Christ Almighty. You people. All they wanna do is be sure that if, at any time in the future …"

"For a second there I thought maybe it was the truth they were after."

"Forget it! I didn't say nothing."

"When all they're worried about is covering their asses. I mean, this is New Jersey."

Of course she's right, he thought, and said, "Wrong. Forget it. I didn't say nothing."

They talked baseball, and a bit later he left. She'd been glad of the company. It kept her mind off Bernice.

Sky-blue and silver, the gleaming behemoth nosed its way down Schweitzer Boulevard, along Pascal Parade and into Demosthenes Drive. Its tinted windows deflected the stares of the curious; unnecessarily, as it happened, for the back seat was empty, the cocktail cabinet closed, the television off and the phone on its hook.

"It ain't the meat wagon," croaked one doughty watcher. "Not that shade, it ain't."

"I seen one like that in Florida, Herb," chimed in the mate. "Robin's egg blue."

"Florida?" scoffed the other; "they won't catch me in one of those pimpmobiles."

"Not as though you'll have much say in the matter," said the younger mate.

Bernice was up front beside the chauffeur. She had chatted most of the way down, but now was going over in her mind again what to say to Rita. It seemed as though she'd been away an age, instead of a couple of days. So much had changed. Like a house that looks the same on the outside, but inside it's all moved around.

Rage, she hadn't bargained for.

"Here I've been worried half to death, imagining all kinds of crazy things, and you breeze up in some fancy limo like a homecoming queen, all smiles and graciousness. 'What's wrong, Rita? Twitter, twitter. What did I do wrong?'" Rita slammed the fridge door and the tinkle of glass sounded ominously within. She wrenched it open: broken shards fell out amid a stream of Bloody Mary mix. "There is such a thing as a phone," she moaned. "You know—ringy dingy. For thirty hours I've been glued to the damn thing. Practically."

Bernice got down on her hands and knees and started picking up the glass. "I did phone."

"Once. One lousy time. You could have been dead."

"I'm sorry," Bernice muttered for the umpteenth time. "I said I'm sorry."

But ruffled feathers were smoothed and curiosity and sympathy triumphed as they began to catch each other up. Though an aftertaste did linger. Rita, perhaps for expiatory reasons as she cooled off, went first, relating her adventures with Otis and Biswekki. Then it was Bernice's turn.

"They took me in right away," she began. "It seemed like he was, well, waiting."

"Who took you where and who was waiting?" Rita was determined to get it straight from the start.

"Oh, the security guys. They drove me up to the house. Well, it's more like a castle. Flowers all over, and a spring gurgling into the bathroom; well, one of them out of nine and a half. And the driveway is electrified to melt snow. And another guy, who said he was his secretary, took me straight in to Taffelbaum."

"Who gave you a personal tour of the premises, I suppose?"

"Yes. And asked me to marry him. But that was later."

"You're kidding."

"I felt kind of sorry for him."

"You what?"

"It's funny to say, but there was a definite, how shall I put it? Well, like we saw through each other. When I first went in he was fiddling with this camera. Some sort of super instant instamatic that just came out. He took me, then I took him."

"He took you—for a sucker."

"We both came out green."

"Who is this? Some kid or something?"

"He's four ten, but he's no kid. He's our age."

"And your height."

"A teeny bit taller."

"Did you shrink? You were four eleven."

"It was important for him to be taller."

"He cheated?"

Bernice looked guilty. "We stood back to back in stockinged feet."

"You cheated." Rita put a hand to her head. "I don't believe this whole conversation."

"Let me finish. First off I showed him the quitclaim deeds. He didn't believe it. Said it was a hoax. That's why I agreed to stay over—so he could check. He had a bunch of lawyers onto it in five minutes."

"He held you prisoner. That's a punishable offence."

"I could have left any time."

"Oh, sure. With elves and armed dwarves patrolling everywhere."

"Well, I'm back, aren't I?"

"I can't think why he let you go, after you found each other. You may be back, but is Miss Annie? I don't see Stewart. And what about us? Did you ask him that?"

"I laid the whole thing out. Except for Otis. I didn't mention Otis. He said it was all news to him. He was mad."

"And the moon is made of green cheese."

"I know, I know, Bernice conceded. "I know what you're thinking."

"I'm thinking why didn't you marry the guy. Hot springs in every room. I could have been Maid of Honor."

"No one over five feet is allowed in. Anyway, there was a conflict of interest. When he found out the deeds stood up, he called me on the intercom. 'Bernice,' he said, 'it's going to a knockout between you and me. I don't care how many rounds.' I said, 'Look, all I want is a fair settlement plus costs.' It was as if he didn't hear. He said, 'I'm going to crush you.' He started out as a boxer, see?"

"The guy asks you to marry him, then he's going to crush you?"

"He was going to crush me first."

Rita looked curiously at her friend. "Are you hallucinating? They give you shots or anything?"

Bernice jumped up from the table where they were sitting and darted across to the couch. "He gave me this."

"*Atlas Shrugged.*"

"His Bible."

"Figures."

"Open it."

"'For Bernice Crickle. When you've had enough, come back and let's talk. F.T.'" A sprawling, childish hand. "He wrote that?"

"He said he doesn't believe in killing; there are other ways of eliminating the competition. That I was the only pebble on the beach, and he was the tide."

"And Otis never came up?" She shook her head. "He fired a half dozen people over the KAY-LEE title business. Just like that, for not catching it. They fairly tiptoe around him."

"KAY-LEE," Rita said. "What about KAY-LEE?"

"He said of all of his operations, it's closest to his heart. His wife's Kay and his daughter's Lee. Isn't that cute? And you know what it means in Chinese? 'Giving strength.' How's that, for a construction company."

"The guy has a wife?"

"Had." They died. About ten years back in a plane crash. He was piloting. That's where he got his scar."

"Scar? He showed you a scar?" She had visions of Taffelbaum pulling up his shirt.

"It's all one side of his face."

"He couldn't afford plastic surgery?"

"It was his fault, the crash. His way of living with it, I guess."

"So what did you do all day, after comparing heights? Wander hand in hand in the woods?"

"The woods are wired. Might have set something off. They have enough trouble with deer. But there's this courtyard I found, with a gazebo all the way from Italy, and a fountain that does sixteen things. I mostly just sat and read the papers.

They get papers and magazines from all over. Financial and stuff."

"Engrossing."

"For instance, did you know there's a dock strike in Australia and they're running out of Scotch? They declared a whiskey emergency. You never know what you pick up."

Thinking of Felix Taffelbaum and how easily he'd conned Bernice, Rita agreed. 'Giving strength', indeed. Yet there was something ... She tried to winkle it out of her subconscious. Biswekki, the previous day. *Somebody, and I mean somebody, wants this whole thing cleared up.* How many strings could Taffelbaum pull, or was the timing a coincidence? "Come on, Bernice, I'll drive you home. You can pick up stuff for tomorrow. Vacation's over."

"Thanks." Bernice looked down at the slacks and top she had on. "Been washing and wearing quite a bit lately." When the Checker wheeled into her driveway, she said, "Tell you what, Rita. Why don't I stay put. I think now it'll be all right."

"You sure now?" But they'd both recognized the warning signals. Friendship is as fragile as a bottle of Bloody Mary mix. "Well, first thing we have to do is find Stewart. Biswekki's no nearer than when you left. We've wasted enough time."

"Wasted?" Bernice's hackles rose, but she kept control. "Oh Rita, I hope not. Well, time will tell." Time, she knew, was what they didn't have.

"Say Josey's, four thirty?"

"You're on."

142

18

By the time she left work for the day at Four, Bernice had set a number of things in motion. She'd met with Kerry 13½; she had bought the least expensive Polaroid she could find; and she'd double-checked that the Lodge in Orange held bingo every Friday night at 7:45.

At lunchtime Kerry was waiting on the bench by the boat basin. Bernice produced the camera. "Ever worked one of these?"

Gravely, Kerry shook her head. They went over the instructions together and, after a couple of dry runs, the girl seemed to get the hang of it. "Good," said Bernice. "Now practice up on your own. I'll call maybe tomorrow, maybe in a couple of days. And remember now: if you see me, you don't know me."

The girl nodded. "Yes, Mrs. Crickle." They arranged terms.

Rita was at Josey's, as agreed. "Bingo, Friday. Are you on?"

"Friday? Sure. But isn't that your HELP night, Bernice?"

"I'm going to have to cancel."

"Where at, the firehouse?"

"The Lodge in Orange."

Muddy tracks three blocks away should have prepared them. In little more than a week, the site on Gunning Point Road had become a teeming mud-hole of activity. Stewart's house looked as closed as it had been on their last visit; except that up close they could hear sounds. The TV was on. Bernice rang the front door bell and waited. No response. Rita pressed her face against the garage window.

"Car's here."

"Is anybody home?" Bernice called up through cupped hands.

"How about I phone? Either he's asleep or away, or he doesn't want callers; which I wouldn't either under the circumstances unless they had good news." Rita walked down towards the corner booth. Bernice strained her ears, listening for the phone. Her watch said almost six.

A car stopped in the road. Someone got out. The car went on. A boy of about six came towards her across the lawn. He walked slowly, dragging a backpack, eyes on the ground.

"Hiya. Ollie, isn't it?" She wasn't sure he'd seen her.

"Oliver," the boy said, in a world-weary voice.

"Oliver," she corrected. "Your Dad not home?"

The boy squatted on the concrete step, rummaging in his satchel. At length he found a key, which opened the door.

"Mind if I come in?"

The boy shrugged.

Rita came trotting down the road. "Hey!" she waved.

"She can't," Oliver growled.

Fair enough, Bernice thought. After all, the last time he'd seen them Rita had beaten up on his brother and broken his glasses. She liked this kid, she decided.

Without a word or a backward glance the boy opened the front door and started up the stairs, still dragging his backpack. A TV blared from the room to the left but he paid no heed. "Anybody home?" Bernice peeped in. And ran back out. "Rita," she called from the door, for the boy's sake suppressing the urge to scream. "Quick. In here."

The room was a mess, chairs and tables skewed every which way. Sprawled half on, half off a couch, his face in a cushion, one knee on the ground, wearing little more than the last time they'd seen him, was Stewart's father.

"Mr. Krabbowicz? Mr. Krabbowicz!" Rita knelt down, fingers feeling expertly for the pulse on his one visible hand.

"Is he breathing?"

Rita grunted. "Sort of." The empty beer cans strewn around told the story. "Get some water."

Together they managed to turn the carcass over and stretch it the length of the couch. Cold water, liberally applied, had an effect. Stewart's father groaned, and unleashed a blast of stinking air in their direction. "I'll go fetch something to wrap him in." Bernice was already halfway across the room.

Rita turned off the TV and pulled a chair up to the couch. She sat down. "So, what in tarnation's going on?"

"Sonofabitch," he mumbled, eyes half open. "I'll get that sonofabitch." He struggled to get up. "I swear I'll throttle the fucking bitch." Exhausted, he collapsed back.

"Take it easy now." They looked at each other. Then the man closed his eyes and the fight seemed to drain out of him. "I know it's tough, but it's no use punishing yourself." By the looks of it he hadn't shaved in days.

"It's her fault. He'd have never run off but for her. You heard what that son of a bitch said, that schmuck lawyer she keeps? If he don't come back, he said, she gets the insurance." His face contorted. He was about to add something, but changed his mind, his wary red eyes suddenly taking Rita in. "Who the fuck are you? How'd you get in here?"

Rita went over and put the phone back on the hook. It was on the floor against the far wall, where she guessed he'd hurled it. A china lamp lay in pieces on the carpet. What's keeping Bernice, she wondered. "We just stopped by in case there was something we could do. We were by a couple of weeks ago, remember, me and my friend? About the old ladies that died. You were watering the lawn."

"Yeah," he said, "that's where I seen you. You seen what they done to it, my lawn?"

"Did Stewart seem kind of depressed at all, last time you saw him?" She decided to wade right in. To heck with Bernice.

The man's mouth twisted into a smile. "I never seen my boy depressed, like real depressed. Sure he was a loner; but he always had something he was into. Know what I mean? Always something going."

"What about lately?"

145

"He was gonna be a reporter. Had his heart set on it. He already got a break with the newstips, winning first prize. There was something he was working on he was real excited about."

"Did he say what?" Rita asked hopefully.

"He said it would make his newstips look like last weeks leftovers. I remember that. He'd get a job for sure on one of the biggies." He chuckled. "That's the way he talked. But you never knew with Stewart. You think sure, sure, but you just never knew." He brightened. "He'll be back. He had too much going for him."

"Did he mention the old barn? What he was doing there?"

"Fixing it up; him and Ollie. Said sooner or later it'd be a gold mine." Stewart's father shook his head. "That's Stewart all over for you."

"A gold mine?"

"See, lemme tell you something." The man propped himself on one elbow, searching for words. "Me and Stewart, we didn't—how do you say—converse. I guess that's it. For one thing," he scratched his ample belly, "well, he's smarter than me. I don't mind telling you. He's got some I.Q." Sounds filtered down from above. He sat up. "Ollie's back."

"They're upstairs, him and Bernice. That's my friend I was with." She called from the door, "Bernice!"

Stewart's father rolled off the couch and groped around on all fours in an attempt at straightening things up. "I don't know what got into me," he muttered. He seemed aware, for the fist time, of the state he was in.

"That's a great little kid." Rita said. "You don't want to lose him." She almost added, 'as well', but checked herself. Bernice appeared in the doorway.

The man seemed pathetically grateful for the visit. To Rita, his thanks were like a sword to the gut. Back in the Checker, she turned on Bernice. "You were a help."

"Oliver showed me Stewart's room."

"Oh, good thinking."

"Poor little fellow. He's convinced he'll never see his brother again."

"You think he's right?"

"He's certain Stewart would have told him if he was taking off. What he did tell him was his reason for not going to North Bergen that weekend. Said he had a 'business meeting' that was extremely important."

"A business meeting?"

"Something to do with the barn, Ollie thinks. But that's all he knows. I said to keep quiet about it. Even to the police. Oh, and there's no sign of a notebook. Oliver says he always kept it on him."

"See anything else?"

"Yes, as a matter of fact."

"Well?"

"Binoculars. There's a view of Miss Annie's from his room. At least there was. I'll bet Stewart knows a lot more about the comings and goings that night than he's let on."

"Knows?" Rita asked. "Or knew? Perhaps Otis was right. I'm almost beginning to wish we hadn't got involved."

"Don't give up now, girl. Just when we're getting somewhere."

"Yeah?" Rita turned the key in the ignition. "You think so?"

After a few blocks, Bernice said, "They did have a cat. Ollie was sure. I should have realized."

"Realized what?"

"The hairs on the bedspread. It'd sure have saved some heartache."

"What are you talking about, Bernice?"

"It was a cat up there, I heard. Not mice, and not the Devil. Yet the room was locked."

Rita stepped on the gas. She could tell by the peculiar smile on her friend's face that she was off again, some place out of reach.

For the next two mornings Rita parked the Checker outside the library at noon and waited with Bernice at Josey's. Bernice spent so much of her lunch hour gazing out of the window that the waitress, a woman of the world, realized she had a

147

bad case on her hands. "Don't worry yourself, dearie," she finally advised, "they're all of a piece. When they're good and ready, they come, but not before. Ain't nothing a gal can do." She winked.

"He's running scared," Rita suggested. "You should have seen him at that funeral. And he trembled like an aspen all the way back. He could have signed by now."

"Oh, guess what came in the mail!" Bernice fumbled in her purse and produced an official looking envelope containing a quitclaim deed in her name identical to the one sent to the old sisters.

"He didn't lose any time." Rita looked it over. "Still the three hundred bucks. Tempted?"

Bernice smiled enigmatically.

"I think our little friend is. He hadn't reckoned on organized crime."

"If he signed, I'd be surprised." Bernice got up. "Mustn't be late back. Not after last week." But she was a few minutes late; on the way to the bank she stopped by a travel agency.

On the third day, Otis took the bait. After Bernice made a quick phonecall, they left Josey's in a hurry. The waitress was puzzled: the same man Rita went off with before, now Bernice was after. A little runt of a guy moreover, who she personally wouldn't have given the time of day. "Beware my foolish heart; take care my foolish heart," she sang over and over till the woman at the register screamed at her to stop or go on to another verse.

When they reached the Monarchburger, Otis was waiting. He seemed in better spirits than they'd imagined possible, and ordered "Californians with everything, my treat." They found a picnic table round the back under a sunshade that wouldn't open near an overflowing trashcan, which a gang of youths on Hondas was using as a turn-around point. But neither noise, nor fumes, nor heat seemed capable of dinting Otis's mood.

"Ever bin there, California?" he asked through a mouthful of shredded lettuce.

"L.A. Sure." Rita said. Her impression of California was roughly akin to what they were experiencing at that moment.

Bernice said, "Here's one gal hasn't been west of Nashville."

He'd waited for it. "Then I'm just going to have to take her."

Bernice said, "Is that a date?" and patted his hand. "When were you in California?"

"A while back. After the war. Oh, I had dreams, once. I was going into chinchillas—breeding them for coats. Boned up on all the literature. I'd have been Chinchilla King of California by now. Could have made a killing. Look at the way fur's took off again. Before that it was Florida. Bullfrog farming."

"What happened?" Rita asked.

"The ponies. I'd save it all up, and lose it in an afternoon."

"I guess the way I see it, life's enough of a gamble as it is," Bernice said.

Otis apologized for not picking up on the signal earlier. "Bin running around all over. I was up to the site where they're gonna put the park. Nothing doing. I keep checking, see. You have to. I got my lawyer all set. Soon as they break ground we slap on the lawsuit. Stops everything cold till it's settled, which could take years. Even if the judge ruled for KAY-LEE, which he couldn't no way, it'd cost them millions, probably the contract. No way they won't settle, the way I see it. Let's put it like this: what's a hundred G when you're talking millions? Oh, and incidentally Bernice, that's fifty apiece—so long as we're partners. Unless," he leaned towards her with eager wide-open eyes, "you want to double your money. One grand each."

Rita said, "You better have a pretty powerful lawyer."

"Oh, he's good. This is how good the guy is. A burglar sets off one of those shriek alarms and gets a heart attack. The lawyer sues the manufacturer on his behalf and wins a five-figure settlement. Can you beat that?"

"He probably split it three ways with the judge. I didn't say good, I said powerful. There's a difference. Taffelbaum would hire the Father, Son and Holy Ghost if he could. He wouldn't need to buy a judge. He'd own him already."

Otis's confident grin sagged to a gape as Bernice described her visit to the lions' den. "Did my name come up?" he wanted to know.

"He didn't say it, and I certainly didn't."

"You know something, Bernice," he said, I'm glad we're in this together. 'Cause that's exactly what that son of a bitch doesn't want. If he could see the two of us sitting here now, he'd flip right out of his tree. So take care," he glanced around, "you never know where the beast'll strike next. Or in what shape."

Out of the corner of her eye Bernice took in a couple of kids at a nearby table, sucking on cokes. One of them had a camera. "The only way to beat him is to stick him with murder," she said. "And that's what we're going to do. Right, Rita?"

"Hey, it's bin real nice." He said awkwardly. "We should make this a habit."

"And risk the wrath of the beast?"

"Rita," she scolded. She planned to see more of Otis.

"What do you do for kicks?" he asked.

"Oh boy. I took American Square Dance 1 at County College last semester."

Rita hooted.

"It was between that and Baby Management."

"Well, I'm no Fred Astaire," Otis said.

"What are you?" Rita asked.

"Not much of anything."

"How about bowling?"

"I'm not what you might call a pro there, either."

"Rita scored 196 in single the other week."

"Way outta my league. How about you?"

"85 the last time, wasn't it Rita?"

"Now we're talking. I'll challenge you."

"You're on." As they got up to go Bernice scooped up the debris the kids had left and added it to the mound of garbage.

Otis turned to Rita. "There's a place down in Delaware any amateur can enter. You don't even have to be sanctioned. First prize is $10,000 or a brand new Cadillac."

"Dream on," she said. And to Bernice as they drove back to town, "The guy's a dreamer, with a kaleidoscope for a brain. Two hundred grand. He's hallucinating."

"I beg your pardon, ma'am, but half of that two hundred's

mine. You heard the man. Now let me see, what would I do with it?"

"Nothing for very long, if I'm your beneficiary. I'd get my hands on it and fast."

"You keep your cotton-pickin' hands away."

"Poisoned toothpaste. A lingering death, I'm afraid, Bernice."

"There, you see. As long as it's in the mind it's harmless. It could even do some good. But a hundred grand in the bank, that's trouble. So let him play with his kaleidoscope. Maybe it's all the fun he'll have."

"You think it's harmless, Bernice?"

"I hope so, for his sake. Tomorrow night, at bingo, maybe we'll find out."

When Bernice walked into the bank at one she was told the president wanted to see her. From the way people looked at her, or didn't look, she knew there was trouble. "Oh oh, what did I do now?" she asked the woman who brought the summons. But the woman busied herself with a file. In the elevator she went over all the things it might be. Finally she settled on the 'sick' leave. Somehow he must have found out. It was the only thing on her conscience.

But it wasn't the sick leave.

The president personally opened the door and ushered Bernice to a seat. He was a kindly man, concerned-looking, in his early fifties, whose picture on the annual report inspired confidence. Bernice had another name for it: worry. And not so much from the husbanding of funds as from the trials of being a husband. Many a Friday night she'd sat, sometimes for an hour or more, the phone cupped to her ear, as a slurred, winey voice droned on to the squeak and plop a cork makes leaving a bottle. The president's wife had a problem.

The president's hand went up and covered his mouth, and his fingers massaged his cheeks. He turned to his desk as if seeking help, and Bernice knew that whatever it was, it was bad. On a scale of one to ten at the bank, if he was ten, she was at the bottom. But this couldn't alter the fact they'd gone to high school together, even, once embraced passionately behind the gym. She wondered if he even remembered.

"Bernice," he sat down heavily in an armchair next to her, "They've got the new computer on line. It's going to replace Central Filing. Everything's going through Philadelphia."

"So I'm out of a job." She said it quickly to cut short his misery, like killing a mangy pet.

"You, er, guessed."

She hadn't guessed. She knew it wasn't any computer in Philadelphia that was taking away her job. It was Felix Taffelbaum. So this is what he meant by 'crushed.' It was certainly what she felt. She looked the president squarely in the eye. "Is it that important—to the bank?"

Relief loosed his tongue. "I'm not about to pry, Bernice. I'm not going to ask questions. You've been with us long enough to know that at County Bank & Trust the Customer Comes First. Well, it's more than just a slogan here, I like to think."

Suddenly he was pleading: "This industrial park. It means … It's one helluva shot in the arm, not just for the bank, for the community as a whole. It means jobs, investment, tax money …"

She stood up, cutting him short. "That's all I wanted to know."

"You'll be all right?" He sounded anxious, now.

"We have to do what we have to do. Each one of us."

He went with her to the door and stuck out a hand. "If there's anything I can do …"

Just give me back my job, she thought. I've been happy here.

In the outer office a secretary handed her an envelope: two weeks pay in lieu of notice.

That same afternoon Rita learned that the normally routine renewal of her cab license was held up. Something about operating a business in a residential zone. There would have to be an investigation and a hearing.

19

"Bingo!" "Start the next card for me, Rita. I'll be right back." Bernice tiptoed to the side of the hall where a woman was setting out food by a coffee urn. "Where's the ladies' room?"

"Right through there, dear. Can't miss." She pointed to a door near the front.

They'd not come in the main entrance under the pillars, where they'd been before. Bingo, organized by the Ladies' Auxiliary, was relegated to a long low redbrick annex alongside the rear parking lot. It had its own entrance—though the buildings were joined, Bernice noted.

She found herself in a no-man's-land of gray paint and cinderblock with the toilets and a flight of descending stairs to her left across from a swing door leading in the direction of the main clubhouse. Here goes, she thought, and pushed it open. The room looked like a school kitchen: sinks and big, stainless steel mixing bowls and a tile floor. Deserted. Yet she smelled cooking. Up the far end was a door with a small window in it, and in the window shone a light. By standing on a milk crate she could see a man in a chef's white jacket slapping something on a counter, hamburgers perhaps. Turning towards her, he yelled over his shoulder, ash from a cigarette scattering like confetti. Bernice ducked. Even should she get past the chef, she'd glimpsed in the murk beyond him a wall

153

of upturned faces like hungry hogs at feeding time. There had to be another way. She went back and tried the stairs.

Down below, in the basement, was a six-lane bowling alley. In deference to the bingo, or for other reasons, it was dark, with only a safety light left on. On one wall were posted notices. She peered at them: nothing of interest. *League Standings*, a sign announced. Teams with names like Avengers, Outcasts, Wildcats, Heart Strikers, Big O's and Lady Killers were doing well. On an impulse she searched for Otis's name, and found it. "Hey," she said out loud, "he's good." Otis, to her surprise, was up there with the leaders.

A passage leading under the kitchen area looked promising. Several doors opened off it, and Bernice tried them one by one in case she needed to hide in a hurry. All locked. Just as well she'd passed up high heels for rubber soles. She normally wore heels to bingo. They'd have clacked like castanets on the concrete floor. Hang in there, she kept telling her heart, as if it was a nervous passenger along for the ride.

A double door separated the newer basement from the old. Beyond she saw an elevator, and stairs up to the left. She took the stairs. From the sound of it she would bob up in the middle of whatever was going on, and with every step the acrid cigar smell intensified. For the umpteenth time she saw, in her mind's eye, the trim retreating figure with the snow white hair. He'd turned right, been gone under a minute, and come back with the postcard; and the card held a thumbtack. That was all she had to go on.

The door at the top of the stairs was wedged open. From where she stood, Bernice could see a couple of feet of passage. She waited. Nobody passed. The noise was coming from the right, like a hundred preschoolers at a party from which the mothers had fled. She said a quick prayer and almost at once it was answered. A chant started: "Lights out! Lights out!" Then came a mighty cheer, though the light in the passage stayed on. Bernice dodged left, then right, into a musty room full of pool tables. A bulletin board was just inside the door, and in the pale light from the window, she saw what she was looking for. Picture postcards, a row of

154

them. She'd unpinned the last three when the noise stopped. Then it started again, wilder than ever, and, she fancied—or was it just nerves—nearer. Yells, catcalls and whoops.

Peering out, she thought she saw shapes at the end of the passage, but the smoke was so thick she couldn't be sure. A door opposite, marked 'throne room', seemed to offer temporary haven. She pushed it cautiously. It was here—installed like a queen, with her feet up—that she read the news she both dreaded and needed. Even when the door thumped open and male voices ricocheted round the hard white space it was more like a radio had been switched on, nothing that touched her directly: "Hey there, Big Liz, howja get them boobiz?" What had been a hunch was now incontrovertible.

Getting out was harder. Each time she made up her mind, a fresh group barged in. The important thing was to pin the cards back up. After that, if they caught her, what could they do? She'd act the flustered innocent. Eventually Rita would come, asking questions. Rita wouldn't leave without her. At last she decided: now. One of the pool tables was lit and a game was under way. She stuck back the cards. So far so good. A door at the far end of the room was open, but as she reached it a voice called out. "Hey, just a minute there! Hey fellas!"

Bernice turned, smiled sweetly as if she'd just jumped out of a cake, and closed the door on a cluster of astounded faces. She was in the paneled hall with the front door to her left at twenty paces. Two men were leaving. They'd about got it open, when the gang from the poolroom, cues leveled like lances, hit the hall. As the men at the door turned, Bernice dodged between them. "Thanks fellas, ladies first." Then, with the fresh air in her lungs, she began to run.

Rita looked up as Bernice resumed her seat. She seemed out of breath. "This is the fourth since you left." She pushed a card towards her.

"Three and five, thirty-five," sang the caller.

Bernice looked blindly at the card that Rita was now tapping with her pencil. "Oh Rita, finish it, could you?" Standing by the side door she'd noticed the greasy individual with the

155

cigar stub from their previous visit. He surveyed the sea of graying hair. His belly heaved.

"Six and four, sixty-four."

"OK, let's have it." Bernice retrieved her card and assumed the mask of concentration worn by all around her.

"Nine and one, ninety-one."

"Bingo!"

Rita gave her card a disgusted flick. "How come it's always the same ones winning?" She glanced at Bernice. "So where were you?"

"Restroom."

"Constipated?"

"You about ready?"

"Hell, no. My luck's got to change."

"Who's dreaming now?"

"Let's wait for the break, at least."

They played a last card and broke for coffee. The greasy man had gone.

"There's just one stop I have to make, Rita, as long as we're here. It won't take but a minute."

In the dissolving light they drove between the sad little houses. Otis's place was dark, the shades drawn as before, the shrubs in their tubs standing guard. A mile away to the west the sky flared orange behind the Watchung Mountains, last burst of a summer's day. Rita stopped the car two houses on and kept the engine idling while Bernice rang the bell and was admitted. She'd just wanted to reassure them that all was well, she'd told Rita.

Next morning Bernice stood on her front porch surveying her tangled garden. My goodness, she thought, it must be August already. The ragweed was in bloom, its tiny white flowers dotting the greenery. Her ragweed never bloomed before August. Because of the mild winter and heavy spring rains the weeds were denser than ever this year. With time on her hands there'd be no excuse now not to tackle them. A hard winter had its advantages: it killed the bugs, and discouraged the weeds. A garden needed a hard winter. Same as a person. Only too many months of it could do permanent damage.

The phone was ringing. "Bernice, guess who's here?" Rita sounded excited. "Uncle Sudeley. His car's been torched. Vandals, he thinks, but I wonder whose vandals." She was mad.

"Is he hurt?"

"Seems all right. He hitched a ride in. I'm running him to the station house to file a report. We'll come on to you. Oh, and Bernice."

"Yes?"

"For us it's one thing; but other people? Suppose he was dead?"

"Well, he's not. I'm sorry, Rita. I don't want to sound callous, but if anyone's life's on the line, it's Otis's and mine. You'll see."

"I don't want to see. I think you should come back in with me today. We're not getting anywhere."

"But we are. We're closing in. If things work out, I'll even give you a day."

"Are you crazy! A day for what? What's got into you, Bernice?"

"The day Miss Annie's murderer comes to justice."

The vehicle that passed the house on Bay Road, hesitated, backed up, and oozed like a slug into the driveway, was not a Checker. Nor did it contain a face Bernice had ever seen before. When, a half hour later, Rita arrived—alone—and pulled in behind a gray Mercedes, she was puzzled by the New York plates with MD on them. A doctor and, by the looks of it, a Park Avenue one. She entered cautiously, through the kitchen.

"Oh Rita! This is Doctor Dranger. He's a friend of Mr. Taffelbaum." Strike one.

A lanky, olive-skinned man, sixty perhaps, bounced up out of a chair in a startling display of energy. Rita touched the eagerly proffered hand, and squirmed to feel its softness. Strike three: his headful of ringlets. Old men with perms, made her gag.

Dranger flashed her an appraising smile. "Norbert."

Bernice said quickly, "He's been kind enough to come all the way from New York City. He's an authority on murder."

"Murderers," Dranger corrected. "Or, more precisely, the murder mentality."

"A friend of Taffelbaum's? That figures." Rita sat down.

"Mr. Taffelbaum passed on what I told him about Miss Annie and Miss Mercy, as well as our ... Well, our feeling it was murder," Bernice explained.

"A textbook case, if you don't mind my saying so," Dranger purred. "A gratifying confirmation of my research over a lifetime. I sensed it at once."

"You know what they say ..." Rita began, but Bernice interrupted.

"Rita's the one I was telling you about, who knew Miss Annie way back; who had her in Sunday school."

"Then perhaps I can briefly recapitulate." Dranger crossed his legs, joined his fingertips and cocked his head. He stared at Rita as if seeking inspiration. She was on the verge of standing up, when he began. "The murdering instinct, you must understand, is present in every single one of us. You, me, Bernice. It's nothing to be ashamed of, nothing to be afraid of, unless," he raised a cautionary finger, "unless it's provoked in the course of an emotionally intense relationship with a victim. Sustained emotional frustration, when it reaches a certain level, will trigger the impulsive act we call murder. So, in a manner of speaking, the murderer can be said not to be able to help himself. Are you with me? It's the victim, so-called, who draws around him his karma like a cloak."

Dranger draped himself in an invisible cloak, and began pacing. "Again and again, I have found, it's the victim who is to blame. It is the victim who is, in a manner of speaking, the murderer. Suddenly the clouds roll away,"—he rolled the clouds away—"and the most baffling crimes appear obvious. Take, if you will, your Miss Annie. An exemplary character in every respect. Kind, good, comforting Miss Annie. What would we do without her? One day, deemed no longer good enough to play piano in church, she's dropped. Her feelings are not considered. Why? She appears to have none. She devotes herself slavishly to her parents and her sister, the teacher; her sister who drives a car, who doesn't dirty her hands with housework, who doesn't milk the cow, who is witty, intelligent, her parents' pet, perhaps with a male admirer. The parents die and Miss Annie slaves only for this sister; till one night the hate which has accumulated unconsciously through a lifetime—quite justifiably so perhaps—reaches flashpoint. Who knows what the final provocation was, conscious or unconscious, latent or manifest, it doesn't matter. Horrified by what she's done, Miss Annie rushes into the street …"

"Get out."

Dranger, caught up in the cocoon of his own rhetoric, blinked, like a man waking. Then he remembered to smile.

"Get out," Rita repeated.

"I beg your pardon?"

"Out," she motioned.

"What have I done?" He appealed to Bernice. "God damn it, I'm trying to help."

"Mr. Whateveryournameis," Rita said, "I have in my purse a gun. I intend to use it. But since, in a manner of speaking, the victim is the murderer, let's call it suicide, shall we?"

Dranger laughed uneasily, glanced again at Bernice, and sat down. But when Rita reached into her purse, he got up, shook his curls, and stalked off. Moments later they heard a car start.

Bernice ran into the kitchen. "Can you back out? You're in his way."

"Like hell." Rita went out and stood on the back porch watching Dranger maneuvering his Mercedes to and fro. Finally he let down the window and looked up at her. "If you don't want it hit, you better shift it, baby."

"You so much as touch my car, you've got a bullet through your windshield." He maneuvered some more, to no avail. Rita stood and watched. She could see—even though the car had to be air-conditioned—that his shirt was splotched with sweat.

Finally, he opened the door. "So what am I supposed to do?" He looked close to tears.

"Walk."

He stared at her, then turned on his heel. On reaching the road, he looked back. "Know what you are," he yelled. "A bunch of fucking rednecks."

"Score one to the Rednecks," Rita murmured.

Bernice came out of the kitchen. "Wouldn't it have been easier just to move?"

"I don't have doormats in my blood. Why'd you let him in, Bernice? You like being crapped on by Park Avenue?"

"I just thought maybe I'd learn something," she said meekly. "And guess what?" Rita eyed her. "I did."

"Not about Miss Annie."

"No, not about Miss Annie."

They were still standing there when a bright red Ford pickup drove in, hooting. "What do you think?" Uncle Sudeley called out. "Anyone for a spin?"

"Go along," Rita told Bernice. "I'll follow."

"You don't lose much time, do you?" Bernice hoisted herself into the cab.

"Had to get out of the infantry."

"I'm real sorry for what happened."

Uncle Sudeley blew out. "Way I see it if you're alive and well after twenty-five, every day is Thanksgiving Day."

Bernice concurred.

"She had a good death. For the cause, though which one I'm not exactly sure. Could have been vandals; could have been the Jersey Devil. It was the death I missed in '44 when I was touring the Pacific at Uncle Sam's expense, and six LSTs, combat-loaded for the Saipan D-day invasion, blew up. Defective fuses, they said. I can still see them fishing out the bodies. That morning I happened to be off with Floyd C. Mondabaugh on Oahu. That night I made my Will."

"Which reminds me," Bernice said, "If I wanted—say Rita—to have power of attorney for me, what would that cover?"

"Most everything, if that's what you stipulate."

"She could sign anything on my behalf and it would stand up in court?"

160

"All-inclusive, they call it. You've got to be mighty careful whom you give a thing like that to. Could be a passport to a whole lot of trouble." He turned off Jasper Avenue and pulled up outside a diner. Rita was right behind. "Say, it's a coon's age since I took a pretty girl out for a hoagie."

When Rita dropped Bernice back off on Bay Road, the Mercedes was gone.

20

"Biswekki called. There's a break in the Krabbowicz case. They're working round the clock. He needs us down at the station house right away."

"Good or bad?" Bernice's heart was in her throat.

"Stay there. I'll be right over."

"They need us. Well, that's a change." She knew it wasn't good.

"Our *fingerprints*."

"Have they …?" But Rita had hung up. Bernice's brain began to spin. She held up her fingers and wondered dizzily what they had to do with anything. She paced the room, listening for Rita, trying not to think. At last, the familiar scrunch.

"Remember the old Model A?" Rita reversed out of the driveway. "They just didn't have a single lead that checked out, according to Biswekki, so they went back to one of the last places he'd been seen in the hopes of picking up something fresh. Did a real job on the car. Inch by inch, and it paid off. It might be just vandals, but they're inclined to think not. If not, it sheds a whole new light on what could have happened."

"So what did they find?" One part of Bernice didn't want to know.

"A couple of things. First, they noticed that the clutch pedal was bent slightly up. Well, they'd seen that before; but this time they took the whole thing apart and found traces of a gray powdery stuff under the metal tread—like from the toe of a sneaker which had gotten caught. None of the sneakers in Stewart's room have that sort of a mark, but he was last seen wearing sneakers. The other thing was a bunch of black fibers caught in the doorframe, like from the back pocket of a pair of jeans. Stewart was last seen in black jeans, and the fibers matched others from his room. See what it's adding up to?"

"I think so." Bernice saw only too vividly. Herself and Rita in the back, Stewart driving. His question: *Where to?* Her reply: *Back in time.*

"They figure he didn't leave that car voluntarily. He was dragged. And whoever dragged him was either Superman, or Stewart was out cold." She swallowed and cleared her throat, then added softy, "Or dead."

Bernice gazed out the window. They passed trees and houses. She didn't see them.

"Oh, and another thing," Rita, said. "The horn."

"It didn't work."

"Yeah, but it looked fine. Now it's wonged up, kind of twisted."

"What do they think?" Bernice had already guessed what they thought. Rita confirmed it.

"That's where it happened. Probably he was throttled from behind. There's a chance he was gagged and bound and carried off, but a slim one. They're going over all the fingerprints, hoping to end up with a suspect. And they're talking to the neighbors again. It's not that simple to walk off with a sixteen year old, alive or dead."

At the station house, Biswekki had other disturbing news. "We talked to the kid brother again. Pushed him to come up with a face, some guy who might have hung around, who knew about the barn and so on. The sex offender angle. Seems like the little fella just pulled down the shade on the whole thing. Finally he came up with a guy who came by and bought a ticket. But all he could say was he was old and he only saw him once. Hell, anyone over twelve'd look old to him."

Bernice thought: Otis. She knew Rita was thinking the same. Neither said a word. Would Otis have left fingerprints? She wondered.

Back again in the Checker, with freshly scrubbed fingers where the ink had been, they both started talking at once. "What do we do?" Rita said. "Sooner or later it's bound to come out. I mean this 'cruise' has got to end sometime. Then what? We can't go on covering up for ever for him."

"I'm sure he realizes that, which is just the point. I'm afraid he'll try something stupid, if he hasn't already." Bernice foraged in her purse. "Mind if I ask you a question?"

"You just did."

"Promise not to laugh?"

"For God's sake, woman, spit it out." She turned the key in the ignition.

"He likes me, don't you think? I mean he's just a little bit sweet on me. Or you don't think so?"

"Oh, he dotes on you, Bernice. He adores you. Now where to?"

"Seriously, Rita."

Rita turned the key again and the engine died. "Bernice, if you asked him to marry you tomorrow, believe me he'd accept."

"You think so?"

"Sure. You're worth a hundred grand, don't forget."

"Rita, you're not jealous?"

"What's gotten into you lately, Bernice? You think I'd touch him if he was served up on a platter with all the trimmings?"

"That's not nice."

"It's not supposed to be."

"You don't go for him, do you?"

"The guy's a nothing. He has all the inner resources of a balloon; he's not in your league. Now, can I drop you off at Sunday school?"

"Sunday school." Bernice forced a laugh. "That's where it all began."

Rita glanced at her. This didn't sound right.

"Jellybeans, behind the minister's back. Miss Annie, all those years ago; riding through the forest, come rain or snow ... Hey, that's poetry! And look at us now." Bernice looked around at the manicured lawns, the tame trees, the new houses in cute designer shades peeking though cute designer shrubs. And the cars, parked and passing on the road. Always the cars, with their poisonous breathe. What had come over her? She'd never felt quite this way before.

"So? Church, is it?"

"Uh uh. They don't want me teaching there any more."

"Bernice! When did this happen?"

"Last evening. They called last evening."

Rita glowered. "That's just about what you'd expect from that holy bunch of shitheads. Pardon my French. You're better off without them."

Bernice was silent. "Can we go by Kerry's? Remember: south, beyond the tracks." For some reason, she'd been putting it off.

"What about Otis?"

"Hands off. You just leave Otis to me."

It was Rita, a few minutes later, who voiced it, but the thought had come that same instant to Bernice. "Mind if we run by the old barn first?"

Being Sunday, the site was deserted; but they could see from the road that foundations had been dug for two houses, and already they were pouring concrete. Building materials were stacked all around; cinder blocks, metal rods, drainpipes, sheets of plywood, with machinery poised at odd angles waiting to spring to life at the touch of a button. A beat-up trailer with wires running into it and a generator looked like the nerve center of the operation. On the further edge, against the trees, a couple of Portajohns leaned together at a rakish angle. Only the barn was the same, though most of the creeper that once doused it like thick green sauce had browned.

"Like an outsize dog kennel, sitting there," Rita murmured as they picked their way through the sandy red mud. The gap in the side had been patched up. A sign said, 'KEEP OUT. CRANBERRY TOWNSHIP POLICE DEPT'. They wandered round, peering in through knots and cracks, but saw nothing, not even the car.

"Don't look round. Palms against the wall!" The voice had the chill of authority. The two women froze. The unmistakable—at least to Rita—sound of a gun being cocked came from close behind. "So what did I do, huh?" Almost a whisper. "What did I ever do to youse so you havta go messing up a guy's life, huh?" Hot breath on her neck, or was it a breeze? "Stickin' your nose in where you've no damn business, huh? Well? Well?"

"Biswekki knows we're here," Rita managed.

"Biswekki, Biswekki. Like a fuckin' priest, Biswekki. Run to Biswekki, tell Biswekki. Lemme tell youse something: in about one minute he better be here. You gonna need a priest."

"You wouldn't dare," Rita said. "Not now, not here." Keep them talking. Isn't that what Bernice does on HELP?

"Oh no? Ever hear of a silencer? No one'll know from nothing."

A wild thought flashed into Rita's mind. "Like with the kid, eh? From behind, with a silencer."

Bernice cringed. No, Rita. She prayed like she'd never prayed before. After the first jolting moments and the man began to brag, she'd relaxed a little. Real muderers, surely, didn't broadcast their intentions. But taunting him like that? No, Rita, no.

A bullet crashed through the wood inches from her ear and she spun round. Rita did the same. In fascinated horror they watched as methodically he unscrewed the silencer and stuffed the .38 special into its holster, then turned stiffly and shambled away. Without exchanging a glance the women made for the road. They didn't run. Self-preservation argued against that. But they covered the distance fast.

"Phew!" Rita spoke first. "Either something snapped or he's stoned out of his mind."

Bernice was suddenly aware of the birds in the trees, the rush of noise from a car radio, the parallel white trails three jets had left in the sky. "Poor guy."

"Wait till Biswekki hears." With several backward

glances they walked to the Checker. "This wasn't such a hot idea. He seems to haunt the place, like a dog with a worry bone. Why not just haul him in? I don't get it."

"We better leave him to the pros."

"They'll let him plead insanity. Very temporary, mind you. They all get off that way."

They found Kerry 13½ sitting on a crumbling rattan rocker on a dusty strip between the front stoop of a tarpapered old house and the road. Spread out on bits of cardboard at her feet was an assortment of junk: chipped saucers, half an aluminum coffee pot, a blonde legless doll, a bicycle chain and three battered colanders. A sign nailed to the porch said: Refreshments, Collecterbles. Next to the rocker, on an upturned tin tub, sat a jar of lemonade and three paper cups. It's all right," Bernice called when Kerry feigned non-recognition. "We're friends again."

Rita exchanged twenty cents for a drink. "The spirit of Ayn Rand is alive and well in Shore County."

"I beg your pardon?" Kerry looked up, a puzzled squint on her freckled face. She had on cutoffs and an old T-shirt.

"She means," Bernice said, "that a little honest enterprise never hurt anyone."

"I'll be right back," Kerry jumped up and disappeared into the house.

"We'll mind the store." Rita installed herself in the rocker just as a car pulled up behind the Checker.

A couple got out and began scrutinizing the goods. "Do you got spittoons?" the man asked.

"Sure do." Rita picked up a hubcap and a colander. "See, this fits right in here like so and you've got yourself a real good spittoon." The man regarded her doubtfully, as if she might take it into her head to demonstrate.

"Bert, Bert, come on down here," the woman called, trying not to sound excited.

Bernice saw Kerry run out from behind the house and walked over. "She's doing great." She indicated Rita.

Kerry produced the camera and an envelope tightly secured with a rubber band.

"What's this?"

"The change."

"Keep it."

"Oh no, Mrs. Crickle."

"Well then give it to your brother—for the gas." She pushed the envelope back into the girl's hand.

Kerry glanced back to where, spaced out among the trees that dotted the small hollow behind the house were the hulks of cars in various stages of decomposition. In another place it might have passed for a sculpture garden. A pair of legs stuck out from under a jacked up van.

"All his, huh?"

"And my daddy's." A flicker—was it shame—passed across the girl's face.

Bernice put her hands to her mouth and shouted, "Thanks, fella!" A leg waved in acknowledgement. Meanwhile Kerry extracted a small piece of folded paper from the envelope. Bernice looked at it, nodded, and stuffed it into her purse. "No problem?"

"It was fun."

"The photo came out good."

The couple was driving off as they rejoined Rita, who handed over a five-dollar bill. "I took my commission in lemonade."

Kerry's eyes widened, "What's this for?"

"Let's see. One orange plate, and was that a butter dish top? I thought they might be Depression glass."

"They were plastic!" Kerry was horrified.

"Believe me, they deserved each other. And I said *might* be."

"Is that honest?" From anyone other than Kerry, it might have sounded smug.

"I'll amend what I said before. Ayn Rand is sadly neglected in this neck of the woods."

Back in the car, Bernice said, "Do you think Rudi of Switzerland would be open?"

"Rudi's House of Beauty? In the new mall? Bernice, what's got into you? You are out of a job. On the discard pile. Being hunted ruthlessly by a mad cop and a power-crazed billionaire dwarf. You can no longer afford life's little luxuries."

"I think it's open Sundays. If you wouldn't mind ..."

Rita sighed. Her friend was in one of her mystic moods.

"As Madame pleases." She was getting used to them.

21

Tap-tap-tap. Bernice put her ear to the door, then tried again. Tap-tap-tap. She thought she heard a noise. "Mr. Olds? Mr. Olds?"

The woman in the office had sworn he was in. His car was there, and his room key off the hook—though that didn't mean a lot. He was always forgetting to leave it when he went out. Yes, she'd known the face right away, even though it was not in focus, greenish and partly obscured by a giant hand tilting a coke bottle. "Sure. That's Mr. Olds. Been here close on a month, he has. Sweet man, nicely spoken, always paid up. Definitely a cut above the usual. You wouldn't believe what gets washed up through these doors." She glanced reproachfully at a tearful heap of a woman occupying the room's only other chair, and embarked on the saga of the place she'd run with her late husband, the colonel, "not a dime's throw from where old Mr. Rockefeller would pass by" on his way to or from somewhere. "Those were the days." Her mottled, purplish face suggested that she'd not lacked for companionship of another sort since the colonel's demise.

Tap-tap-tap. Cautiously, Bernice tried the knob. Locked. Reluctantly she headed back towards the office. But at the last moment, instead of going in, she walked out between the buildings onto the road. Finding the Whippoorwill Motel had entailed an expensive cab ride. She was darned if she'd give

170

up that easily. To say nothing of the hairdo. Rudi of Switzerland—not her usual hairdresser, and she felt sure now, a frustrated pastry chef—had whipped up an elaborate coiffure all held together with spray. She prodded it gingerly. Already the heat was having its effect, not to mention the flies. She had on her head what felt like a leaning tower of Pisa in cotton candy. Certainly there was no way she could sleep like that. It was a one-day stand, and the day was today. "Snap to, Bernice," she admonished herself. "Up and at 'em!"

She picked her way across the beer can and glass strewn no-man's-land between the motel and its next door neighbor, J & G Transmissions, which appeared to have gone out of business. Somewhere she thought she heard the wail of a train, a plaintive cry that matched the mood of the place. Must be tracks nearby. Seven windows along. She counted. This must be it. The drapes were closed, but the air conditioner pounded and wheezed away like a hippo in heat, its stale breath further threatening the hairdo. And the window—when she got up close she saw it—the window, though pushed to, was unlatched. She hooked a nail under the rim and pulled.

Back in the office the woman listened as Bernice outlined a theory. "Yes," she chimed in, "he *was* on some sort of medication. Pills. For his heart, I think."

"Of course it's much worse than he lets on," Bernice continued, with an air of including the other in a confidence.

"Don't tell me. Like big babies that way, they are. Take the colonel. Wouldn't believe he was going till he went, know what I mean? A mail-gram wouldn't have convinced him." She opened her mouth again, no doubt to enlarge upon the circumstances of the colonel's going, but Bernice had other ideas.

"Did he seem, well, you know, at all jumpy, kind of nervous, lately?"

The woman shook her head. "Just like always. Keeping himself to himself. I'd be lucky if I got the time of day. Sometimes, some of the time, it was like he had a wall round him. Couple of times he asked if anyone came looking for him. But that was nearer when he first came."

171

"He didn't have any visitors?"

"Uh, uh." She pulled an enormous bunch of keys out of a drawer. "The thought of him laying there on the bed, helpless. Know what I mean?"

"Or worse," Bernice hinted.

"Lord a'mercy!" The woman eyed her with alarm and heaved herself up. "I'd appreciate the company, dear. Never was one for this sort of thing." She helped herself from a bottle in a cupboard behind her, then offered it to Bernice who declined. "A word to the wise: if you're on the squeamish side, stay out of this business. Know what I mean? 'Genteel', he promised; 'befitting a lady of susceptibility.' His very words. How I stuck it all these years is beyond me." She locked the door from the outside.

Bernice indicated the tearful lady. "Is there …?"

"Her?" She tapped her temple. "If the worst comes to the worst it wouldn't be the first time. I'm telling you. More liquid's come out of that woman one way or another. They let 'em out of the nuthouse, first thing they check in here." She grumbled her way across the yard.

Otis's room contained no body, dead or alive, just a dip in the bed where one had lain. The woman closed the window and turned off the air conditioner. Bernice checked under the bed and in the closet. He was traveling light, she noted; just the old green suit, a tan windcheater and what looked like a mailman's blue-gray outfit. The pants had cat hairs around the turn-ups. She wondered just how strapped for cash he was.

They were walking back across the yard, where five or six cars baked like potatoes in the afternoon sun, when they spotted him. "Oh, Mr. Olds," the woman called out, relieved. "You have a visitor." To Bernice, she said, "Take care now," and lumbered off, moving more sideways than forwards like a vast crab, keys clanking.

Otis hid what Bernice knew must be astonishment with aplomb. "Bernice." He wore a golf shirt and seersucker pants and came in past the office as if from an afternoon stroll. "You come alone?" His glance flicked over the cars. Closer up, she decided she'd been wrong. He had the eye-blinking look a nesting bird gives an intruder. And he was wearing slippers.

"Mr. Olds," she said, smiling. Then, lowering her voice in case the woman could hear, "It kind of suits you."

Otis continued to look uncomfortable. He was doing a lot of swallowing. "We can't talk here. Just wait." He fetched car keys from his room. And changed his shoes, she noticed. "She bin in there?"

"We were worried when you didn't answer; she didn't see you go out."

"I'll give the bitch something to worry about." His vehemence surprised her. "How many times I told her to keep away."

"You should have said to go in any time. Reverse psychology, remember?"

He grunted, "You in there too?"

"A second or two."

They were on a busy highway, going nowhere in particular. The motel was ten or twelve miles north west of Neptune Grove, she reckoned. It worried her she hadn't been generous enough with the gas money for Kerry's brother.

"I cannot tell a lie," he said at last, with a sort of amused awkwardness she liked. "I jumped out the window. Had it all planned. One of these days I figured they'd come for me. Soon as I heard the knock, I figured this was it."

"I'm sorry," she said, and meant it.

"So why did you have to come? How'd you find it? Rita drop you off? How'd you know you weren't followed?" Questions tumbled out. "Jeez, that jalopy of hers is ..."

"Like a red rag to a bull. No, I took a cab. No skin off your back, I promise. Not even Rita knows. Nobody does."

"Nobody? Well, that's something." He sounded relieved, though she saw his hands on the wheel were trembling. As if aware of her scrutiny, he tightened his grip. "So why? Why'd you come?"

"I was worried." She told him about Biswekki and the fingerprinting of the Model A, and how the police might eventually trace some to him. "As long as you've been a federal employee they have you on file some place; so it might be better to come forward now."

173

"The car?" he said. "That old thing? I didn't touch it. No way. I swear to God I didn't touch it."

"Then that's all right. It's just that when the boy, the brother, said ..."

"Sure, I paid my buck. But I never touched the car. No sir. It's his prints they should be after, not mine; that rogue cop's. What do you gotta do to get arrested in this state? Shoot the Governor? They should have picked him up long ago."

"They may still," Bernice said, "and then they may not." She described the incident at the barn that morning, and Otis's spirits seemed to lift. "What did I tell you?" he crowed.

"Yes," she said, "and you were right about Taffelbaum. The gloves are off. I got fired from my job."

For all his talk of the terrible vengeance of KAY-LEE, which, after all, was what he was hiding from, Otis registered genuine surprise and shock. "My God, Bernice," he said hollowly, "they did that? They went and did that?"

"That's just for starters."

She told him about Rita's problem with her license and Uncle Sudeley's car.

"I'll tell you what," he said, taking a moment to collect his thoughts. "It's gonna be all right. You and me, Bernice, we're going to stick together. See what I'm saying?" The road was jammed with weekenders beating it back home from the shore. "Tell you what," Otis swung the car out of the mainstream and pulled up in front of a diner. "This calls for a celebration."

The diner looked like a Vegas version of the summerhouse of a seaside Roman villa: crazy stone work, curly red tiles and wrought iron dolphins. "Two light n' sweets!" The waitress relayed their order to an unshaven man with bulging biceps behind the counter. The place was almost empty.

"Sweets for the sweet," Bernice laughed self-consciously, flipping open a greasy menu.

"How about that?" Otis looked up as if a pearl of pure wisdom had fallen from her lips. "You know what, Bernice? You know what I'm thinking?"

She glanced at him and a smile quivered around her mouth.

"No." She knew perfectly well what he was thinking, and wished he'd get on with it because the waitress was balancing her cigarette back on the ashtray and the light n' sweets were hitting the counter.

"Bernice," his hand went out in search of hers and closed around the ketchup bottle. "How about if the two of us ..."

"Alrighty!" Mugs of coffee splattered on the Formica between them. The waitress, pad in hand, eyed first one then the other.

"Chef's salad, I guess," Bernice said eventually and the waitress unleashed a verbal barrage of dressings. "Italian. No Russian. Oh wait, what's in the House? Does it have garlic?" The woman assumed an exasperated demeanor. Bernice surrendered. "OK, Thousand Island."

Otis ordered the Fisherman's Platter with all the trimmings, and tucked a paper napkin under his chin in anticipation. With the waitress back at the counter, he picked up his thread. "Take me, for instance. I never bin what you might call a married man, see? Not that I haven't had what-do-you-call, *experience.* I ain't no three dollar bill. But you, you're different. You bin hitched already, pardon the expression."

She tried not to wince from the pain he was putting himself through.

"What I'm saying is, between us we got a few years left and maybe some spending money coming in. See what I'm saying? Two is better than one."

"Except at tax time." She was teasing.

Just to be sure she understood, he spelled it out: "I'm talking marriage here, Bernice."

"I'll drink to that." They clinked mugs.

"I'm not saying tomorrow or the next day," (Was he backing out already?) "But, like, when it's all over, see. We shouldn't even tell anyone, not till it's over."

She squeezed his hand and their knees brushed. "I promise. Not even Rita."

"Then we'll go away." He took her in with his eyes, suddenly aware that he'd done it and it wasn't hard, that what he thought would never come about was now almost within his grasp. There seemed nothing more to say. He excused himself, got up and, napkin fluttering at his neck, went to find the men's room. His hand was to his breast pocket even before he got there.

Bernice sat and thought about what she'd done. For one thing, she felt safer. She stared at the reflection in her mug and fancied she saw, staring back, the frowning features of her husband. He'd always been absurdly jealous. "Don't mind me, Earl. Don't be mad," she murmured. "You gotta do what you gotta do, remember?" His last words to her, practically. Dunking a napkin in her water, she set about polishing the stains off the menu.

The salad came, and the Fisherman's Platter, which, the menu's lush rhetoric notwithstanding, consisted of two thawed fish fingers and some wilted lettuce. Poor Otis. The waitress hurried back to an interrupted argument at the counter:

"I don't smell nothing." She bent over a customer's cup. "Perfume? What sort of perfume?"

"If I get trench mouth, I'm gonna sue you."

"You can't sue me. I just work here."

"What sort of detergent you been using?"

"Ask him."

Otis was coming back. Bernice found herself humming *The Teddy Bears' Picnic*. He did remind her of a teddy bear. He walked round behind her and kissed the top of her head. "What you do to your hair, Bernice?"

"You noticed. Well, about time."

"It's sticky. You give it a honey rinse?"

She said coyly, "Isn't it funny how bears love honey. Buzz, buzz, buzz, I wonder why he does."

Later, Otis drove her home. En route they stopped at a tavern where the sign said, 'Happy Hour, 5 to 7. Drinks half price. Ladies free.' The champagne was flat, but even diluted with orange juice it went to work on Bernice. She called Otis 'smokey bear' and kissed him on both cheeks when the bartender wasn't looking.

"Jeez, I should give you something for a souvenir; you

know, till it's official." Otis patted his breast pocket where his pills were. "So when you wake up tomorrow you'll know you weren't dreaming."

"I thought of that." Triumphantly Bernice pulled the menu from the diner out of her purse.

Otis scrawled on it, 'With all my love.' "I'm not going to sign till later." He chuckled, "Oh oh. I'll bet you're a regular packrat."

"Three of everything."

"Me too." Yet his room had seemed bare.

He dropped her off and watched as she scurried across the road, turned, blew a kiss, and was swallowed up by the bushes. For the first time in a long long time he felt a twinge of real contentment.

22

Rita was no packrat. Her rule of thumb was: after a year's non-use, out. So when Detective Gus Biswekki slopped beer on *A Guide to Australian Cheese*, which had sat on her coffee table since Christmas, she didn't have to wait. "Don't worry. I was going to donate it to the Home for Old Cops anyway."

They resumed their seats. Rita, Bernice, Biswekki. "Talking of which," Biswekki said a little too casually since it was what he'd come about, "I guess I'm telling tales out of school, but Scag's been temporarily suspended."

"What, from the Force?" Bernice sat straight up.

"No, the Boy Scouts," Rita snapped. She turned to Biswekki. "For his fastest-gun-in-the-East act, I suppose? Did they find the bullet?"

"I didn't say nothing about a bullet." He tried to look mysterious.

"What about his prints on the car?"

"They found everybody and his uncle's prints on the car. That don't mean nothing."

"Including his?"

"Sure, including his. He told us they were there, didn't he? He was going to buy it, so he had to check it out."

"He said."

Biswekki leant forward and his mustaches fluttered in the

breeze from the fan. "It's nothing to do with finger prints. But in one sense it's about that bullet and the hole it made. Yes."

"What is this? *I've got a Secret*?"

"Hell," he looked at Rita, "you blew his scam sky high, didn't you? If I'd a been him, I might not have missed."

"We did?" Bernice blinked innocently.

"The guy's a psychopath. It's obvious," Rita said.

"I couldn't say about that, but he's like this," Biswekki held up two fingers, rubbing them together, "with the Hanratty clan. Just like you said. It all checked out down to the fine print. The bottom line is, the guy's in hock to Mob elements. But don't worry. He won't be bothering you again in a hurry. They got him in Trenton, talking to the State Police and the FBI. And I mean talking. So you can rest in peace."

"Yeah," Rita said, "that's what I'm afraid of." But Biswekki didn't get it. "So you're saying that organized crime has infiltrated the police?"

"Jesus Christ," Biswekki implored. "You sound like some kind of a reporter, twisting words every which way. The guy wants to buy a house, right? He needs cash up front, which he doesn't have, right? So where does he go? His folks? His bank? No, his loan shark. He's from up north. That's where he knows the ropes; that's where he goes. And that's as far as it got."

"He's financing his Cape Cod with Mob money?" Rita whistled. "The Pilgrim Fathers would turn in their graves."

"Scag's the one who'll do any rotating," Biswekki shot back. "These Charlies, once they've tasted flesh, they don't mess around."

"So what about the house?"

"Guess it'll be back on the market. That's no concern of mine." Already he had alerted his brother-in-law. "Too bad, the whole scene."

"Too bad?" Rita rounded on him. "Is that all you can say?"

"The guy was only trying to do right by his family. Give him a break. Working two, three jobs. Just couldn't seem to hold it together. Who can these days?" He sipped from his beer. "They practically set the play swings in cement already." But Rita, he could see, wasn't buying. "OK, OK," he held up

179

a hand, "Only there's no proof."

"Miss Annie didn't have a family, so she's expendable, right? Let her molder in the grave, while Scag goes marching on. And Stewart ..."

"Jesus Mary and Joseph!" It was Bernice. The others stared at her, amazed; then round the room to see what was wrong. She was on her feet, bouncing her head between her palms like a beach ball, eyes popping like studs.

"Bernice, you got religion, or what?"

"Jesus Mary and Joseph," she repeated, quite calmly. "You dummy, Bernice. Oh you dumb bunny. I bet I know where he is."

The sandpit that had been 151 Gunning Point Road had lain empty when they arrived, like a gash in the jungle where civilization had mysteriously died. The construction crew was gone for the day. But as a little knot of policemen worked away, probing and digging, at a point near the back line beyond the newly cemented foundations, a crowd started to gather. At first they stayed near the road where the sign said 'KEEP OUT'. But after a while the more adventurous kids edged forward till they were within a shovel's throw of the hole that was slowly opening.

"Hey, mister, why don'cher use the excavator?" one smart alec yelled.

"That's it!" Biswekki bellowed. One minute he was pacing around, apparently intent on the digging; the next he was waving everybody back to the road and posting a man to keep them there.

"What's up?" enquired a man in a suit who looked like he was coming home from work.

"Nothing to interfere with your dinner," Biswekki answered, an attempt at humor that bombed. "Jesus Christ," he muttered, picking his way back to his men, "next thing they'll have the press here." Bernice and Rita stood off to one side, watching. He strode over to them. "You better be right, you just better be, or I'll be laughed off the Force." The real estate option suddenly loomed large.

"I was just thinking," Bernice piped up. "It was what you said about the play swings in cement did it. That's what Stewart was raising money for—a playground. That and the I—80 overpass. The association, I guess. Plus what Rita said about John Brown's body."

Biswekki stared in disbelief, shook his head and walked away. "For a nutcase," he threw up his arms, "I throw away my career." Rita couldn't help but smile, knowing the workings of her friend's mind to some extent, and knowing how he felt, too.

Lightly, it had begun to rain. Thunder, breaking miles away, bespoke a storm. "I remember one night sitting in Grandma's outhouse when a storm broke," said Bernice. "I must have been just a little thing because I was too scared to move. There was a praying mantis, quite still, on a box, and the way the lamp was set, it threw its shadow on the door. We just sat there, it and me, waiting out the storm, till Grandma came looking with an umbrella. She was convinced I'd fallen in."

"How far down, do you think?"

"Dunno. But it must be years since they dug a fresh one."

"Ten feet?"

"Could be."

But the digging went on and the sky darkened, and a canvas cover was rigged up against the rain. Rita and Bernice huddled in the front seat of a squad car that had its lights trained on the hole and the growing mound of dirt beside it. A man shouted, "Fifteen feet!"

"I guess they didn't have that much in them, just the two of them," Rita remarked.

Biswekki's streaming face appeared at the window. He passed in two containers of coffee. "We got our friends from the press here," he said glumly. "If they wanna know anything, just a flat 'no comment', got it? I'll do the talking." He smiled grimly: "One way or the other, shouldn't be long now. Oh, and Bernice, they got a vacancy for clairvoyant over at the asylum."

"Take it, you may need it," Rita shouted after him, but the splash of rain on the roof and the rumble of the engine drowned her out. "He'd be cute, if he wasn't a bastard."

They were a few sips into the coffee when the atmosphere tensed. Sensing a change, Rita switched on the wipers. When the windscreen cleared, they saw the work had stopped. Men with shovels were standing around, some peering into the pit, some with paper cups. One guy started towards them, dirt streaking his face. He looked wiped out. "Find anything?" Rita yelled. The man nodded, wiped his chin with the back of his hand, and lurched away.

They heard shouts, and over towards the road an ambulance that was parked there came, beeping and flashing, importantly to life. A cop stuck his head in the driver's side window and grabbed the radio receiver next to Bernice. "Ten-six, come in ten-six, this is four zero. We got a body." The speaker barked back. "About a half-hour," said the cop.

Rita had her door open and one foot on the ground when Bernice put a hand on her arm. "No, Rita. No."

"Why?" But she pulled the door to.

Suddenly their spotlight teemed with men in plastic gowns and masks and surgical gloves. Like a scene from *M*A*S*H*, Rita thought. A stretcher appeared, and slowly, painstakingly, an object, dark, bedraggled, uncooperative, was hauled up and loaded onto it. The light brightened to a fierce white. "Shit," Rita said, "it's the TV." With the cameras following, the men in green stumbled out of sight with their burden, over which some thoughtful soul had thrown a police raincoat. Stewart Krabbowicz would meet his final deadline: the eleven o'clock news.

Somewhere out of sight, above the hubbub, Biswekki's voice droned on: "We had a lead. We followed it up. Simple as that. Why did it take so long? What can I tell you? Everything's relative. That's the name of the game. No, not at this time, we can't. We'll have to wait for the autopsy. Not till the next of kin have been informed. I'm sorry, I'm sorry. Listen, I got work to do, same as you, right?"

The siren sounded fainter and fainter. The thunder, too, seemed to have lost interest and wandered away up the coast like some demented bum, taking the rain with it. Rita and Bernice pressed their backs to the old barn, warm still from the sun, which was where the squad car had left them. From the road, parents called to their kids to come home this instant or else, and the kids called to each other, mocking their elders. They thought of Stewart's brother and his father. For a moment their house had been trapped in a harsh glare as the camera rolled; but it was empty. Biswekki had seen to that.

They heard the put-put of the electric generator which someone had gotten going so a cable could be strung to the pit. The light was still on, shining up out of the hole, reminding Bernice of an illustration in a book of Bible tales, *The Light from the Tomb*. A shadow moved to and fro across it like a giant, trapped moth. As they watched, a face appeared above the dirt line, then arms, then torso, then legs. Biswekki.

"Jesus Christ," Rita hissed, breaking their silence. A while later they were all three squashed in the front seat of his unmarked Torino for the ride home. "Take a look." Casually Biswekki pulled something from his top pocket and tossed it into Rita's lap. Through the clear plastic, in the light from the streetlamps, she saw a soiled, swollen, twisted, curling notebook. "That the one?"

"Sure could be." She made as if to take it out.

"Don't break the seal. But I'll tell you this right off. Some pages at the back are gone. Ripped out."

Near the back, Otis had said, *not the last page but near the back*. Her own words came back to her: *Find the notebook and you'll find Stewart*. It had happened. If not quite the way she'd hoped.

Bernice said, "Oh boy, I sure did underestimate him."

"Who?" But Bernice didn't seem to hear. "No use looking for prints on these, is there?" Rita passed her the soggy evidence. Bernice quickly returned it to Biswekki.

"Let's see what they come up with at the morgue." He dropped Rita at Carefree Village and doubled back with Bernice. Bay Road wasn't that far from the station house and he still had work to do.

"I know it's late and you're not through yet, but could you

do something for me?" She put the question tentatively, just as the car pulled into her driveway. "Oh, not tonight. Just when you get a chance."

"Bernice," he said expansively, "after tonight, could I deny you anything?"

"It's probably not important, but then you never know."

"You never do," he said, and meant it.

She took a large envelope from her purse and handed it to him. "Should be a set of prints in there. If we knew whose they were, it might help some."

23

A length of cord still circled Stewart's mangled neck. Tied to the other end was an old coat. It had once belonged to his father. The morgue confirmed what had, till then, been speculation. The killer had worked from behind as they sat in the car, then yanked the body by the neck the few yards to the pit which was all that was left by then of the burned-out privy. Saturday or Sunday, it had happened, because on the Monday, by sheer luck—or uncanny foresight—the bulldozers had filled in what must be one of the deepest graves in the whole state. By Tuesday, when Stewart was finally reported missing, he was under fifteen feet of earth and any trail which might have led the sheriff's bloodhound to the pit was bulldozed over.

Next morning, a further search of the site turned up a bunch of rusting house keys and a pair of broken spectacles; Stewart's spectacles. From the condition of the keys, and their position under the body, it appeared they'd been there longer, but not much longer, than Stewart. Two weeks, five at the outside. Nothing else of interest was found on the body itself, nor did the notebook seem to offer up anything beyond a pathetic reckoning of one boy's summer with death as the bottom line: the figures on his paper route, the *Star* prize money, the takings from the haunted barn franchise. Stewart was clearly Triple A, an all-American achiever; in other words, he could hustle a buck. Which, Bernice reflected, was probably his undoing. The last third of the notebook was missing. If a section for license numbers had existed, it was gone.

"A beaut of a job." Biswekki gave rein to his professional judgment. Rita pounced. "A psycho. A cruel, sick beast. God, the poor kid." Perhaps she was trying to compensate for all the things she'd said when he was alive, or perhaps a scene on the same stage came to mind, with her purse and Stewart's glasses the props.

They had found Biswekki in an upstairs cubicle at police headquarters, more of an interview room than an office. On the table were a tape-recorder and a copy of that morning's *Star* with the headline visible: *Body Found in Lost Kid Mystery*. A man got up to leave, thin, sallow–faced, who'd looked at them with interest. Biswekki introduced him as the county assistant prosecutor.

"Whoever it was had to want those numbers pretty bad," Rita said, pointedly. She had no doubts.

"And had to know about that hole," Bernice added.

"Don't think I don't know what you're saying." Biswekki lit a cigarette and shook out the match. (It occurred to him that he should switch to a pipe, purely an image thing.) "But we can't go around arresting people on a hunch, without hard evidence. This isn't Africa, right? Every pinko politico between Philly and New York would be jumping down our throat."

"You ever heard of circumstantial evidence?" Rita asked.

"Now don't go telling me my job, sweetheart, 'cause that's one thing little Gussie ain't gonna like."

"I'm not telling, I'm asking. And here's another question. You've got Criminal Prevention Unit written up all over this place. What's that if not your job?"

"Hold it, hold it hold it." Biswekki waved his cigarette, sprinkling ash like holy water. "Let's get our parameters aligned here. 'Cos that's a whole different avenue you're barking up. OK Scag, right? No problem." He lowered his voice, "The boys in Trenton have been apprised. Like I said, they're keeping an eye on him."

186

"They better be keeping more than an eye," Rita said. "After last night."

Bernice changed the subject. "How much was he carrying?"

"Stewart? Couple of bucks."

"And the figures on the barn business?"

"Pretty good," Biswekki sounded impressed. "Fifty, sixty bucks. For two weeks, at a dime a throw, not bad."

"Adults a dollar," Rita reminded him.

"Did he total by the day?" Bernice persisted.

"Yeah, weekends was when he cleaned up." They talked about Stewart's family; his mother had come from North Bergen. Biswekki looked at his watch. "Gotta get back to the site. If you have any more brainstorms, let me know. Give you a ride home, Bernice? Be going right by." It was just past four in the afternoon. She was hoping he'd ask.

"So," Biswekki said when Rita had left. "Something bothering you?"

Was it that obvious? "The envelope, last night …"

"Oh, Jeez!" He clutched his head. "I left it with the duty officer. Wait right here. They should have processed it by now."

She picked up the paper. At the top of the page, a picture of the ambulance men leaning into the rain with the loaded stretcher. Further down, a headshot of Stewart's father, matted hair, wet face and the caption: 'Distraught father awaits word.' Near the bottom, another headshot: 'Det. Gus Biswekki, human bloodhound.' There had to be a hero, and he was perfect: modest, dogged, good-looking, single, 'the cop who led the search party to the scene of the crime,' 'old-fashioned stick-to-itiveness.' The clichés flowed.

"Good set of prints, there, Bernice. Gave SAMMI no trouble." He handed back her envelope. Clipped to it was a card with a name and address. SAMMI, the new crime computer, was hooked into the FBI fingerprints network, among other things.

Bernice examined the card. "That's right," she said, "It really worked."

Biswekki stared at her. "If you knew already, why …" He gave up.

"I had to be sure."

"Oh, just checking, eh? Well, SAMMI's no slouch."

"Hard evidence, right?"

Biswekki sat down. "Right." So the woman comes across like a nutcase, but she's batting a thousand. He had to pay attention.

"Check out this address." She handed it back. "It may be your lucky day."

He stared at the card. "I can't just waltz into someone's place. I need a search warrant from a judge. What am I going to tell the judge? 'Bernice sent me, your honor, to go get me some hard evidence.' It's not in the county even. It's way the hell up north."

She wasn't hearing him. "There won't be anybody home."

"What am I supposed to do? Break the door down? Know what you could get for that? The shaft. And lose my pension. You want me to lose my pension?"

"Do you want me to tell you how to do your job?"

He drummed his toe on the floor. "What evidence?"

"Enough to make an arrest."

"What exactly?"

She took back the card and started writing. "Say you were going to kill your best friend, how would you go about it?"

He erupted. "What is this?"

"An attempt to prevent another murder." She wrote some more and handed back the card.

He glanced at it in disbelief: "Some shopping list."

"I'll explain later. Meanwhile you'll have to take my word. But if it's not enough, there's a back-up plan, a trap kind of. But risky. It could mean someone's life."

"Whose?"

"Someone's."

Her own, perhaps. He looked at her doubtfully for a few seconds. "This 'back-up plan'. When would that be?"

"Depends."

"On what? The weather?"

"You got it."

Though the room was as cold as a meat cooler, Biswekki

ran a silk handkerchief across his brow, a gesture of resignation.

"I've checked up, and as near as they can tell me it'll be Saturday. This coming Saturday."

"Wednesday, Thursday, Friday, *Saturday*?"

"Of course," Bernice added brightly, "It may not come to that. I mean, those missing pages; wouldn't that be enough?"

Biswekki shrugged. "Depends." A light-colored van blocked the entrance to the driveway on Bay Road. Biswekki pulled up across the street. "Looks like you got company. The phone company. Shall I stick around?"

"Oh boy, I forgot. The wedding! It's tomorrow."

"Getting married?" As far as Biswekki was concerned, with this woman anything wasn't just possible, it was likely. Talk about a spitball.

"Oh, not me." But he saw the blush and wondered. "My cousin Harrison, in Texas."

"Aha," he said. It made perfect sense. "I'll check out that address if I can tomorrow. No promises."

She scurried across the road, turned, and gave him the thumbs up sign.

The man from Ma Bell was packing up. He pointed at a rectangular black box on the living room floor with switches and wires sticking out of it. "You didn't indicate location." He waved some papers.

"That's fine. Gee, I clean forgot."

"Door was off the latch. Figured you meant for me to go ahead." He showed her what to do. "Red light means on. Receiver hooks in so. Just sign and I'll pick it up tomorrow."

As soon as he left the phone rang.

"Perfect timing," she said, sinking into a chair. "No, I just got in. Sure, I'm alone. You called twice already? Oh, the man from the phone company. About the wedding. Oh gee, I'm sorry. My cousin in Texas. I thought I told you. Listen, we shouldn't talk on the phone, right? So how about coming tomorrow? One o'clock. Just you and Rita. No, I haven't told her. Yeah, yeah, preview of coming attractions, that's good. See you then. I love you too."

189

I love you too. Well, well. Who'd ever have guessed? She felt drained, clobbered, incapable of movement. Her eyes took in the flotsam of her life, piled up around, that one tide or another had beached. Harrison's little pail and shovel from when she'd first had him; a mock-up of the front page of the *Asbury Park Press* with his photo inserted, taken on the boardwalk; and, from his storm trooper period, a plastic helmet. Harrison and Stewart, she mused. Two of a kind. Loners. Hunting outside the pack. Herself too, now, she supposed. Oh well, if she could just get through tomorrow. The place must be neatened up for the ceremony. Rita liked everything neat. And Otis? She wasn't sure, but she fancied he did too. It was, wasn't it, perfect timing.

When Biswekki got back to the station house, he found a message. Trenton had called. Sergeant Thomas Scagiola had walked out of police headquarters that afternoon, a free man. No charges would be pressed.

"Goddammit!" For once in his life, Biswekki was genuinely mad.

24

"You shouldn't have."

"I had the girl gift wrap it."

She carefully removed the paper and a box appeared. The label read: *Rainy Days Musical Figurine. Revolving Childhood Scene. Made in Poland, $13.95.* Bernice covered the price with her thumb and pulled from the box an object in pastel shades: boy, girl, dog, umbrella. "It's beautiful."

"You wind it here, see?" Otis gave a couple of twists. It did, indeed, revolve, and to music.

"You are my sunshine, my only sunshine ..." Bernice sang along. She put the figurine on a chair, grabbed the startled Otis, and together they polkaed across the room. Almost at once the tinky-tonk gave way to the crunch of tires on gravel. Bernice had just time to hide the thing before a familiar voice sounded from the kitchen.

"Bernice, I swear I was followed." Rita started across the room towards the window, but stopped short at the sight of Otis. "Hi there." Her lips froze in a smile. They were unusually red. She wore a red pantsuit with a white corsage at the shoulder. It was, after all, a wedding. "You got here already. I didn't see a car."

"Transmission trouble." Otis was out of breath. "Took a cab."

"Don't I know," she condoled.

191

"Would one of you mechanics figure this out?" They all three bent over the black box. "The man said to put it in there when it rings."

"Is it on?" asked Otis.

"See the red light? I had it on all night warming up." She trotted out to the kitchen for the iced tea. Rita followed. "Don't mind me, I'm a bundle of nerves."

"Hold still." Rita pinned a corsage on her. "There was this guy in a gold Toyota," she whispered. "I got the number. I couldn't shake him. He sat on my tail like I was a tow-truck."

The phone rang. "That's it!" The ice tray Bernice was holding clattered into the sink. In a flash she was on her knees inserting the receiver into its cradle.

"Make sure it's them," Rita called after her. She *is* a bundle of nerves, she thought.

"Hello? Hello? New Jersey? This is Houston. Come in Bernice."

"My God, it works," Rita exclaimed.

"What hath God wrought," boomed the voice.

"Harrison?" Bernice said feebly, still on hands and knees.

"Howdy! This is Craig Tetronelli, your host, the man with the ring who makes the wires sing. I guess Harrison mentioned his best man. Ha ha."

Rita said: "Is there any way to turn it down?"

"We got a couple of minutes to Showtime, here on the fiftieth floor of the Texas Commercial Tower in downtown Space City. Ladies and gentlemen, I'd like for you to welcome Bernice, a very special person in Harrison's development. Heeeeer's Bernice!"

A drumroll was followed by a chorus of "Hi, Bernice!"

"Hi," said Bernice as Rita nudged her.

"In case you're wondering, Bernice, besides all of us here at the office, that was Melanie's aunt in Fort Wayne and family, and her Aunt Connie and Uncle Phil in Corvallis, Oregon. From sea to shining sea." He prattled on.

They sat in the hot room in their Sunday best hardly daring to sip iced tea lest the ice clink coast to coast. Rita pried off her high heels, and Bernice padded to the front door and wedged it open. She signaled to Otis to take off his jacket, but he declined.

Instead he tiptoed towards the kitchen. His shoes squeaked. Bernice held her breath, wondering which would come first, the exchange of vows in Houston, or the noisy flushing of her toilet. With luck they wouldn't know it was hers. Presumably they had flush toilets in Fort Wayne.

"The future is open," intoned Houston. "We affirm our newness and the possibilities which await our lives. Give me your hands."

Bernice heard the familiar squeak of the screen door, then the creak of the porch. She slumped with relief and composed herself for the solemn moment. "Harrison, Melanie, do you here, before your friends and in the secret places of your hearts, promise each other faithfully and lovingly to live together for the extent of your natural lives?"

"We do."

"I hereby pronounce you ..." The words were lost in an ear-splitting crackle.

At first Bernice thought it came from the box; that someone out there had let off firecrackers at the joyful moment of union. Rita had no such illusion. She was practically out the door before Bernice realized her mistake. Pulling the plug on Houston, she followed Rita.

A faint whimper came from behind a stack of storm windows that had rusted on the back porch for years. Otis, ashen faced, was crouched against the railing, clutching at his left side. "God help me. I bin shot."

Bernice knelt beside him on the boards. "Just relax. Where does it hurt?" Gently she pried his arm away from his side. A tiny bloodstain showed on his shirt, just above the belt. She pulled the shirt up. It was only a graze. "It's your lucky day."

Rita, who had been peering around, sniffing the faintly acrid air, glanced over Bernice's shoulder. "I'll call the doctor."

"No, please." Otis scrambled to his feet. "I'll be fine."

"What happened?"

"I came out for some air. I'd taken off my jacket and was

193

stretching a bit, when, well, you heard. A car opened up from the road."

"Was it gold?" Rita asked.

"Could have been, yeah."

"Oh!" Bernice gasped. As if on cue, a gold Toyota swung into the driveway.

Rita reached into her purse. "Get inside."

"Whatever you do don't shoot."

"Both of you. Inside."

"Rita, I mean it." It was an order.

A man was getting out of the car. "Everything all right?" He started slowly towards the house.

"Hold it right there, Mister." She pointed her pistol. He stopped. "Now turn around and get your ass out of here and everything'll be fine."

The man laughed. "If that's the way you want it." He walked backwards, keeping an eye on the gun. "I hope you got a license for that toy. You could get five years." He held up what could have been a police badge, got into the car and reversed out.

An insane urge to pull the trigger possessed her. In the three years she'd had the pistol, she hadn't fired it once. Aiming at the tops of the tall oaks behind the house, she squeezed in the way she'd been taught. Nothing happened. And remembered: she'd not replaced the bullets KAY-LEE's thugs had emptied out.

"Rita?" Bernice was at the screen door. "Did he go?"

"For now. He waved a badge, like he was an officer."

"Maybe he was. You know something? Maybe he was." She lowered her voice, "Biswekki may be stopping by later. He'll deal with it. Could you drop Otis in town?"

Rita shrugged. "You're the boss."

"We gotta get away, Bernice." Otis said. "Right away, where no one will follow. Monday, I'm going to take you away."

"Where?" Rita was waiting in the Checker.

He thought for a moment. "Atlantic City. For some beginner's luck."

194

Later, she noticed the lid was off the garbage. Raccoons? She wished it were Monday.

The place, when Biswekki found it, was in a rundown section of Bloomfield, a town that merged into East Orange, which merged into Orange, which merged into West Orange. He parked a couple of blocks away and walked along under the trees, semi whistling bits of half-remembered tunes, and every now and then stopping to sneeze. The day was hot, with a light breeze and low humidity, a perfect pollen day. The ragweed count must be in the high eighties. It was on days like these he thought about moving to Florida.

He had come alone for a number of reasons: to attract less attention, to make a quicker getaway, above all to be sure to leave no trace. Because he'd neither the time, nor inclination, to get a warrant. He wasn't planning on doing any buying, not this trip, just checking inventory, so to speak. If there was any. Her list was in his pocket. A preview before the grand opening.

Casually he cased the building for escape routes. An eight story apartment house in an area of one and two family homes, maybe fifty years old, dull red brick, two wings close together with the entrance in the cleavage, up a narrow walkway flanked with privet. He looked up. The fire stairs ended at a point immediately over the entrance. Perhaps there were stairs at the back. He hoped so: the narrow passage made a sitting target of anyone entering or leaving. Two cheap metal chairs sat by the door, which was locked. Biswekki administered a sharp jab with his backside, which had the desired effect. The lobby was cool and dark and smelled of rancid floor wax.

The black plastic coating on the elevator button was worn through to the metal. He pressed it and looked around. The sort of place where a person could come and go and no one be the wiser. His eyes skimmed the mailboxes, noting one, in particular, stuffed, reassuringly, with more than a day's worth of paper.

When, at last, the door slid open, a small girl—Indian or

perhaps Arab—dashed out, brushing him with the fleetest of glances. He pressed five. The ascent was creaky and slow, like being cranked up a well shaft in a bucket. The smell of spicy cooking, growing stronger, somehow enhanced the effect. It was coming from the apartment right next to where he was going. He listened, knocked lightly, and listened again; and wondered when the girl would be back. Probably she was just on an errand to the store. If the lock was pickproof, he was in trouble. He'd have to try a window, climbing down the fire stairs from the roof in full view of everyone. But the lock proved a burglar's dream. It would have stopped a pro for all of thirty seconds. Biswekki took an extra minute because he didn't want to leave too many marks.

A wall of warm, sickly air hit him as he stepped inside, so that he caught his breath and almost gagged; like someone had died and been forgotten. The vestibule was tiny and dark. He found the light switch. The kitchen, off to one side, wasn't much bigger. Garbage spilled from a paper bag onto the floor, the sink was piled with dishes, on the drain board a banana skin, black and dry, curled up beside a shriveled tea bag. A pan on the stove held something noxious. As he opened the oven door, roaches dropped off and scuttled for cover across the greasy gray tiles. He had to tiptoe to avoid them messing up his new brogues. In the living room, the sight of a rubber plant, furry with dust, made him sneeze. And the bed-sized bedroom beyond was dominated by a voluptuous pin-up on a calendar two years out of date. The place had an air of someone having suddenly left, long ago.

Some of the items on his list Biswekki found right off: a can of white paint, open, in the bathroom, some legal-looking papers squirreled away in a shoebox in the closet. But search as he might, in pockets, through garbage, under the stained and torn mattress, he failed to turn up the missing pages of Stewart's notebook. And there was no sign of a cat. There was, however, an interesting white substance in a can in a kitchen cupboard. He took away a sample in an envelope.

On the way back, he called for Bernice on Bay Road. "Not a wasted trip. Let's put it this way: I've seen enough to want to know more. If there's a next time, we'll get a warrant. In fact, I'll say this, Bernice: if you ever start a religion, sign me up. You got a believer."

They sat at the station house and talked. Bernice laid everything out the way she saw it. Biswekki listened, questioned, made some calls. Wednesday afternoon became Wednesday evening. He had two full days to fix things up; he'd need them, every minute. For Bernice, there was little to do but wait. Saturday would come. And the reckoning.

"Don't worry about me, Rita. I took out insurance. It's Uncle Sudeley I'd worry about." The phone was ringing when Bernice got home.

"You think I should go down?"

"It wouldn't hurt. For a day or two."

"A day or two?"

"Just in case. Then Saturday, Biswekki's giving a party. Sort of Hail and Farewell, I guess. We're all invited."

"Is he out of his mind? Where?"

"Check with him. And Rita, don't bring the Checker. Otis is right. It stands out a mile. Maybe Uncle Sudeley'll let you have the pickup." God forgive me, she thought. She was sure Rita wouldn't.

197

25

From the depths of the warehouse, Bernice stared out on what could have been a screening of an overexposed film. The water flashed, the sky was an opaque glare, and way over to the left, rising through the haze like two ghostly matchsticks, the twin towers of the World Trade Center pinpointed the tip of Manhattan Island.

The ship hove steadily closer—its deck cranes like folded pairs of legs, a giant, floating praying mantis—till she could just read the name on the prow: *Stella Princess*. And soon water and sky were blotted out and the rust-stained black hulk filled the opening; then a short blast of a steam whistle signaled to the nudging tugboats that their job was done. Fore and aft, the ropes were thrown and fastened. Port Newark, New Jersey.

The warehouse gave little relief from the midday heat. It smelled pleasantly of wood from the boxes and crates that stood about, stenciled with exotic names: Cartagena, Valparaiso, Yokohama. In the rafters under the roof, birds twittered and screeched; black-headed sparrows too small for the sound they made, vied with the belly drone of the ship and the roar and whine of the jets over Newark International Airport, a mile or two away.

From a few crates off, Biswekki's walkie-talkie crackled to life. "Gatekeeper to Bozo. Red Ford Pickup, repeat Red Ford

Pickup approaching." It was the biggest day in his career as a cop; a combined operation of four police departments, and he was in charge. "Roger. About time."

The sign at the gate of the Stella Lines dock said, 'STOP. Authorized Traffic Only. SHOW PASSES.' A ramshackle mobile home did double duty as security checkpoint and customs clearing house for passengers arriving by freighter. At the window an official in shades examined passes. Behind him on this particular Saturday, Bernice knew, was a Port Authority policeman with a two-way radio and instructions on certain special vehicles that were to be admitted. Parking for the Unauthorized was beyond a wire mesh fence topped with a double strand of razor wire.

Through the end opening of her warehouse, Bernice saw the red pickup wheel left and disappear into the dark interior of the companion warehouse across the loading bay. It was obvious why Rita was late: Uncle Sudeley was driving. She'd had her work cut out persuading Biswekki to let her come at all. There was always the chance the carefully orchestrated plan would backfire or go off half cock, and Rita, in his mind, increased these odds. So when she hadn't shown by eleven, then eleven thirty, he started to fume. And Bernice, feeling guilty, worried for her friend's safety.

No need for that now: a small law enforcement armada flanked Rita. Word had gotten out about fun and games on the docks and it looked—as she remarked to Uncle Sudeley—like a Smokey Convention. An unmarked car from the Cranberry Township police, a state trooper or two, a cruiser from Bloomfield, Sheriff's department guys from two counties, even, for a reason unclear even to Biswekki, guys from the Bureau of Alcohol, Tobacco and Firearms.

The gangplank was being lowered. It came down slowly, hugging the side of the vessel, its orange safety net already in place. Bernice, straining her eyes upward, saw tiers of railings and a row of cabin windows and one end of a lifeboat; then, crowning everything, striped red, yellow and green, a thick funnel from the tip of which curled a plume of thin, gray smoke. And there were people: standing, walking, shouting to one another. She wondered if he was in the crowd and whether she could pick him out. It wouldn't be long now: they let the passengers off first, she'd been told, before unloading began in earnest. A blue and yellow Port Authority police cruiser nosed its way along the railroad tracks that ran along the narrow strip between the warehouses and the water.

Biswekki came and stood next to her. He squinted through binoculars at the small crowd gathering on deck. "Could be that's him there," he told Bernice. "Draw a line down from the flag till it bisects the lowest lot of railings. Right there, in the Hawaiian shirt." He handed her the glasses.

She adjusted the focus. "With the beard?"

"It's been a while."

"Too tall. See the one nearer the gangplank, talking to the woman in the Panama hat? Say, I think they're letting them off."

The radio spoke again: "Lookout One to Bozo. Lookout One to Bozo. We got three guys in a black limo just pulled in dockside. They our guys, or what? Say they have a pass."

Before Biswekki could answer, another voice cut in. "Bozo this is Gatekeeper. On the limo: it's clean. It has a pass. The guy here's good buddies with the driver. He's a regular around here."

"Bozo to Gatekeeper: Find out who they are."

"He's in and out the whole time." Pause. "Taffelbaum's people. They got stuff coming in ..."

Biswekki exploded. "Fucking right, they got stuff coming in. On two legs. I'll tell you what you gotta do. You gotta expedite them out of there now, and I mean now. Get your guys onto it."

"Gatekeeper to Bozo: That an order?"

"It ain't poetry."

"Roger."

From where Bernice stood, an angle of the warehouse hid the limo. She followed Biswekki to a better observation point as the screech of a siren started up. "Jesus Christ!" Biswekki raised his arms in an appeal. "What is this?" The blue and yellow squad car squealed to a full stop inches short of the limo. "What is it with these cowboys?" If they wanted to wreck the operation, they were going the right way about it.

In ones and twos a straggly group were starting to disembark. The men from the limo had lined themselves up like an honor guard waiting for them. For one of them. Bernice guessed what had happened: Taffelbaum wasn't taking any chances. Perhaps he'd known all along. She saw the cops amble over and the men start to remonstrate. The long arm of Felix Taffelbaum, palming big bills no doubt, would be used to getting its own way.

Then Bernice saw him, less than a dozen yards away. She pulled back, though even looking right at her he'd not have seen her. The glare was that intense. He too, as he threaded his way between the waiting hoists and dumped containers, was intent on the altercation near the foot of the gangplank.

"Lookout One to Bozo. Lookout One to Bozo." Biswekki's radio crackled. "Custer on foot. Custer approaching on foot."

Otis hadn't planned to go forward. He'd parked on the far side of the barrier and planned to meet his friend as he came through customs. But the limo with the three men had unnerved him. He'd watched suspiciously as it slid past the guard. When the occupants got out and approached the ship, he'd decided to act. No one challenged him as he walked through the gate, a drab-looking man in a golf shirt and seersucker pants; they had eyes only for vehicles, it seemed. If this was some ploy of Taffelbaum's—and he suspected it was—ten to one they wouldn't know the quarry by sight. How could they? For sure, he wouldn't know who they were. As long as he saw a friendly face he wouldn't get into a car full of strangers. No way. But what if they persisted? Tried to follow? Could he lose them? He'd have to. Jeez, why hadn't he thought of this before!

The cops, at least, seemed on the ball. He'd heard the siren and seen the squad car careening along the tracks. And as he closed in, trying to blend in with the unloading preparations but not get in the way, he saw the men were back in their limo. Then both vehicles passed him, one escorting the other out. None too soon. He quickened his pace. The moment so dreaded and so planned for had come. Halfway down the ramp, looking buoyant as ever and boasting a tan, there he was. The sighting was simultaneous.

"Hey, Ote!"

"Artie! Artie Olds!"

A jet roared overhead, coming in so low they were forced to look up. Then handshakes, backslapping and a scramble for the bags.

Minutes later, Biswekki's radio signaled: "Gatekeeper to Bozo. Gatekeeper to Bozo. United States passport in the name of Phinney, Lamar Otis, hometown, Orange, New Jersey."

"I read you." What Bernice had known for days was now official.

"Subject entering green Pontiac, a 'seventy two, I'd say." He gave the plate number. "Do you read me?"

"Loud and clear. Who's at the wheel?"

"Custer, repeat Custer. They're pulling out now."

"All Stations alert,"

"Roger."

Biswekki ran out onto the loading bay. Already cars from the other warehouse were nosing into the light, revving their engines; like bloodhounds straining at the leash. Someone yelled—it might have been Gatekeeper on the walkie-talkie or Lookout Two, the unmarked tail along the road: "The limo, they're after him!"

"Great. Just great." Biswekki spat out the words. "We're going to have to choke 'em off before they altogether fuck up this whole operation. Keep 'em muzzled, till we're through."

A State trooper and one of the sheriff's cars were dispatched for this purpose. They roared off, lights flashing. "Holy Jesus." Biswekki shook his head as he watched them go.

Next to leave was the unmarked car, then all the others. Biswekki climbed into a radio car. "The lab report just came through," the driver said. "It's a dead ringer."

"Open and shut," Biswekki sat back, slamming the door, but he sounded anxious. The car took off.

Bernice stood on the dock. She felt sweat trickling down her body, and when she licked her lips they tasted salty. The feeble sea breeze did nothing to temper the heat waves pulsing up off the tarmac. Shading her eyes, she peered into the chasm of the other warehouse and saw nothing. Blackness. More or less the way she felt, now that it was over. For her, at any rate. A verse from Scripture bounced around in her head: *And they laid their hands on him, and took him.* Yes, she'd kissed him. She ran into the darkness, blotting out the thought. Rita, where in the world was Rita?

An engine was straining to start. Above the roar from the ship she heard it. Shapes began to loom around her. Then, with a clatter, it came to life. "Bernice! Over here. Where in tarnation have you been? Get in." Rita opened the door and hauled her into the cab. "Climb over to the middle. My knees get in the way."

"It's the sea air," Uncle Sudeley announced. "She's not used to it."

"Sea air my foot. He got stuck with a lemon," Rita scoffed. "Now, will somebody kindly tell me: what the hell's going on? What kind of a party is this supposed to be? Gunfight at the O.K. Corral?"

"Custer's Last Stand, more like," Bernice said bleakly. "Anyway, it's over. For us." They chugged out the gate.

"We were up with the sun and drove three hours in this red lemon—for *this*? To sit in a stinking shed with a bunch of boy scouts playing cop, birds crapping on our heads and jets skimming the roof every three minutes? Come on! Was that an Otis look-alike wandering about out there? And where's Biswekki, I'd like to know?"

Bernice took a deep breath. "OK, where shall I start?"

"The middle; you usually do."

"Well, to answer your question: no that wasn't Otis you saw out there. It was someone else altogether. Otis was on the ship where he's been for the past several weeks."

"Australia? He made all that up?"

"He didn't. He said he made it up. Besides, they never made Australia. On account of the dock strike, remember? The ports there were backed up. They ran out of Scotch. That's what tipped me off. They turned around at Auckland."

"What are you jabbering about, Bernice?"

"That ship, the *Stella Princess*, is full of New Zealand lamb."

Rita slumped back against the seat. She could feel a migraine coming on. Then she sat up and prepared to pull teeth. "Do me a favor, Bernice. Try to take it from the top."

26

Somebody once characterized Uncle Sudeley's driving—possibly himself—as molasses flowing uphill in January. The red pickup crawled by mountains of rock salt and scrap iron and forests of round gray storage tanks and here and there, against the sky, hovering cranes. The port went on and on. But for all Bernice and Rita noticed, they were on the boardwalk in Atlantic City.

"The person who ran down Miss Annie, who possibly killed Miss Mercy, was the person who strangled Stewart. Because Stewart knew too much. He'd seen a man in a car hanging round 151 Gunning Point Road that night and written the number in his book. His mistake was trying to sell what he knew for cash. My guess is that's what he was up to when he died."

"We know all that." Rita said impatiently. "Scaguiola, right?"

"Wrong. It wasn't a blue Impala that Stewart jotted down. It was a green Pontiac. Scaguiola was the scapegoat; what we were *supposed* to think. It was a setup, and it fooled us right down the line. And the man behind it is the man you saw meeting the *Stella Princess*. A man called Arthur Olds, who had us believing he was Otis Phinney."

"Arthur Olds?"

"Phinney and Olds were buddies. Both worked for the post

office; both belonged to the Lodge; both are bachelors with no family to speak of. Only, one of them is a bowling ace, plays Santa Claus for the kids, likes a party, and cats. The other, well, you know the other. And where Otis Phinney's been lurching around in the Ocean for the past few weeks, Arthur Olds has been here in Jersey conducting a wild goose chase."

"That little squirt? A murderer?"

"Why not?"

Rita flushed an angry red. "So did they pick him up yet?"

Bernice looked at her watch. "Give them a half hour. By then they should have enough evidence."

"What evidence?"

"They have to catch him red-handed. It's the only way."

"Doing what?"

"Killing his best friend. Oh," she hurried on, "it's quite safe. Biswekki says they'll get him on intent. Open and shut. Unless he drinks it, the iced tea."

"What iced tea."

"Right now they're on their way to Orange—Otis's house with the tubs in front. Arthur Olds will drop him off. He probably won't go in, so as not to compromise himself; because the first thing Phinney's going to do on a day like today is fix himself a glass of iced tea."

"Don't tell me the tea's poisoned."

"Exactly."

Uncle Sudeley kept quiet, concentrating on the road.

"The rest of the poison's at Arthur Olds's apartment, in Bloomfield. Biswekki found it. They've been watching him for a couple of days now. This morning early he slipped into Phinney's place. He has a key. When he left they went in with a warrant and took samples for testing. The report just came in. Rat poison. In the ice tray."

"Just let me get my hands on him."

"I'd have told you sooner, only …"

"He spooked me out. The creep."

"I know. I kind of liked him."

"Kind of! Your teddy bear, remember? You'd have hitched up with the creep given half a chance."

"Well," Bernice admitted, "he did ask. We're engaged, I guess." At that, Uncle Sudeley took his foot off the gas completely. "It was insurance. For him the whole thing started when that quitclaim deed came for Otis Phinney. He opened it—Phinney had left and he was getting his mail—and thought he saw a hundred grand, ripe for the plucking. Then along comes Bernice with her claim. It must have thrown him at first, till he saw the chance to double his money. I knew at least I'd be safe till after the wedding; and as there wouldn't be one ..."

"You're crazed. And him—how could he have gotten that money if he wasn't Otis, let alone if he was?"

"Legally speaking he had no problem. He had Otis's power of attorney. Unconditional. Biswekki found the papers in his apartment. He was handling all of Otis's affairs, plus he was sole beneficiary if he died. It must have seemed like fate dealing him into a game he'd given up on. He did his homework, found out about KAY-LEE's involvement in the industrial park, and decided to up the ante—when the time came. Probably figured a hundred grand could buy a new life. He tracked down the sisters. I don't know when he made up his mind to kill, but after that ..."

"I went to a funeral with him—alone." Rita recoiled at the memory.

"Two funerals. When he first saw us he assumed we were relatives—more of the competition."

"His big mistake."

"When he found we weren't, he thought he could scare us off with painted skulls and the kiss of death and threatening calls, and make us think that KAY-LEE and the police and goodness know who else were out to get him. Scaguiola played right into his hands, buying that lot, and then when it turned out he was in debt to a loan shark. He went as far as tinkering with the tail light on his car to make it look like one I thought was following us the night we stole the Bible. He must have slipped the cardboard skull into the trunk at the same time. And he staged that chase when you spotted him from your kitchen, in a rented car like Scaguiola's."

"Having himself a ball. And all the time we were busy protecting him from—no one."

"The night we drove to Perth Amboy in the Eldorado he'd just come from strangling poor Stewart."

Rita flinched. "How long have you known—who he was, I mean?"

"Bingo night at the Lodge; that's when I knew who he wasn't. I checked the postcards. If he'd written them up ahead of time, as he claimed, they wouldn't mention the dock strike. But they did, and that the ship was skipping Australia, taking on New Zealand lamb, and sailing back from there."

"What made you go back to look?"

"Taffelbaum. Telling me I was the only pebble on the beach, and he was the tide. I said, 'The only pebble?' And he said, 'On the beach. The other one is still far out to sea.' I thought, 'Boy, Otis has really done a job on him.' Then later I got to thinking, 'Wait a minute, Bernice, this guy knows. He's powerful.' And, of course, he did. His people were there just now to meet the boat. They weren't taking any chances on getting Otis Phinney's signature on that deed."

"And his real name; how'd you get that?"

"I fixed with Kerry to get a couple of Polaroids of Otis at the Monarchburger, and leave one among the garbage at her table. That's what I showed the neighbor in Orange. 'No way that's Otis,' she said. Meanwhile Kerry and her brother had trailed him back to where he was staying. The woman at the motel knew him right away, 'That's Mr. Olds.' Then I got his prints on a menu. He'd been a federal employee. He's on file. Biswekki did the rest."

They had left the docks and were negotiating a sort of no man's land between the port and the town of Newark—a landscape of swamp grass, railroad tracks and elevated highways snaking off into the haze. Uncle Sudeley gazed ahead, stabbing the air with a finger. "Get out the compass, Rita. Take your bearings. Bernice, fill the water bottles."

"Here's why we were late," Rita said. "Figuring out this cloverleaf."

"Cloverleaf! This here's no cloverleaf. This here's a pile of

208

wet spaghetti." A slew of major roads writhed together in a Gorgon's Head of loops and twirls, on-ramps and off-ramps, some engineer's mad folly. Uncle Sudeley ploughed on into it, full of grim determination. Rita and Bernice left him to it.

"Then how come he was shot at during the wedding?" A few things needed straightening out.

"Simple enough to shoot a hole in your shirt before you put it on, then scratch your side."

"But the bang. We all heard that. And I was followed."

"Firecracker; it was in the garbage where he threw it. Just in case anyone had any lingering doubts. Which means, incidentally, he keeps a gun. And the tail *was* a cop. Scaguiola was on the loose and Biswekki wasn't taking any chances."

"I could have shot him."

"Rita, you wouldn't ever fire that thing. As it turned out he didn't have to worry. Scaguiola's on his best behavior. The FBI needed a handle on that loan sharking racket. It'll be business as usual for that one."

"With a Cape Cod on Gunning Point Road."

"Till they prosecute. Then he disappears. Federal Witness Program. California, Hawaii, some place nice."

"And crime doesn't pay? Wouldn't Otis have loved that. I mean Arthur Olds."

"They were both of them gamblers and dreamers."

"Were?"

"I can't help but think of them as gone."

"How about that?" Uncle Sudeley pointed. A limousine had burst partway through the low roadside barrier. One side was badly bashed: the limo they'd see fifteen minutes ago on the docks. It looked empty.

Ahead the road peeled into three; large green signs offered an array of destinations, none of which Uncle Sudeley quite wanted. He peered, blinked and held the pickup in a swooping curve, down, under the road they had just been on to where massive pillars stood Samson-like; then up, up, arching into the light between slopes of wavy grass, searching for the next opening. He was lost. Somewhere a siren bleeped. Then another. Lights flashed, closing in, it seemed, from all sides.

Biswekki held the radio receiver in a crushing grip so that his knuckles glowed. White blotches spread unhealthily at his temples and his mustache hung limp. Sweat oozed through his shirt. He was fighting to contain his fury, and losing. "Bozo to Q Four, Bozo to Q Four. "I'm gonna need an ambulance at the I-9-78 intersection. This thing's pin wheeling. It could explode. Make that a couple. Pull 'em from the airport if you have to."

He had his driver stop. No point in running with the pack. There was as good a view of the intersection as any right where he was, and he could pass on the word as to which route they were headed out on, though at that moment, no one was headed anywhere. Just round and round like bumper cars: a half dozen police vehicles chasing their tails. Keystone cops on wheels, the screech of tires punctuating the chopped-up chatter on the radio. Biswekki reached into the back seat for his high-powered rifle with telescopic sights. Where was the Pontiac now? For the moment, he'd lost it. He got out.

Up until Taffelbaum's goon squad put in an appearance, the operation had run smooth as silk sheets. The tail had picked up the Pontiac heading out of the port, but the limo had held on like a leech however much the trooper flashed at it to pull over. After minutes yapping at its heels, the trooper and its cohort tried to squeeze it out at an intersection. Still no dice. It was after that they flipped out—the way Biswekki saw it— and ran it into a side rail at fifty miles an hour. Amazingly, with no casualties. For a while, in the confusion, they lost the Pontiac. When they picked up on him he'd doubled back to the cloverleaf from the New Jersey Turnpike that ran nearby, all twelve lanes of it.

What chance the guy thought he had in the face of so much law and order, Biswekki couldn't fathom. Who could tell what was passing through his mind? Sheer panic, probably. It had been a madcap venture from the start. Then came word that he was holding a gun on his pal. Trying to draw out the heat from the situation, Biswekki ordered everyone to calm down, not to bottle him up. Let him breathe, let him out of the intersection, let his mind work. Chances were good he'd give himself up. The gun alone would be enough to book him on. But he wasn't cooperating, just round and round in a holding pattern. Either he'd run out of gas or, at that speed, crash land; one false move and over the edge.

Biswekki climbed up on the concrete parapet and looked about. He felt the rush of a general surveying the field of battle, which marginally improved his temper. Fortunately it was Saturday and there was little other traffic about. What there was, he'd attempted to divert. Then he saw it: grinding in on the port road, the red pickup. Almost at once, the Pontiac reappeared and circled to the crest of a rise some fifty yards off. He watched it careen to a halt, flinging itself half round like a skittish horse at a jump, so it straddled the road. Had one of his men gotten too close, he wondered.

Ducking back inside the squad car, he grabbed the bullhorn. But the Pontiac didn't stop. When he looked again it was headed back the way it had come, down a one-way curve, hugging the inside. The pickup was also into the curve, going a good deal slower. They were on a collision course. Biswekki waited for the crash, his brain fixated on a single thought: he was taking them all with him.

Instead of completing the turn, the Pontiac shot across the road missing the pickup by just feet, and embedded itself in the outer guardrail, one front wheel spinning over the edge. Biswekki trained his binoculars on the driver's door just as it opened. First he saw the gun, then the man behind it. "Police. Biswekki speaking," the words rumbled across the mass of twisting highway. "Drop the gun, Arthur Olds, and start walking."

The pickup had stopped. Rita could hardly believe that the lunatic with the ugly-looking weapon, weaving and twisting towards them like a pro, screaming at them to get out, was the mild little man she'd known as Otis Phinney. In less time than it takes to say GTT she was standing on the hot road with her hands in the air, and so was Uncle Sudeley. "Not you Bernice. You stay put." Then, waving the gun at Rita: "Get your purse over here."

211

The purse was on the front seat, where she'd left it, but instead of her own, Rita took Bernice's, tossing it at his feet, not daring to catch her friend's eye least it alert him. Grabbing it, he lobbed it over the side of the ramp before jumping behind the wheel of the pickup. Perfidiously, it started like a dream and took off at a pace she'd hardly thought possible. Only then did Rita grasp that the thunder filling the background was Biswekki's amplified voice, and that it had stopped. The next moment squad cars swarmed around her, and strong hands hefted an inert form along the front seat of the disabled Pontiac.

They rode, at first, in silence. Then Bernice said, "We going any place in particular?"

"Just going," he said. "Keeping going."

"They're not out to hurt you. They just want to talk. Why not stop and listen?"

"So the sharpshooters can pick me off? Ha! You're a crafty little number, Bernice. To think, I trusted you, and all the time … It was you, wasn't it?" Steering with one hand, he kept the gun trained on her.

"Couldn't I say the same about you?"

"You know what? I hope they pull something. I hope those dumb cops pull something, so I can squeeze the trigger on this here."

"Go ahead," she said, "but don't forget, if you do, who's going to stand between KAY-LEE and that industrial complex. No one. 'Cause now there's only me left."

"Ote—you think he's …?"

"Seems like you're good at something after all. Taffelbaum's going to love you."

"You'd hand it to him on a plate, so what's the difference? Ote'd have done the same."

"He was your friend."

"Some friend. He told the jokes. I laughed."

"He trusted you."

"Which goes to show." He forced a laugh. They passed a squad car pulled over to the side.

"I liked you better as Otis."

"You and everyone else."

"Tell you what," she said. "I'll give you my word. If I get out of here, I won't let him off easy. I promise."

"Taffelbaum?" She sounded so convincing that the pistol drooped. "A hundred grand. You'll hold out for that?"

"Yeah." It was a new thought to her. "Why not?"

He tossed her the gun. "So shoot me." It landed beside her on the seat.

She picked it up, took a quick look, and dropped it out the window. "If I'd wanted to, I could have done it by now." Reaching into Rita's purse, she produced the little .22. He lunged for it. Too late. It was on its way to join the other.

The pickup slowed. The man at the wheel seemed to sag. "I can't figure you out, Bernice. What do you want? You know something? I'll bet if I'd a met you before ..."

"Before?"

"Before it was too late." He jammed on the brakes. "Get out!" A bullet slammed through the windscreen dissolving it into a million silvery slivers. "Move!" she heard him shriek, and half fell into the road.

The pickup bounded forward like a horse stung by a hornet. The last she saw was its tail end tipping away from her, over the edge. She braced for the explosion. It didn't come. And in that second, when everything went still the wail of an ambulance sounded.

He had the feeling he was in a vehicle going some place fast, but when he opened his eyes he saw nothing. Funny. He swore he'd been behind the wheel; recalled the red pickup, and in it, eyes staring with reproach, Bernice. He'd known then it was *her*. Or was it all a dream? Were they in Atlantic City after all?

When he woke again, an earlier memory seeped back. Again he was at the wheel. It was dark; the night from which there'd be no turning back. She loped into the light, blind and foolish, like an old jack rabbit. A gentle pressure on the gas was all it took. The barely felt tremor had knocked her clear of the wheel, and knocked him—well, further. He'd gone back for the other. The bedspread came in handy, though he wasn't sure she wasn't dead already. It was all too easy. But he couldn't take the risk. They knew he wasn't Otis. Then, days later, worried about fingerprints, he'd gone back with a match.

If she hadn't tried to trick him, saying no, they didn't get no letter, had no people left, nothing like a Bible. If he hadn't said he was from the post office, tracing a special delivery. If. When he'd searched the kitchen, she'd said, 'It's upstairs. Only door's locked,' and given him the keys. A great bunch of them. He'd said, 'Show me.' But the stairs were too much for her, or so she said. And while he was up there, fumbling with the locks the dam cat brushing his legs, she'd slipped out. Not to the neighbors, thank God, to a phone booth on the corner, and stood there in the light, and after a while he'd found her.

He inched his right hand across his chest to the bulge in his shirt pocket. Still there. Six, should be. He scratched around a bit, then moved his fingers to his mouth. His pills, his luck and his money … A little later, when the trembling started, a voice said, "He's coming round." But he wasn't.

27

"You made the front page." Rita had stopped by to pick up Bernice for Sunday school. "Again." She tossed the paper along the front seat and began backing out of the drive. "Go ahead. Read it."

"There was a bucking bronco, a hayride, four marching bands, the Kornblumen Queen of Philadelphia and the Garden State's own Tiny Sweetheart of Sea Girt; but the real star of Cranberry City's annual Founder's Day parade was Queen for a Day Bernice Crickle, 51, of Neptune Grove. Riding on the theme float, emblazoned Spirit of Our Forebears in paper flowers by the Neptune Grove Fire Company Ladies Auxiliary, resplendent in a champagne silk gown hand sewn with seed pearls and matching crown, the petite brunette waved, smiled and blew kisses to the crowd as to the manor born.

"Behind her rode her court—Maid of Honor Rita Bonney of Carefree Days Village, and Maid in Waiting Kerry McKelvie, 13½, a student at Cranberry City High."

Rita said: "At least they left off my age."

"Leading the Cranberry Township Police Department contingent was Detective Gus Biswekki, 33, newly promoted to lieutenant, who headed the successful investigation into the disappearance/murder of *Star* newstip two-time award winner, Stewart Krabbowicz, 16, of Scoop Creek. In the course of the investigation, Mrs. Crickle, a lifelong resident of the township,

215

became something of a local celebrity. Her abduction at the hands of the principal suspect in the case, and subsequent hair's breadth escape, is well known to readers of these columns.

"At the Jayceeettes Dunking Booth, following the parade, the Queen for a Day was presented with three baseballs to throw at the target. A direct hit would have dropped Founder's Day Chairman, County Bank & Trust President Claude R. Peyser, into a tank of water. 'Guess it's my lucky day,' he quipped dryly."

"You didn't even try, Bernice. I'd have dunked the bastard."

"Asked what she had gotten out of the ordeal, Mrs. Crickle replied, 'My job back. And I mean to keep it.' Mrs. Crickle is employed at the bank.

"As reported earlier, her share of the one hundred thousand dollar figure put up by KAY-LEE Enterprises, main developer of the township's proposed 1,235 acre, multi-million dollar industrial park, was divided, at her request, among the original heirs to the Good Estate now living in Texas."

"It must have killed Taffelbaum," Rita exulted, "but with all the headlines, what could he do?"

"It was Mrs. Crickle's surprise emergence as a claimant to the estate that led to her involvement with the Krabbowicz case. Another heir, Otis Phinney, a retired postal worker from Orange, who said he was down for the day, said the balance of his share of the settlement would go towards a Stewart Krabbowicz Memorial Fund so a playground for youngsters could be built on his block. Mr. Phinney had his arm in a cast from injuries suffered a month ago during the high speed auto chase which led to the apprehension of the suspect.

"An investigation into the deaths of two elderly spinsters, Miss Mercy Good and Miss Annie Good, both of Gunning Point Road, Scoop Creek—who were also heirs to the estate—is continuing, police say."

"Funny thing," Rita broke the silence, "pathetic creature that he was, there's no way they're ever going to pin it on him. That, or Stewart."

Bernice sighed. "I told him he was good at something. Still, he'll be paying—for a long time to come."

"He's dead, Bernice." She paused. "Oh, you mean ... Let's not get into that."

The Checker stopped at a light. Somebody pointed. A kid waved. "Your public," Rita said.

Bernice smiled. "They want me to run county-wide—for Grandmother of the Year."

"Without grandchildren, that could be a problem. It's a bit late to start now. Besides, no way will I be the same age as any grandmother of the year."

"Well, in a few months, maybe Harrison'll ..." She wanted to be Grandmother of the Year.

"Which reminds me: *did* they get married?"

"Didn't I tell you? I had a postcard from the Grand Canyon."

"Oh, guess what. Uncle Sudeley stopped by. They deputized him: temporary wild dog warden at a dollar a year. He actually got a buck out of the state. He was so happy. He said to say hi. You know, Bernice, I hate to say this but he kind of likes you."

"Give me a break, Rita. I can't handle another romance." She looked out of the window. "Not this summer."

THE END

Praise for the novels of J.N. Catanach

Brideprice

"...sophisticated whodunit....in a style that is detailed and subtle and in a tone that is quietly, beautifully haunting."

Marilyn Stasio, The New York Times Book Review

"...a rare sensitivity and understanding of Africa gained through keen observation and residence."

The Drood Review

White Is the Color of Death

"Mordantly witty, extremely complicated and challenging, this is a first novel by an author obviously familiar with the setting....Catanach's debut offers rich entertainment..."

Publishers Weekly

"...sure-handed and evocative descriptions of the jungle locale; crisp, convincing dialogue; and varied characters drawn with a few witty strokes—including a certain Vellu, one of the zanier second fiddles of recent fiction."

Aaron Elkins, *Mystery Scene*

"Catanach knows Malaysia, and especially the lovely Langkawi Islands—where the somewhat languid, yet entirely appropriate action takes place....he has a shrewd eye for both social and physical detail."

Robin W. Winks, *The Boston Globe*

The Last Rite of Hugo T

"If you are looking for something different in the way of espionage novels, try *The Last Rite of Hugo T*....something of a fable, written with charm and sympathy."

Newgate Callendar, *The New York Times Book Review*

"J.N. Catanach's care with language and his eye for detail are the strongest elements....It's these talents that enable the author to make Hugo's world, even as it nears death, come alive for the reader."

Rex Burns, *Rocky Mountain News*

"...an unusual thriller....'Last Rite' is rich in supporting roles, dense with the atmosphere of its two cities, and nicely layered in both style and content."

Michael Harris, *The Los Angeles Times Book Review*

91361090R00133

Made in the USA
Columbia, SC
17 March 2018